Worlds
Apart

Carol Puhl-Snyman

This novel is based on a true story of events on a small wine farm in Stellenbosch, South Africa. Names and dates have been changed to protect people's privacy.

To farmworkers and farmers in South Africa

CHARACTERS

Catherine and André Steenkamp – owners of Bellezicht Farm

Isaac Jacobs – farmworker, older generation

Laetitia Jacobs – wife of Isaac

Sheryl Jacobs – daughter of Isaac and Laetitia, later briefly married to Reggie Syster. She had four children: two older, Trina and Godwin, two younger, Quinton (Reggie's son) and Jannie

Reuben Jacobs – son of Isaac and Laetitia, husband of Susanna. They had two sons, Danie and Jaco

Neela Jacobs – daughter of Isaac and Laetitia, wife of Henry Botha. They had two sons, *Klein* Henry and a younger son

Tommy Jacobs – son of Isaac and Laetitia

Godwin Jacobs – grandson of Isaac and Laetitia; farmworker at Bellezicht

Esta Stoffels – girlfriend of Godwin

Marina – adopted daughter of Susanna and Reuben Jacobs

Anna Solomons – domestic worker in the Steenkamp home

Frankie Steenkamp – brother of André

Arno Landman – labour consultant

Mostert Muller – cousin of André

Frans Brown– colleague of André

CONTENTS

"I (too) had a farm in Africa."

PART ONE

~ 1 That meeting ~

At the agreed time, in the dusky hiatus between the close of the work day and the serious start of evening, Esta Stoffels and Neela Jacobs, two matriarchs from the farmworker's extended family living in the cottage on Bellezicht Farm, filed into the main house's dining room. Godwin Jacobs, the one and only farmworker, followed them in. The two women had approached André and Catherine Steenkamp, the farm owners, the day before and asked to meet.

Catherine felt anxiety rise in her throat. Something was brewing, that was for sure. Growing up a city girl in America, she never quite knew what to expect on a farm, let alone one in Africa. She felt a dash of excitement too.

André, still in office attire, positioned the chairs for everyone around the oak table. Catherine welcomed each person with a nod and a smile that extended to her green-blue eyes. She set on the table a pot of tea and some rusks. Their two dogs, a big ridgeback named Lola and a small terrier named Jonty, knew everyone on Bellezicht and wagged their individual greetings. More smiles and nods as the people sat down and planted their cell phones neatly beside each place mat. This meeting was not routine but it was not unusual either.

André took charge. He was used to taking charge. He felt that it was his duty as boss of the farm, a duty which lay heavily on his shoulders. He looked at Godwin to begin the discussion. Being a gentle soul, Godwin looked at his girlfriend Esta. "Ladies first," he said, using English rather than their mother tongue, Afrikaans.

But before Esta had a chance to speak, André jumped in, playing his familiar tune. "When are your visitors leaving?" Smiles around the table evaporated like morning dew on the grapes in Bellezicht vineyards. A red flush rose from André's neck to his cheeks.

Catherine's one eyebrow lowered, as it did when she was annoyed, and her mouth went taut. Why oh why did he have to say that now, when they were just getting started?

The visitors. The visitors to the cottage were a very young couple and a toddler – was it their child? There seemed to be some doubt. How were they related to Esta? Was the young woman her niece, as she had said before? Or her daughter, as the young woman herself seemed to imply? Or just a friend? Catherine could not get answers. It was clear that they were not related to Godwin. The fact that their "visit" had gone on for months indicated that these "visitors" were putting down roots, and it was clear that those roots were watered and fed.

They seemed to know they weren't greatly welcome on the farm. They avoided contact. Neither Esta nor anyone else had brought them to meet André or Catherine. The young couple were like ghosts, floating in the the background. Most requests for information were ignored. No ID books were shown; names differed every time Catherine asked.

"Friday," said Esta, annoyance in her voice. "This coming Friday." Just as she had responded many times in the past. Fridays came and went but the visitors stayed on.

Catherine and André had bought the farm 16 years earlier, 10 000 grape vines and all, with a worker Isaac Jacobs and his wife Laetitia and their family already living there. After Isaac died, the farm job had skipped a generation and had now fallen to Godwin, who unfortunately did not take after his grandfather Isaac where vine-tending was concerned.

A pleasant chap, Godwin tried his best to please. He was tall enough and strong enough, but he just couldn't make himself work with the vines. Eventually, André realised that this was not just adolescent rebellion, and he gave Godwin work on the farm as the gardener. Bellezicht did not sport a wine tasting room so there was no need to cultivate an upscale look, but Godwin's work did help to keep the farm looking cared for. More importantly, the job gave the farm family a reason to stay on at Bellezicht, especially seeing that farm jobs and farm housing were getting scarce.

Esta, short and round with spirit in her bright eyes, kept speaking. She looked at André. *"Ons is hier oor my ma.* It's about my mother. She lives in Robertson and she is ill and I am considering moving back there to help her out. I'm not sure yet what I want to do, just thinking. Maybe Godwin could come with me." Robertson was quite far, about two hours if one had a car.

Godwin looked down at his rough farmworker's hands.

Esta had been Godwin's girlfriend of two or three years, his only one ever. When he first brought her to the farm to visit openly, Catherine invited them both in for tea, to get to know her. She didn't have children, she'd said. Catherine had been impressed that she'd waited; most farm girls fell pregnant quickly as teenagers. She was shy then, at that tea visit, but now she was anything but shy. It was obvious that she was quite a bit older, maybe 15 years older than Godwin, who was 26.

Esta continued, now in Afrikaans. "Neela and her family will stay." She looked at Neela, who nodded. Neela was Godwin's auntie. "Sheryl will stay too." Sheryl Jacobs was Godwin's mother. She was around but not at the meeting, keeping a low profile at the moment.

"Ons wil net seker maak. We want to be sure that *Meneer* knows and that everything will be all right for the others in the cottage."

When he heard "the others in the cottage," it was too much for André.

"Which others? If you mean the visitors who have been here for months, there is no future for them here in any case."

"Meneer, hoe bedoel Meneer?" Esta gave a quizzical look, asking what that is supposed to mean. Perhaps to buy time.

"Julle het my gehoor. You heard me. The visitors must go." André's voice went up two notches. *"En as Godwin trek, dan moet almal trek. Dis hoe dit is, en klaar!"*

Neela, quiet, droopy-eyed Neela who had not said a word thus far, erupted to her feet and threw her hands toward the ceiling. *"Ek wil nie!* I won't leave! I can't! I can't go back to the bush! No, no, no! Never! *Ek kan nie! Nooit nie!"*

Her chair flipped over backwards and crashed to the floor. The others jumped to their feet too. Esta and Godwin shouted in sympathy as they pushed away from the dining room table, knocking over other chairs, and, along with Neela, made for the door. The two dogs barked in confusion at the sudden scraping and crashing.

As Esta left, with a flippant toss of her head, she whipped out a dramatic line, in English: "My lawyer will be in touch."

It had all happened in a matter of seconds.

Catherine and André stood there as if flash frozen, jaws agape, as Godwin and his family stormed out and marched the few metres from the manor house back to the worker's cottage.

"André! What?" Catherine raised her hands in a gesture of shock, as if to protect her racing heart.

He shook his head. "What did she say? 'My lawyer will be in touch?' What?"

Catherine felt distress on top of the anxiety. She acted quickly, striding out of the door after them. *"Wag, asseblief!* Please wait! There must be some misunderstanding. Come back! Let's sort it out."

But they were several steps ahead of her and not to be seen. It was as if the cottage had swallowed them up. Catherine knocked, and then banged on the doors, first one and then the other. No response; the doors were closed tight. She stood there and knocked hard again. Lights were on behind the curtains but nothing moved there.

"Please! Come and talk!" Silence. Silence like a giant blanket. What a contrast to the bedlam of two minutes ago. She knocked again and again; she stood there a long while facing the closed doors, but in vain. Nothing else to try. Back to the house.

André was still standing there, his face like a thundercloud. He shook his head. "What's going on?"

Catherine shook her head also in disbelief. Then she looked long at him. "André, please repeat what you said, in English, that led to this." She knew she was making a subtle accusation; André with his temper could have said just about anything. She had mastered much of the Afrikaans language but still she missed things spoken too quickly for her.

"Esta asked for this meeting; it wasn't my idea." His mouth had a grim set to it. "Who made her the boss of the cottage anyway? She's only Godwin's girlfriend."

"She hasn't been here that long," said Catherine, "only a year or so, but it's amazing how the others just go along with her. Including Godwin." She could understand how Esta might be the stronger partner in her relationship with Godwin; being older, obviously she had had more life experience. It remained a mystery to her how Esta could dominate the women older than she was.

André spoke. "You would think Godwin would be more influenced by his mother and his auntie. Anyway, Esta was telling us her plans, that if she and Godwin move away, including the one jobholder, then the others will stay here. You heard it."

"Yes, I heard that part, but I didn't quite get your part; your Afrikaans was too quick for me. You just rattled it off." Her frown deepened. "If someone was thinking of leaving the farm, that should have been good news for us, with the serious overcrowding. Twelve people now in one small cottage!"

"Well, I didn't see it that way at the moment."

"No, you were already in fighting mode. When they came in, you started up again, 'When are the visitors leaving?' That probably got their backs up."

"Their visitors." André scowled, his hazel eyes almost green with anger. "They've been here for months. They can't stay here permanently. I won't have it."

"They played their familiar tune too," observed Catherine, "not meaning a word of it, about when the visitors were going." To lie must be the first rule in some clandestine Farmworker's Survival Handbook, she thought. It could be that the truth doesn't always make you free. In fact, they seemed to know that the truth, whatever that really is, could cost you dearly.

"They asked what would happen to the others if Esta and Godwin move out," repeated André. "Esta said her mother was ill and she was thinking about going back there to Robertson, with Godwin in tow."

"I heard that part too. And you, instead of taking the question thoughtfully, spat out something … in Afrikaans … what exactly did you say? It all happened so fast."

"I said, 'If Godwin leaves, then everyone leaves.' *Dan moet almal ook trek.*"

"Oh my word! Just like that? 'Everyone leaves. *Almal.*' I missed that. No wonder they erupted!"

She sat down heavily, elbows propped on the table and forehead tilted into her fingers. André sat down at an angle to her, looking at her. He spoke slowly and deliberately, forcibly suppressing anger behind his words.

"Catherine, I didn't tell Godwin or Esta or Neela or any of our own farm family that they have to leave this farm."

"Then how did they get that message? You said everyone; *almal.*"

"No, I didn't. Well, yes I did, but in the context that they put up, that Godwin would leave. I never said Godwin had to leave, and I never said anyone except the visitors had to leave."

"No," she agreed, drawing it out. "But the wider context is there. Some farms have thrown off their farm families. It seems to be a current trend, a brutal one. Maybe that's why they spooked at the word leave."

"We aren't throwing anyone off this farm. Not even the visitors. We are asking them to leave, just the visitors, not throwing them off."

Catherine looked at him, then buried her face in her hands.

André got up and paced to the kitchen and back. He was thinking hard. "On the contrary, Catherine; I don't want Godwin to go. It would create problems for us on this farm if he left. Problems with security; problems with stability. We've accepted his family living here because of his job here, a job we created for him. That's the only reason."

She looked up at him. "André, we aren't dealing with logicians. Didn't you know that words like 'go' or 'leave' could set them off?"

"Well, I was just responding to their issues, that's all. Isn't that what they wanted?"

"It seems they heard a different message. Maybe they thought you were talking about eviction. 'Everyone leaves.' It's such a political hot potato right now. It's all over the news. 'Those horrible farmers are putting their loyal workers of many years out on the street. Resist!'"

"But I said 'if', Catherine. I'm sure I said if. *As. As Godwin trek.*"

Her mouth was set. She looked at him for a long moment. "If. Seems they just heard the 'leave' part."

"Well, if they want to leave, that's their fuckin' choice. They don't have to go anywhere. If Godwin were to leave, I'd have to replace him. We would have to house a new family here. So why should I want them to leave?"

"Have they forgotten that farm housing rides on a farm job? One would think that farm people understand that only too well."

"Not anybody in Godwin's family who has been living here all along, has to leave, as far as I'm concerned. Just the three visitors."

"So it's two issues here: the issue of visitors and the issue of Godwin."

"Hmm. True. They are mixing up these issues. What does Godwin want to do? Stay or leave?"

"He didn't say."

Poor Godwin, Catherine thought. How could he even begin to decide what he wanted, living day in and day out with these overbearing women, especially Esta. After his grandmother Laetitia's funeral, and before Esta became a big part of his life, he came back to his job but he couldn't work. For days he stood around, repeating to himself and to anyone near, *"Ek is alleen in die wêreld.* I'm all alone in the world."* He was so vulnerable.

He had a half-sister who loved him but she lived on the other side of town, and Esta had cut him off from her. Indeed, he seemed all alone.

Catherine went to the sink and drew two glasses of water. They moved to the lounge and stood side by side in front of the large window. As they sipped the water, they watched the lights of the traffic moving along the tar road below. In the valley and up the opposite hill, lights came on in the deepening dusk. It looks so tranquil out there, Catherine thought with a sigh. She re-tied her scarf and adjusted her denim jacket against the winter cold. She looked at André.

"Did Neela say 'Back to the bush,' is that what I heard?"

André nodded. "Where did that come from?"

Catherine looked away for a moment. "I wanted to reassure her, tell her no, no, we'd never make anyone live in the bush, least of all that wild place near the airport where she used to live. But she wouldn't stay to talk."

They knew about that place, where Neela's husband, Henry Botha, had her and the child living with him in a shack on open land, among bushes and scrub trees. Along with homeless people like the *bergies,* other people living there informally, not much of a roof over their heads. Probably with thieves all around and cheap drugs and despair. With screaming in the night.

"We'd never send anyone into that," said Catherine. "Especially not a woman with a child."

The child *Klein* Henry, when he was small, was the centre of Neela's life, maybe because husband Henry came and went, along with his occasional jobs and his love for the night life of the shebeens. The child gave her meaning. She was certainly a caring, even doting, mother.

It seemed so easy for her, so easy for all the farm girls and farm women, to fall pregnant. Neela had another boy a few years later. Catherine had tried for a child until she was beyond heartsore. She and André had been hopeful. The doctors did what they could, without success. André was gallant about it; they just had to accept that there would be no children of their own. For Catherine, it made her relationship with her husband all the more important, all the more central to her life.

André turned from the window to look at Catherine. He shook his head, hesitated, and said, "Neela didn't give us a chance to talk it out."

"No; she just jumped to a conclusion and wham. Just as you did, at the start."

André looked taken aback.

Catherine sighed and ran her fingers through her hair. "Well … we should be able to straighten this out, when tempers cool."

"*Ja*," he sighed, "we always have before." He brushed back his hair too, exposing the silver in his hairline.

She knew there had been clashes; not so many, but now and again. The biggest clashes always involved who could stay on this farm. Only one had been really serious, but it too had worked out. Things would be said in the heat of the moment. In a few days tempers would cool and a talk around a table, any table, would sort things out. On one or two occasions André even brought himself to apologise.

"André … do you get the feeling that something is different this time?"

"Not really. Our farm family is here and that's that. The problem is the visitors. Esta and Neela are just being difficult. Maybe they just want to get their own way. They'll get over it."

"You think so. I don't know … . Well, let's just give them a little space. After all, we've had such good working relationships on this farm, for so long."

"They'll come right."

But they didn't come right. The next few days set the tone. They came and went on the farm as usual, right along the little brick pathway between the cottage and the main house, right past the house's windows, but the adults did not speak to Catherine or André. When addressed, they would keep walking and avoid eye contact. Godwin went on with his garden work cheerfully and communicated about farm details as needed, but nothing about any plans of anyone, to stay or to leave. Nor would he be drawn.

The six farm children went on as they normally did, speaking, helping, accompanying the owners on the daily walk with Lola and Jonty and Godwin's dog Ringo. It seemed that the adults allowed them to remain children and did not draw them into their own larger conflict. The teenage boys surely could figure out what the issues were but did not give any indication. They surely had been coached not to discuss farm matters with the owners. Catherine, always careful not to undermine parental authority, did not press the children. Nor did André.

So it was a waiting game.

One evening after work, Catherine was making food at the hob as André poured them each a glass of Thelema chardonnay. He took a seat near the hob for warmth. Lola and Jonty drowsed in their doggie beds close by. As Catherine browned the chicken pieces, she brought up the subject.

"It's been two weeks, André. The folks have been ice cold toward us ever since that meeting."

He sipped his wine and just nodded.

"This morning I saw Neela heading out of the farm and I was going out too. I asked her if she needed a ride to town. She never even looked at me. Just kept going down the road."

"Don't you get it, Cath? They don't want to talk to us at all."

"I'm not used to being snubbed. I feel insulted." Snubbed. Not much experience of that for Catherine, and even less of it in her repertoire of behaviours.

"Well," said André, with a twinkle of mischief in his eye, "it's been rather nice ... ." They both laughed because they shared some resonance to what he implied. The farm people were often knocking at the door for something. The dreaded knock-knock, Catherine named it, because it meant she or he had to stop whatever they were doing immediately and give out something or arrange or plan things that mattered in a different world.

"Not nice, André." She shook her head but smiled in reluctant recognition, and then got serious. "But it's true, in these few weeks there haven't been many demands on us," she said. "That's for sure. For things like small change, loans, taxi money, things for the children for school. Even for flu medicine and headache pills. In fact, none."

"I wonder, Catherine, if they aren't giving us the finger. 'You think we actually need you? Forget it. We can manage on our own, thank you very much.' Asserting independence."

She studied André for a moment. "Maybe. If so, that can't be all bad."

She turned over the chicken pieces. She tried her best to prepare healthy food, to keep those kilograms from piling on to their bodies. The scale always seemed to show a few kilos too many; it was another of life's constant battles.

"Not that we don't want to help," she continued. "We do. Especially when it comes to the children, and to everyday medicines." She offered preventive care as well, supplying disinfectant and cleaning materials to help keep germs at bay.

"*Ja*, you always have something. You are too good to everyone. Still, they must be really full of anger. But why, exactly? I mean, can't they see that if the worker leaves, the one worker that we have here on Bellezicht, everything changes for them? Isn't that what they came to prevent?"

"They seem to believe that we told them all to leave the farm. Which we didn't. But they won't hear that."

"Seems that minds are made up and don't bother with facts."

"A real lack of listening. A lack of trust. After all the years of good relations on this farm." She shook her head. Even the decent wine in their glasses couldn't revive their flagging spirits.

"Well," said André, "we are going on in any case. There is no need to push for anything to happen now. If they still want to play a waiting game, fine. We can wait too."

"I'm not so sure, André. Waiting for things to happen gives me the creeps. It's like an open wound; infection could set in at any time."

He looked at her. "That's you, making a catastrophe out of anything."

"André," she said in exasperation, "we aren't a small isolated farm any more. The whole atmosphere of farming feels like it's changing all around us."

"Well, if so, that's just too bad. I'm not giving in. Not even to you, Catherine."

She ignored "even to you." She knew he could be stubborn. But a trickle of fear rose up inside her. Had something between them changed? "What's this talk, giving in? We have to see the world as they see it. Maybe even adapt."

"That's you, the softie. They just have to live and learn. Finish and *klaar*."

But the fear grew from a trickle to a flood, like red wine spilt on a white blouse. Catherine remembered what had happened to her in Pennsylvania. From a breakup she had thought would never happen to a pain she had thought would never end. Is this how it begins, she wondered, with words thrusting the tip of a threat: "not even to you"?

She knew André was being the boss as best he knew how. She understood that he simply could not allow himself to be seen as weak. Maybe he felt he would drown in other people's demands. Just how do I cope with that, she thought.

Not now, she told herself. There was dinner to get on the table.

~ 2 Some weekends ~

The early years on the farm functioned for Catherine and André as a baptism of fire. Neither had grown up on a farm. But André's grandfather had. As a child, André and his family made occasional visits, but that was all the farming experience he had had. When he and Catherine moved to Bellezicht as owners, running a farm was a new challenge for them both. Catherine wondered if perhaps they had been blinded by the beauty of the mountains and the vines, been too gobsmacked to pay much attention to the dynamics of the farmworker's family.

She was blinded by André too. How amazing it was to live with someone as attentive, as caring, as he was. He would pour a glass of wine for her every evening, after making the glass shine, and he watched to see when to top it up. He always held the door for her and carried her books and her packages. Sometimes when she was going to an evening meeting at the school, he would get her car for her, get music on the radio, and stand patiently to hold the car door and help her in. Then wave until she was out of sight. He was the kind of guy who would lay his coat over a puddle so that she didn't have to step into it.

She loved to be physically close to him. When they drove in his uncle's 1961 Peugeot, which was parked at the farm until Uncle decided what to do with it, she sat in the middle of the bench seat and kept her hand on his knee.

The work week took a lot of their attention. Catherine taught every day at a primary school about 40 minutes away, and tended to after-school activities as part of her job. André drove into Stellenbosch to his office. Both got home late in the day and they were out early the next morning. Isaac and his wife Laetitia and their family were alone at Bellezicht.

It had been so nice, so good, she thought, when we did work together, especially in the old days. Friendly greetings in the mornings and evenings. Isaac, Godwin's grandfather and their first worker, always looked up from his work among the vines to note comings and goings, to give a wave, to come and receive a delivery, to help carry packages inside. People didn't enter the farm unchallenged. He and Laetitia kept their eyes on things to see that the manor house was properly closed and locked while André and Catherine were at work or away. If a drain blocked up in the middle of the night, Isaac would be there, working it open again. When rains came down too heavily, Isaac in his rain gear would be out in it, sloshing through the mud, to be sure the runoff did not burst its banks. Besides flooding the vines, the rainwater could seriously erode the farm roads, carving deep ruts that made them impassable even by tractor. But not on Isaac's watch. The older generation, Isaac and Laetitia, were something special.

But weekends were another story, with constant churning Friday evening to Monday morning, and often that churn spilled onto their veranda and into their lives.

It was never quite clear where the *dagga* came from, the marijuana that seemed to grow nowhere and yet was everywhere. Or where the tik was bought. Or even the alcohol, after André stopped giving it to Isaac along with the weekly wages. It was not clear how they paid for it all. The women were not party to getting drunk or drugging, definitely a plus. Nor did they work outside the home anyway, except now and again, mainly in the few weeks when there was harvesting to be done. So the money didn't come from them.

Somehow, the men must have managed to keep some money back. They must have sent down to the shebeen, an open shack under the bluegum trees of a neighbouring farm, for their "special takeaways". They did not seem to go there themselves. One could see the bar counter and a few chairs dimly from the tar road when driving back home from Stellenbosch. The shebeen sat within the grouping of informal shacks near the small cash store down the road. Of course, farmers never went there. Obviously it was easy for the farm men to order what they wanted.

Some weekends in those early years were downright horrible. One drama-laden weekend loomed large in Catherine's memory. That Saturday brought huge fluffy clouds strolling along just above the mountains. André and Catherine had had a bit of extra sleep and, after brunch on the veranda, they were sitting there making plans for the week. Suddenly there were sounds of shouting, of doors slamming.

Catherine was startled. "What's that noise?" she said, glancing around anxiously.

"Don't tell me there's fighting again!" André frowned. "Now what. It sounds like Isaac ... yes, it's him. He sounds drunk as a lord."

He got up and strode to the back, Catherine right behind him. Isaac stood on the little rise beside the cottage, glaring at the *werf*, the yard in front. His small compact body was tensed up. In his hand he held an upraised panga. The rust on the huge machete-like knife made it look even more lethal. Laetitia faced him from a safe distance.

"*Baas, jy moet ons help!*" she screamed. "Help us!" The other women stayed inside the cottage, and the children milled in and out, frightened looks on their faces.

"He's beyond all reasoning." André in his protector role assessed the situation. "Go back to our house and be sure everything is closed up. I'll handle him."

"Please, André, be careful! Don't get too close. Please!" She knew that being macho was not part of his nature, but even innocent protectors can be drawn in. Despite her pleading, André waved her back down the path between the garage and the cottage. Then he stepped slowly to one side of the rise, his eyes on Isaac. He picked up a large stick. It was nothing against a panga, but it was there.

Laetitia moved carefully away from the cottage, away from Isaac, away from André. Isaac's eyes followed her. Then he turned to go after her. She moved quickly down the same path Catherine had taken, Isaac after her, but not able to move so fast. The panga became heavy against his arm. André moved to stand on the little rise near the cottage, the better to see, and the better to protect the people still holed up in the cottage.

Sheryl stepped tentatively out of the cottage and scooted the other way, around the garage, and met up with her mother. Together they drew Isaac down the path beside the rows of vines. Laetitia was too large a woman to run, but she turned into the driveway and half-ran, half-walked out of the farm property. The ends of the yellow *doek* on her head flounced along behind her. Sheryl ran out between the rows of vines, parallel to her mother. The weeds and uneven ground slowed her down, as did her long flowered skirt. Isaac seemed confused – which one should he follow? He chose his daughter and it was not easy going for him either, with his heavy boots over the small plowed mounds of earth.

Catherine watched from the window. Sheryl was just like a mother *kiewiet*, the small plover that they'd seen on evening walks, pretending to have a broken wing and enticing the dogs after her, then taking to the air, luring the danger away from her nest on the ground.

Between them, Laetitia and Sheryl led Isaac on a not-so-merry chase through the vineyard and up the farm road. Isaac shouted some obscene words, lifting the panga high. Finally he stumbled on a stone or a root and fell heavily to the ground. The panga landed just beyond his easy reach. He did not get up.

Catherine and everyone else emerged. She went back to gauge the effect of the threat on the children. "*Is almal ok*? Is everyone all right?" To her surprise, they nodded. The children's eyes darted around nervously but they did not seem terrorised.

"Time for some *koeldrank*, with ice," she said. Then there were smiles as she gathered them into her house.

André walked up to where Isaac lay. He found the panga, picked it up and moved away. Laetitia and Sheryl waited nearby. Eventually, they got Isaac to his feet and, between them, walked him back to the cottage and put him to bed.

There was no need to call the police that day. But on other days the police were the only solution. On another late Saturday morning, Laetitia appeared at the low dining room window, which was at the smaller stoep at the front entrance to the house.

"*Baas, Isaac raak mal!* He's acting crazy! He's drunk!" André went back and spoke softly but forcefully. Talking to him calmed him a bit, but any logic was wasted.

"Let's see if that works," André said. "Cheers, again." They resumed their early lunch.

Catherine took a deep breath. Her heart went out to the farm family, having to live with a breadwinner who gave his kindness and his salary to them during the week but on many weekends took it all back.

Shortly afterward, Laetitia was back. *"Isaac het 'n knopkierie en hy maak ons bang.* That club of his could really hurt us." André went back again, and managed to coax the club from Isaac. Actually it was a walking stick but so thick that he could use it as a weapon. And worse, one of his sons was also out of control, ranting against the women and children.

"Do you want us to call the police?" asked André.

"Nee, Baas, kom ons gaan aan met probeer. No, let's just keep trying."

"That poor woman," Catherine said, when André came back.

"I don't know why he does that," said André.

"That's the trouble with family violence. They always take it out on the women, on the people who are their nearest and dearest."

"I don't know what to do about it," frowned André.

"We're getting desperate for a social worker. The police surely have someone."

André shook his head. "But if you want, I'll phone them on Monday."

Catherine nodded. It wasn't much use, she felt, but worth a try. "Maybe the drinking is the problem. Isaac only does these things when he's drunk. In the week he is the most pleasant of persons."

"Well, we drink too," said André. "The last time I talked to him about his drinking, he got defensive. He said to me, 'Look at all the wine that comes into your house!' "

"He's right in a way," she commented. "Can't we tell him that we drink but we don't get drunk and fight?"

"That's true. If you drink a little too much, you just go to sleep."

"You – you just get happier."

He chuckled to see the truth in her observation. "Alcohol use but not alcohol abuse."

As they lingered after lunch, Laetitia showed up at the window for the third time, her face drawn, her eyes with dark circles under them. She had exhausted her options. *"Baas, ons is moeg. Bel die polisie."*

So eventually the police came, three o'clock on a Saturday afternoon, two young officers from different language groups. They went to the cottage, assessed the situation, and took Isaac in. Things then got quiet and peace returned to Bellezicht. The police phoned the next morning.

"Meneer, u kan vir Isaac kom haal. You can come now and take him home. He's slept it off."

André drove back to the farm, with a hung-over and sad-faced Isaac sitting beside him in the bakkie. Back Isaac went, into the forgiving arms of his wife.

Unfortunately this was a pattern for many weekends. It never really stopped but, as Isaac got older, the violent part seemed to fade and by that time Godwin had stepped into his job.

When the farm family had a problem, Catherine and even André would go to hear and try to help. When Neela's husband came home with a big gash in his foot from a bicycle gone wrong, Catherine sat him in her dining room while she brought a container of warm water to soak the foot. She cleaned it and gave it a gentle wrapping before she persuaded André to drive him in to the emergency room.

André had said, "Catherine, are you like Jesus washing the feet of his disciples?"

"Rather like Mary, pouring myrrh on his wounds." They knew their Bible, and so did the farm family. That was a bit of common ground. Henry smiled beneath his pain and lapped up the attention.

Catherine's mind flipped back to the present, the grim present. Maybe now, the parting of the Red Sea would be a good image, she thought, with us on one side and them on the other.

That is not the way she wanted to think. She tried hard to be inclusive. Despite occasional glitches, farmers and workers on this farm enjoyed a certain unity, working together in their own ways for a successful farm.

Granted, the farmers were in the more powerful position, but that shouldn't make them the baddies. There is always somebody more powerful, no matter who you are; that's just the way life is. As Bob Dylan sings, "you're gonna have to serve somebody."

Had they ever abused that power? How would we know, she asked herself. She couldn't imagine a farmworker or anyone living in the farm cottage coming to her to complain of abuse of power. Especially not to complain to André.

There was an incident in which Neela did come to complain, about pay. Her husband Henry had made an oral agreement with André. Henry wanted Neela and himself and their son to stay in a small outside room attached to the manor house that in the past had been built as a maid's quarters. André used it as a storeroom. It was small but it had electricity and maybe offered some privacy from life in the cottage. Henry said he would work a few hours on Saturdays for the use of the room. One Saturday, after his work on a warm day, André gave him a cold beer. Neela came angrily to the front door and confronted André.

"He works all morning and all he gets is a beer? I need money for food."

"What did Henry do with his pay yesterday?" Henry worked elsewhere, sometimes on a farm and sometimes as a painter's assistant.

"I don't know. All I know is Henry worked this morning and all he got was a beer." She repeated, "I need money for food. For the children."

André realised that Henry had not explained their informal arrangement. To his credit, he saw that she was asking for something basic, and not just for herself but for her family. He got his wallet and found something for her. After that, he just allowed Henry's family the use of the room gratis.

"At least Henry did offer to work for it," he told Catherine.

André was generous. However, he did hold power. Yes; but was the fact of power also an abuse of power? Catherine felt troubled in her soul by the inequality of farmer and farmworker. She'd heard of white guilt; was it that? She often wondered how people can have so little and she can have so much. Such a distressing thought; she confronted it daily. But what could you do about it? What could you do in a lasting way?

She had grown up in a struggling household that had less than her friends had. Her mother somehow managed so that she and her brother and sister had what they needed, however basic. The lesson was to work for it. She started working in a nearby shop after school, at age 14, with her parents' legally signed permission. She gave her wages to the family. Her mother gave her about a dollar back, to save, which she did.

She saw so many farm men work long hours every day. There seemed to be always so many people to take care of that saving was not possible. How could their work give them what they wanted? She could not see a way out of their dilemma, even with excellent wages for unskilled work. How could they and the owners become more equal? Could this be termed abuse of power?

Somehow this trouble with the visitors was much more than a spat. The world of us versus the world of them. Maybe it was not so sudden. Maybe fault lines were lurking under the surface all along, and an earthquake struck, like a meeting gone wrong, and the underground chasm surfaced, with huge damage. Farmers on one side and workers on the other. It was deeply disturbing but there it was. How she wished it could be different.

~ 3 Godwin ~

Godwin was born to Sheryl while she was still living at Bellezicht. He modelled himself on his grandfather and what a blessing that was. Isaac had shown Godwin how it's done in the vineyard, giving a day's work for a day's wages. Isaac used his wristwatch and was on the job promptly at 06:00, the usual starting time on farms. He stopped for farmworker breakfast time 09:00 – 09:30, went back to the job until break at 11:00, on to lunch 13:00 – 14:00, on to break at 16:00, on to *tjaila* at 18:00.

Godwin was a gentle fellow. He patterned his own workday to be just like Isaac's. Now it was 2005 and André got modern and reduced the workday to 8 hours, not 10 hours. Godwin seemed neutral about it – work is work. He was on the job promptly at 07:30, took proper breaks, and finished at 16:00. He kept to this schedule despite the conflict over the visitors. Like his grandfather, he did not let differences interfere with his job.

When Godwin was little, Isaac had drawn him into farm work just as a parent (or grandparent) includes their child in whatever work they are doing. Godwin never knew his father, but Isaac filled that role. One day when Godwin was about nine years old, Catherine arrived home to see the two of them working on the lawn, sitting there bent over hand tools, leaning a bit toward each other as over an intimate space, and popping out broadleaf weeds. This warm human scene, framed by a blue dome of sky above, crystal-clear mountains in the background and thick green grass as a carpet, made Catherine run for her camera to capture the moment.

Another time, a moment she was too late to capture, Isaac had been working with a rented tractor at cultivating time. Bellezicht was too small to own such an expensive item; when one chugged onto the farm, the power and noise of it pulled everyone in. Up the road the tractor rattled, and perched there high up, sharing the driver's seat in front of Isaac, was an ecstatic little Godwin.

As he grew older, he began to help Isaac more and more, with watering the flowers in gardens and pots, sweeping up the leaves, and hosing down the front stoep and the veranda. He was happy in this work and he tried to do it well. Catherine began to pay him for his gardening work. She even stopped Anna Solomons, the woman who helped her in the house one day per week, from sweeping the stoep so that young Godwin would have another way to earn some cash for his pocket. Anna herself took an interest in Godwin. She got him to help her in the house when using the heavy polisher, as he was tall and strong for his age. He loved it. She would scold him if his hair was not neat enough and he would smile and immediately go and make it right.

Catherine herself had grown up in America with such a tradition of work. It was not child labour; nothing related to farming was expected of young Godwin, and of course school came first. But she saw it as the beginning of autonomy, as a way for a young person to understand that first you work and then you get money and then you can do with it what you like. "Don't ask for money; ask for work," was her mantra. "Then you are free."

But this sequence wasn't in the farm tradition. There was more of a dependence. Ask and hope it would come your way. Ask for a loan and hope the farmer would give you what you wanted. Promise to repay it but hope he or she would eventually forget about it.

Whatever few rands Godwin earned, his grandmother Laetitia, who ran their household and who was in the place of mother for him, would take the money. "For bread," she explained. For the group, not for the individual. What could any boy say to that? How could he be encouraged if he never felt the benefits of his labour? Catherine looked for a way around it. She wanted to contribute to their lives but not take over. Children always wanted things. She discussed it with Laetitia and Isaac.

"If Godwin does his chores, perhaps you could let me save his money for him. That way, if he wants something like a music player or trendy shoes, he can buy it for himself. Then he won't be asking you for these rather expensive things." They nodded.

Catherine wondered if it was a rather new way of thinking. They were used to living from hand to mouth, spending everything that came in. Perhaps they did it so that others could not ask it of them. Perhaps it was just the way that poor people think. Of course, they needed the money. Doesn't everyone?

That was one thing that André approved of – saving. "Every time Godwin saves, he creates wealth," he told Catherine.

"Wealth? With just a small number of rands?"

"Yes. If he doesn't consume it, it is there, and it is wealth. Just multiply his saving behaviour and then we will have a wealthy country."

"Like Japan?"

He laughed. "That's the idea."

So Godwin's money added up. Catherine kept meticulous records of every rand Godwin earned, including dates and job. She also knew not to wait too long for payoff. She got André to agree that they could add to it. When Godwin was about 12, she looked around for a bicycle.

They had already bought a bicycle for farm use. The children were quite excited and they all had to learn to ride it. Which they did, right in Bellezicht's driveway, tilting over, falling off, but eventually learning to balance. They were thrilled. Every child wanted to work and save money for their own bicycle. But with just one bike there had to be turn-taking, and there were inevitable squabbles of who could ride when, for how long. The best thing was to manage a bike for each older child, starting with the oldest, Godwin. Private ownership would bring about responsibility, Catherine assumed.

Catherine shopped around and found a bike, a second-hand one that was within financial reach, and brought it home in their bakkie. She called André to come to the front door, and asked Laetitia, Isaac and Godwin to come into the house, the day being windy and cold. Such a meeting was not usual and no one was quite sure what to expect. She was ready for the ceremony. They all stood in the entrance hall.

Catherine wheeled out the bike from its hiding place in the laundry room. "This bicycle is now Godwin's. He has worked for it. He has earned the money to pay for it. We have added some money also, and now it is his to use, his to take care of, his to lend or not."

André joined in. "Owning a bike is very nice. But it takes responsibility too. The owner has to keep the tyres inflated, keep the chain in good order, keep it clean and oiled. Are you ready to do this?"

Godwin and his grandparents chorused, "*Ja, Meneer.*" Almost like a wedding. Do you, Godwin, take this bike, to have and to hold … ?

Godwin's eyes shone. He reached over slowly, respectfully, and took the handlebars in his hands. He adjusted the feel of it. Then he looked at Catherine and uttered a soft and deeply heartfelt "*Dankie, Missus.*"

Smiles all around. Even André was touched.

Godwin spent his first 10 days in hospital, with some of that time in an incubator, before his mother Sheryl brought him home to the farm. Sheryl, like so many farm girls, was probably the object of pursuit by the local boys. With her flirty eyes and her lithe figure, she didn't seem reluctant to be caught. Her mother could not see her everywhere. Farm country had lots of bushes and trees and often girls just got "taken" and they were helpless to do much about it.

While still living at Bellezicht, Sheryl had borne her daughter Trina and then Godwin and while they were still little she left the farm and her children as well to seek her fortune elsewhere. These two chidren never knew their fathers.

Sheryl had tried to be a good mother. When Godwin was an infant, she cared for him as her life style would allow. When it was harvest time, every adult in the family was needed to snip off the bunches of grapes. There is an optimal period when the grapes are ripe and they can't wait, when the sugar rises and the acid falls and the balance is right. Every day, every hour, makes a difference.

At that harvest time when Godwin was just a baby, Sheryl harvested along with her family. Even Laetitia snipped quickly, many harvest years of practice to her benefit. Each hour got hotter under the summer sun. This kind of work is no joke when the day gets long and the sun gets strong. Catherine knew this from experience; she herself helped to pick in the first harvest she spent at Bellezicht. Of course, harvest wages were good.

That harvest year, no one remained at the cottage so Sheryl carried her infant to the vineyard and laid him in a grape crate. Not in a manger as for husbanded animals, but in a small, orange-coloured plastic crate for gathering newly-harvested grapes. As she clipped off each bunch, she tossed it into her own crate for grapes, which she would get paid for, by the crate. As she worked, she pulled the grape crate behind her, and she also pulled behind her the crate cradling her baby son. She made sure to keep both crates in the shade of the fully-grown leaves of the vines. Godwin was a cared-for baby.

But now, Godwin was a man. Sheryl's life had moved up and down and around and she was back at Bellezicht. You would never know they were mother and son, despite the fact that they shared the small cottage. Sheryl had never succeeded in bonding with Trina or with Godwin. Catherine wondered if there is a critical period for such bonding. If it doesn't happen when children are small enough, maybe it doesn't happen at all.

This new time of trouble with the latest visitors, this time of shouting and strife, of anger and fear, made Catherine reflect all the more on Godwin and his life and his history at Bellezicht. He was born here; surely he belonged here, even as an adult.

But the circumstances had changed. The older generation had died. Laetitia had passed away the year before, and Isaac, a year before her. Bellezicht was struggling to get help with farming the vines. It seemed normal to André that Godwin would just take over. But there was little chance of upward mobility on such a small farm. The real question for Catherine was what Godwin could do to make a decent living, outside of vineyard or garden work.

When Godwin was in primary school, he struggled to learn and was not passing his standard. Sitting down with him to deal with homework did not seem to help. Catherine had him tested at the psychology unit of the University. They found he really couldn't do the work; the problem was something cognitive. Yet he went to school every day, he was cooperative and even very helpful to the teachers and to his peers. His gentle spirit, his kindness to other people, rose to the fore. He was, as the testing people called him, " *'n ware heer,*" a true gentleman. He was also known as *"die ou wat spaar,"* the chap who saves. Obviously he was proud of himself for that.

When he finished primary school, having repeated a few years there, the high school deemed him too old to attend there. They advised him to get a job. But what sort of job? Catherine took him again for tests, this time for aptitude. Results showed that he liked working with plants, and he liked working with bricks, perhaps because he had helped André lay a brick path. Yes, even André the economist got his hands dirty from time to time.

The plant aptitude pointed to vines. Despite his closeness to Isaac, Godwin was not interested in the job that Isaac had held for 18 years at Bellezicht before his retirement. Isaac had been working on the farm when the Steenkamps bought it. It was the work he had done on many other farms before that. He had come to love vines and he just seemed to be in sync with them. If she had been in Godwin's place, Catherine thought, she would have loved the vines but she would also have found it overwhelming to be responsible for 10 000 of them, not to mention taking out weeds, treating for pests and managing all the pipes and sprayers and wires and taps that go with farm irrigation. Even though Isaac had done all that and more, maybe to Godwin it felt an impossible task.

Well, the aptitude testing showed also that Godwin liked bricks. What about training as a paver? Catherine phoned around and discovered courses at a technical college in Cape Town. Yes, he could get a tailored course and the fee, okay, she and André would pick it up. The training even included some bricklaying. Transport, always a problem for farm people, could be worked out.

Laetitia and Isaac were not so enthusiastic. "What if he is in trouble, so far from home? How could we protect him?" Catherine realised that farm families stayed near one another. Isaac, living at Bellezicht, lived within ten kilometres of where he was born. The idea of going away to study anything was just not in their way of thinking. But for paving it was the only option. So she arranged a visit to the college for Laetitia and Isaac and showed them around, showing them where the train stopped, very close by.

"The train! No. There is so much violence on the trains. We can't let Godwin do that."

Catherine could feel Godwin's training slipping down a muddy slope into the sea. So she drove him to and from the college for several days, and meanwhile found an instructor who also drove this way and who agreed to pick him up and drop him off daily, for a fee, of course.

Godwin finished the course and then it was job time. Again, Catherine phoned around locally and he had a few jobs, but for various reasons each job didn't work out. Catherine noticed him at home. It turned out he just quit going. No discussion with anyone. Why?

First, he had to find very early transport from the farm into Stellenbosch, not easy, and then get back at the end of the day. There were no easy taxi routes along that road. Then, he didn't like the work situation. "They swear," he said.

"Farmworkers don't swear?" asked Catherine.

André was astute. "They probably swear at him," he said later.

"Poor Godwin. He tries so hard. It's just that he is inexperienced."

"In paving and in the ways of the workplace. He has never really worked anywhere but the farm."

"He needs a father or a kindly uncle to take him under his wing."

"Fathers on farms are scarce, and uncles too."

There may have been another reason. It was not work requiring much education, education against prejudice, and prejudice comes in many ways. Many of the other workers spoke another language, another one of the 11 official South African languages. Godwin came from a different, Afrikaans-speaking group. How to fit in, when those old apartheid-based groups still seemed to thrive with a life of their own?

Well, what else could he do to earn a living? Whatever the answer turned out to be, she knew he would be helped by having a valid driver's license. So she phoned around once more.

Catherine herself wanted to pay for individual tutoring and driving practice for him to get his driver's license. She did that. She very much wanted him to find his work niche in life. His future, she felt, must be better than his past. Not to control him but to help him be able to stand on his own two feet.

Getting his license was quite a story. He really couldn't read the training manual, so the driving instructor, retired from the traffic department, came regularly and took him through it bit by painstaking bit. The two of them sat at the dining room table in the afternoons at Bellezicht and worked. When the instructor said he was ready, after many weeks, Godwin sat for the written test. Being a slow reader, he said he didn't have time to finish the test, even though it was multiple choice. He didn't pass. So the instructor said to ask for an oral test.

Catherine took Godwin to the traffic department to ask. She knew she couldn't send him alone. Many farm people can be put off too easily by bureaucracy. Come back tomorrow, the right person is in Cape Town today, sorry but it's lunch time and we are closed until two o'clock. And so on. Even stalwart Anna, who helped Catherine in the house, said that if she had to go into a bank and talk to an official there, even if she had only to walk into the bank, she would just cry. It was much more stressful than drawing money from the ATM outside the bank.

Godwin and Catherine were told they had to see a certain officer, please wait. When he finally arrived and sailed into his office, passing them sitting on a hard bench waiting, she could feel the ill-tempered vibes. She decided they had to go in on their knees. She put on her most obsequious manner and at least they got a hearing. What power an angry government official can wield.

After all that, the officer said that he could not give permission for an oral test but that they had to write a letter to the department in Cape Town. She wrote the letter. Many weeks later the reply came denying the request; only if the learner was illiterate would they give an oral exam. So after getting Godwin's consent, she wrote the next required letter and many more weeks later, they had a yes. Eventually Godwin passed the "written" part.

Then came the driving part, with the instructor putting his own car forward for Godwin to practise. He failed the first test as often happens to learner drivers. After more coaching and another go at it, Godwin had his license and with it, more access to future jobs. The whole process had taken over a year.

Godwin was now more empowered in the workplace but jobs were still not easy to find. A bit here at a lawn company, a bit there at a plant nursery, but it wasn't enough and there was no future, it seemed, anywhere. So André kept Godwin on as gardener, and along with him, the whole family. Change brought instability and keeping farm things stable was high on André's list.

By now, with the older generation gone and their sons off to other farms, Godwin was the breadwinner for the cottage, the only steady one. But he still didn't seem to have much say inside the cottage, not with strong-minded Esta around. Catherine thought about her daring André to stop the farm family taking in three more people. She did it by playing games, saying the visitors would leave but they never left. The teenage visitors had dropped out of school probably after primary school; facts were hard to get, especially when there were various versions of the story. There was no real history for them at Bellezicht.

Truth. In war, truth is the first casualty, said Churchill, often quoted by André. Was it always war on the farms? Did workers and their families need to hide continually from the farmer? Was a story really necessary for survival? In the end, it can happen that no one knows the truth, not even the person speaking. If this kind of objective truth really does exist.

Two of the three visitors seemed to be basically adults. They were not employed and hardly employable, except for farm jobs, which were getting fewer all the time. There was no effort to go back to school for evening classes or even day classes. There seemed to be no reason for them to live at Bellezicht except for Esta's insistence. Their background was not shared with André or Catherine. They stayed phantoms, quiet and behind the scenes. The future did not look good for them. It looked even worse than for Godwin.

So Godwin went on gardening at Bellezicht and the impasse continued.

~ 4 Night ~

S omething wasn't right. To Catherine, coming home from her job late one evening and driving in between the rows of grapevines, she heard what sounded like a furious chorus of 50 people shouting. With antagonism now on the farm, she felt a trickle of fear; what was happening?

As she approached, she realized there were only two voices, soprano and alto, point and counterpoint, and it was not a happy song. It seemed spontaneous, yet somehow well rehearsed, perhaps through years of complaints repeated around evening fires at the hearths of farmworker cottages. It got louder as she approached, varying only from intense to more intense.

It was Esta and Neela. The two women waved their arms, lifted and bent their heads, and stomped their feet, each one in a separate dance but still partnering the other. What were they shouting? Catherine could not make sense of it. One would start, then the other would interrupt, and then the first one would interrupt the second one. They rolled out continuous waves of loud sound, centimeters from the closed door. Coming home from a long parent-teacher event at the school, she felt immensely hungry, tired and cold in the wintery August night. Her adrenalin heightened. They are right at our door, she thought; must I turn around and drive out again?

The white terrier ran out to the car, with Lola following, both wagging their tails in delight. Not worried by the shouting, they gave her courage. She climbed tentatively out of the car and stood watching, shielded by the open car door, the dogs licking her hands and legs. The women ignored her.

The ends of their *doeke* flowed out as they turned around and thrust their heads this way and that. It was as if they were toyi-toying, these two short plump women, Neela wearing slippers and Esta in jeans and lace-up boots. Their words were unintelligible but anger spewed out from their tone as well as their actions.

Like nearly all farmworking families in the Western Cape, they called themselves Cape coloured, descendants of people white, indigenous, and black, whose relationships have mixed the races for hundreds of years in the most human of ways. Catherine saw them shouting toward each other, but she knew that the two women were really shouting at André, and at her too.

Shouting at the farmers! That was definitely not usual for Catherine and André in the sixteen years since they bought the farm. A wedge of light widened onto the farm women as André, inside the house, opened the door. "What the eff?" she called to him, feeling her brow contract. The women kept it up, a whirl of shouts spinning around the two of them.

The atmosphere felt heavy, dark and most of all, foreign. André waited for her, and after a long look, she slipped carefully around the angry dancers and melted into the cold house. Still not safe. The shouting followed her, first louder, then muted after André slammed the door. But ominously still going on.

The sky above was clear, the southern cross big across the African darkness. Millions of stars seemed to stand there like spectators transfixed, as if also seeing something strange. Inside, the simmering curry stew made her long for a merciful end to the conflict. She tried to move on, loosening the clip and shaking out her honey-toned hair. A bit of relief, a bit of display, as if she were shaking off the shouting.

"The nonsense started earlier this evening," André said. "First they came to the door in anger and demanded a report. A report of that meeting a few weeks ago."

"The meeting that went horribly wrong."

"It was a strange request. Of all the meetings we've had, now they come and ask for a written report. They've never done that before."

"A report. Hmm. Actually, Neela had asked me in an oblique way, but I just didn't take it seriously. She wouldn't say who the report was for, or why they wanted it. I couldn't understand what kind of report they wanted and then just didn't get around to finding out more."

"Well, tonight they were demanding, not asking. Really annoying. Who the hell do they think they are, coming to the door and demanding?" A flush of anger started up his cheeks. "Just to get them off my back while I was waiting for you, I dashed off a one-page report as best I could recall."

"Ah. Seems like it hasn't worked." Seeing his frown, Catherine softened. "But why now?"

"I don't have a clue." The outside chants grew louder. He should have a clue, Catherine thought, but she didn't voice it. Better at the moment to keep a united front.

She walked to their bedroom at the back of the house to take off her boots. She thought of that meeting weeks ago that went so wrong. It was definitely strange. They had held many meetings with the farm people in the course of the work year, as needed and as requested by either side, worker's family and owners. There was a yearly meeting in January, the farm's little Annual General Meeting, in which any issues were discussed and at which the yearly raise in wages was happily announced. All the adults were invited and most pitched up. Catherine made *rooibos* tea and offered rusks, *beskuit,* with it. She usually drew up an agenda in Afrikaans, cleared with André for correctness, and took the meeting's notes.

Growing up in America, she'd never heard of Afrikaans. By now, she'd learned enough to ask, toward the end of those meetings, "*Is daar nog iets wat op julle hart sit?* Is there anything else that bothers you?" She'd been teaching long enough to know that there's just no alternative to dialogue when it comes to getting people to work together, be they little people in the classroom or big ones anywhere else. On this small wine farm, shared goals were needed if they wanted to live and work harmoniously.

Yes, harmony. It had to be possible, somehow. Everyone getting most of what they want, making their peace, yet still striving for something better. Wants keep us striving, says André the economist. Needs are basic and can be filled, but wants ... never filled. Needs are finite, he preaches, but wants are infinite. People have rights about basic needs, but not about wants. Economics is about needs, he says, but cannot deal systematically with wants. Especially in the context of Africa, this distinction seems crucial. Governments can address needs, even overwhelming needs, but wants, no. There are too many wants; simply out of the question.

They now had a report. Why hadn't it satisfied them?

Absent-mindedly she set down her tote bag with rosters and lists of marks, with folders for the learners, with more classbooks to be evaluated. Dinner stood ready on the hob, thanks to Anna, dear Anna. Anna lived in the town and when she came once a week, she cooked in addition to all the cleaning and ironing. This afternoon she'd made a Cape dish with lamb and potatoes, its Malaysian aromas filling the dining area, just off the front door. It was very late. But there seemed to be a mountain to climb before they could spoon the curry over the yellow rice and be warmed and filled.

"Surely we can sort this out," Catherine said as she returned to the kitchen. André just leaned on the counter, saying nothing. "Let's try again, let's invite them in, let's sit down and talk." He glared at her, his hazel-green eyes like bullets, but didn't say no.

She turned and strode to the front door, yanked it open and tried to speak, but the waves of angry sound tumbled her words like bathers caught in the surf. What they were shouting wasn't clear but there was no mistaking the hostile tone.

She waved her hand in a gesture of come in, welcome. They just ignored her and kept on. Yes, she thought, standing at the door, her head tilted as she struggled to comprehend, this is our home, our territory; to come in would ask politeness, and politeness tonight was out of the question. They came to the stoep but still they are ignoring us. Definitely not usual on a wine farm in South Africa.

The ranting was in Afrikaans, the mother tongue of most farmworkers in the Western Cape, and also one of the two mother tongues of André, along with English. Catherine was a speaker of English (or rather, of American but not English, as friends teased). She took classes in Afrikaans whenever she could find them. She could manage normal conversation, but this conversation was definitely not normal and she just could not make sense out of the menacing stream of words coming their way.

"Even I can't make sense out of all this shouting," said André, rubbing her shoulder sympathetically. It's an avalanche full of ice and rocks."

"It's got to be about their belief, mistaken as it is, that they were told to move out. But let's try again," she urged André. His body angled away from her; his face was a picture of disgust. He kept glancing toward the stew.

"André, I know you're hungry, but I know also that something radical has to be done here or worse things might happen."

On TV she had seen pictures of mob 300 action, of people stoning the homes of others, of chanters raising knobkerries in a threatening gesture. Burning tyres. Things like that had been unknown on farms, but … there was a new ambience of rising militancy, of unions gaining a foothold, of a culture of demanding rights, whether one has them or not.

There was certainly some justification for general anger, she could see that, given generations and even centuries of farmworkers being treated as if they had no rights at all. No one can escape history. But that was then; things were different now, more than 10 years after President Mandela took charge. New laws, new policies had been put in place to favour the people who had been so disadvantaged in South Africa's troubled past.

"André," she said, "you know that I believe in dialogue, so that needs and wants can be addressed. We have to talk with them. At least they have finally burst out of their silence." He turned his head away.

She went on anyway, a speaker to a hostile audience. "Come on, André. We mustn't let things get even worse, so that that dialogue becomes impossible."

But impossible it looked, late that evening. Even her husband had become impossible. Try, she kept saying to herself; try again; try to find another approach.

"André, talk to them in Afrikaans, so that we can begin to understand what the issue is now." She opened the door, to that avalanche which seemed to roll them flat.

André strode over and slammed the door again. "For the first time I'm flummoxed. I can deal with a board room full of difficult business executives, but this … ." He turned and stomped down the passage deeper into the house.

Catherine stood there looking at the chanting, stomping women through the window. Was she the only one not stomping? André walked back into the kitchen and began to set the table. She reluctantly drew the curtains, shutting out the sight of the angry women.

Then – the ranting died into silence. After a minute or two, she peeked out of the side of the curtain and there was Neela, flanked by Esta, standing there with a paper in her hand. "André! Come quickly."

He came dragging his feet and opened the door again. The ranting resumed but this time it morphed into more comprehensible shouting. "*Hierdie verslag is sleg! Waar sê dit ons moet weggaan! Ons wil dit hê, swart op wit!*" ("This report is bad; where does it say we have to move off the farm? We want a report that says it clearly; in black and white!") Neela slapped the paper with her hand as their eyes threw flame, mouths twisted down, hands and feet still churning. He closed the door quickly.

"Neela, the shy, unassertive one, with the heavy-lidded eyes. The one with not much to say. Look at her now. She's unrecognizable."

She looked at André for translation. He said, slowly, "They want a clear statement that they have to move off this farm. They want us to say something that we didn't say."

It took her a moment to realize the situation. "So they want us to say we are evicting them. They obviously want to fight it, but whatever activists are behind this resistance, this anger – they want a clear fight. They want proof of eviction before they march, or whatever they plan to do."

They looked at each other with dawning comprehension. "Yes," he replied, "they're no fools."

She opened the door yet again, cautiously, and tried to speak loudly to the noisy pair outside. "Can we discuss this tomorrow, around the table?" They answered by resuming their actions. "Can we talk now? We didn't tell you all to leave." She waited, and waited some more, but their minds and bodies were set along a certain path. André pushed past her and closed the door firmly and snapped the lock into place.

He poured two glasses of red wine, then sat down for dinner and waited elaborately for her to join him. Finally, finally, the sound and fury moved away toward the cottage, to one side of the main house. Other people from the cottage joined the two women, making the shouting louder. The words were indistinguishable but there was no mistaking the messages in the tone. They all kept it up, led by Neela and Esta, for a long time.

Catherine didn't feel like joining André. He was with her, and not with her. But the hour was late, the aromas were seductive, and tiredness drew her to the chair. "André, isn't this strange – most farmworkers would put up a fight if they were told to leave the farm. Now, our people are fighting because they were not told to leave the farm." She looked past him for a moment. "Whatever politicos are behind this want a clear fight."

André glanced at her as he piled his fork high. "Let's see how things look in the morning." She gave him a stare. He kept his eyes focused on his plate, and then took his first bite. She picked up her knife and fork.

André stacked the dinner plates in the dishwasher with a vengeance, ignoring the continuing shouting, while she tidied up the kitchen, nervously keeping one eye on the window.

"André, those dishes are going to break, the way you are slamming them in."

"All this ranting, and you are worried about the stupid dishes?" he responded. "Let them bloody well break!" For emphasis he pushed the silverware into the basket with a loud clank. A teaspoon slipped onto the floor. Red in the face, he stamped it flat. She stood there, dishcloth in hand, glaring at him.

"Hey, that's my spoon! I know you are on edge, André, but really. You're getting scary." Her voice quavered as she looked at the flattened spoon.

She had never seen him so out of control. She realised with a start that he must feel pushed to the edge. Would his temper ever come her way?

After a moment he turned toward her. "This is something new, Catherine," he said, his voice less sharp. "Everything has changed. There is aggression here and I don't get where it's coming from."

"Everything has changed. Still, we have to try to talk to them at some point."

"Not if they behave like that." His face reddened even more, his eyes narrowed. "Shouting at the farmer! It's unheard of. Where is their respect? In the old days, the farmer would just take the *sjambok* to them and give them some lashes. Show them who's boss."

"That's assault! Don't even think about it! We have to clarify their issues and then address the root cause."

"How are we going to do that, when they won't talk to us?"

"I don't know. But we have to find a way out of this mess, and it takes both sides. It doesn't work to impose solutions."

"Oh, so now we are in negotiations? Forget it!" He went on. "This nonsense has to stop, and now."

"André. This is a side of you that I don't know. So unlike the kind and sensitive man I married."

Her doubts kept getting stronger. He had been distant for a while, she realised, before this incident started. It's like he was developing an alter ego. She could understand how pressures could weigh on you, but this felt like more than pressures. She knew him in his off moods, but not this. This was something new.

"André, maybe they are scared," she said. "We hear a lot about evictions these days. They've lived on some farm all their lives and that's all they know. If they get thrown off this property, where will they go?"

"Oh, so they think that this toyi-toying will make us keep them here?"

She sat down, put her elbow on the table and put her hand under her chin. "André, this isn't the first time we've had a conflict with our farm family. Remember the baby incident?"

The owners hadn't wanted Isaac's family to take in a baby that they felt was not cared for well enough. But it was only one person who ranted, Laetitia. And she did it at the cottage, not at the front door.

"As I recall," said André, "we gave in."

Catherine nodded. "That fight was with the older generation. Now the younger ones are doing the same thing."

"But this time," André proclaimed, "we are not giving in."

"This time," added Catherine, "we have them not just ignoring us, but getting political and legal activists to back them. 'Our people,' Esta said. It's in a different league." She considered for a moment, her voice heavy. "Laws have changed. Who knows how this will end?"

Things changed quite a lot after Esta worked her way onto the farm. She had been visiting more and more, she made herself useful by sweeping up and helping to care for Laetitia in her dementia, and then ... she was there. Just wormed her way in, Catherine felt.

"She's a little trouble-maker," said Catherine. "She's small in stature but she has an awful lot to say. She flashes her bright eyes and works up the others as well. Neela has definitely taken up the banner."

"Look," André continued. "We have never told everyone to leave. In fact, we need them here. Crime is getting worse, and every pair of eyes is a lookout for criminals. We have years of trust between us and the Jacobs family. We've stood by one another against crime. We all have dogs, all for security. Thieves these days will kill you for ten rand."

She was putting dishes away, trying to ignore the aggression outside. Like a fire, it flared up and died down, flared up again and just kept on.

He went on too. "All the security on this farm – motion-sensitive lights, house alarm, alarm monitoring, dogs, security company – it protects them as well. And they pay nothing for it. We even buy the food for their dog. It gets more expensive all the time."

She put the last glass away, enjoying for a fleeting moment the way it caught the light. "Now, we have to protect ourselves against them, Bellezicht's own farm family." She shook her head in disbelief. "How weird is that!"

He stopped as if to catch his breath. "And one more thing. I just don't need you taking their side. I just don't need that."

"What?" she exclaimed. "Taking their side? When I ask for the chance to engage with them? How in the world can you say that?"

He looked at her with cold eyes. "I know you bleeding hearts. 'The poor workers.' Those so-called workers don't take the opportunities they already have, and then they blame everyone else. They just sit around and don't work – not Neela, not Sheryl, not the visitors. There are plenty of jobs that women can do in the vineyards, and in the wine farm restaurants nearby, and in the packing shed across the road, just for examples. But no – it's nicer just to sit around. Now you. You want to hand everything to them. I've just had enough of that."

She was speechless. Something told her not to argue with him further. There was something not rational about him now. Something chilling.

As they moved from the kitchen to the other end of the house, still she could hear the steady rhythms of the shouting, like the pounding of a war drum.

~ 5 André ~

The bathroom door leading from the bedroom never balanced properly. One evening a few weeks later, André went and closed it lightly, but it still slowly swung open. In the mirror he saw Catherine in the bedroom, putting away laundered clothes and getting ready for bed. He spoke to her through her reflection.

"I'm getting so grey." He appraised himself in the mirror. "You think these silver temples are sexy but I don't. They mean I'm getting old. Already 51 and what have I got to show for it? Debt, bills and ranting. No discipline on this farm. Just trouble."

He took a drink of water and sighed. "Too old for this nonsense at the cottage." He ran his hands through his thinning hair and sighed again.

The phone in the study rang, the landline they still maintained. Catherine called to him, "André, it's your brother the night owl."

"Who else, at this hour?" He slipped into the study that they shared.

André motioned for her to come in and have a seat on the little sofa there. She noticed that, as he chatted, he looked at the pictures on the walls, one a very large photo of their farm Bellezicht from above. An enterprising surveyor had seen aerial photos of the whole country, all free for anyone to use. This surveyor had zoomed in on each farm in this area, copied the photo, block-mounted it and marketed it with great success to the farm owners.

"What? You're getting low on your sauvignon blanc?" André repeated for Catherine's benefit. The brother Frankie knew that Bellezicht being in the wine industry could get some good wines at a serious discount. He was always keen to have André get his special wines. Sometimes he would drive out from Cape Town and the two brothers would make a party out of buying at the wine farms and then enjoying a long afternoon lunch.

"Okay, next week." More chat.

"Listen, we've had some trouble here on the farm." He recounted recent events.

André put the phone on speaker mode for Catherine's benefit. Frankie's voice boomed out. "Why the hell do you keep on going at Bellezicht? You know you're happier lying in bed reading than bleeding irrigation pipes or playing macho on a tractor." André often commented that Frankie wasn't called Frankie for nothing – he was always frank, even brutally so. Catherine could imagine his light blue eyes starting to flash.

He went on. "You say it yourself, you're not good at supervising people. You hate it. They get away with murder and you can't seem to stop them. Now it seems like you have a revolution, right on your own doorstep. Let's see what you do with that one." He paused, probably to sip his sauvignon blanc. "Why did you ever get into that farm business in the first place?"

"Come on, gimme a break. I bought the place with Catherine, mainly for somewhere to live, and of course, as an investment. Except for harvest time, it seemed to run itself."

"Hah. That'll be the day."

"Just listen, will you? How hard can it be, we thought – just five hectares, with grapes, in the Winelands, and with a spectacular view. We could buy in consultants, and there was already a worker on it, Isaac, staying in the cottage down by the road. Before his wife decided they should move up to the apartment near our house."

"How hard can it be, indeed."

"Frankie, I've got to figure out what to do here. The farm still has its beauty, the mountains and a bit of sea, but I hardly see that any more. Bellezicht has become an albatross. This trouble from the farm family – it feels like the last straw."

Frankie was still.

"The costs of fertilisers and sprays keep going up. We just replanted three years ago, new poles and wires and irrigation pipes, a huge investment. We're still paying for it. The new vines still need lots of care, and we've even lost a few of them. No money coming in yet from the vineyard; it's all going out, not coming in. Not much for at least another year. You just bury your money, they say."

"*Ja,*" agreed Frankie. "They also say there's a lake of red wine in the world. I read just the other day about the global glut of wine. Supply outstrips demand. Although as we speak, we are doing our bit to reduce that lake. Even if we're drinking a white."

It was André's turn for a scornful laugh. "A lake of red wine, indeed. The winery we've been selling our grapes to, bullied the farmers into planting red wine grapes, with their Project Red Alert. They convinced us that we all could make more money in reds, not whites. Our previous vines gave us white grapes, but those vines were at the end of their productive life anyway. So we went ahead and put in four hectares of cabernet sauvignon. Red wine grapes. But if there's no market for wine, then there's no market for wine grapes. Year on year, we're not sure who will buy our grapes. As if we had any grapes yet to sell."

"When you get them, can't you export them as eating grapes?" asked Frankie.

"No, wine grapes are different. Their skin is too tough and the pips are too big." He paused. "Frankie, this farm is becoming a nightmare."

"Then why did you go organic? That's asking for more trouble right there."

"We thought that's where the future was. At least at the time there was a demand for organic grapes, if not for conventional ones. But every year it gets harder to meet the organic certification rules. Let alone the costs of the certifying company. Certifying is now a profession in itself. Everyone wants a piece of the action. For a hefty fee, of course."

"You probably picked the wrong star to hitch your wagon ... er, your grape bin to."

"Too late now. We just have to make the best of it.

. "What? Just make the best of that place? Sell it, man."

"Naw, in for a penny, in for a pound. Can't sell it now."

"Why not? Are you daft? You can always find a buyer and you know it. I mean, it's Stellenbosch – the best place in the country."

"*Ja*, well, we'd never get our price now. But thanks for the reminder. It sure doesn't feel like the best place."

Frankie paused again to sip his wine. "Well then, don't come crying to me if you won't act."

"Frankie, why can't things be the way they used to be, like when we were kids, when we went to visit our grandparents on their farm? Everybody knew their place."

"Well, you know what Bob Dylan said ... .

"The times they are a-changing?"

"No – the answer, my friend, is blowing in the wind."

"Well, up yours too, and have a good night."

They both laughed. "Till next week."

André looked over at Catherine. "Yes, it would be a relief to get out from under this farm. But we still need Godwin and the farm family, even though they're part of the burden. "

Catherine shook her head. "But we've made a long-term investment. We'd never recoup it now; it's too soon. And the view. And our friends. They all love to come here for a braai and to enjoy the mountains, enjoy the peace and quiet we usually have. Seems like fighting moves away whenever we braai. Where else would we braai, if not here? Where else would we live?"

"It has already become a burden, and now this ... this ... this rebellion. Who do they think they are! No."

"Give up the farm? Just for a quarrel? Look, this trouble might blow over. We are not telling Godwin or his family to leave. If he decides to leave, however, that is a new situation, one of his choice. Then, other realities come into play, involving housing and family. But the basis is the job."

André shook his head.

"The problem is," continued Catherine, "many farmers are putting workers off their farm. But not us. Godwin can stay and his family can stay, no problem. Once we get it cleared up, that it's only their visitors that we want to leave, things can get back to normal." Her eyes drooped and her brow furrowed. "If normal again is possible."

"So what should I do? I can't let them get away with this nonsense. Who knows – where will it all lead?"

"Frankie says you have to act, but … let's not be hasty. We're in this thing together."

"Catherine, the farm people can't see me as a pushover. I've got to figure out what to do here." She saw he was in a loop. Better to hold your tongue, she felt, and stop the discussion now, before it too got out of hand. Who knows, she thought; the waiting game might be good for everyone, to give them time to consider the situation more carefully.

André fixed his eyes on the large aerial photo of the farm. He stood up resolutely, took it down off the wall, turned it around and stashed it behind the sofa.

~ 6 The baby ~

In the days following the shouting episode, Catherine did some serious thinking about where this conflict had started. In her mind she went back to one of their early days at Bellezicht, when they had been there just a month or so. That evening was Friday and time to pay the wages. She was setting some flowers on the dining room table, just inside the entrance, when she heard André's angry voice.

"Isaac, put that spade away. And that hosepipe – why have you left it lying where people walk? And the vineyard; you should have finished the pruning by now. Why the delay?"

"*Baas,* my shears were broken and I couldn't finish."

"Then why didn't you tell me? And why don't you take better care of those shears? They cost money and a lot of it. I'm tired of paying for all the broken tools on this farm. That spade will be broken too if you don't put it back."

André carried on. Isaac knew to remain quiet and just take it. Finally André went quiet too. As he handed over the week's wages to Isaac, he even stood on the top step and Isaac stood below. Isaac got the point.

Catherine was upset to the point of tears.When André came inside, she had a big question for him. "André, how, just how, can you treat Isaac like that?"

"What? What's wrong?"

"You shouted at him. You even harangued him. That's just not right. He didn't argue or fight with you. You just went on and on."

"So what should I do, coddle him? He's here all day and doesn't do things right. It's Friday and he's already started drinking."

Her eyes flashed anger. "Whatever he is doing against your wishes, of course take it up with him, but not by haranguing him."

"So you want to let them walk all over you? Well, I'm the boss of this farm and this is how I do it."

"You – we – need him to work with us, not against us. We are gone all day and we trust him with this place. We need cooperation, not antagonism."

"He better not dare to oppose me." He glared at her. "Do I detect a lack of loyalty here?"

"Lack of loyalty? What a question! How can anyone be loyal to that sort of treatment? I have to oppose it, for the good of the farm."

He turned and left the room.

She was already a stranger in a strange land; now she felt like running away, running back to Pennsylvania, where she knew the rules. She escaped into the lounge, as far away at the moment from André as she could get. The shouting was bad enough. Worse was Isaac's submission. To be put into that situation!

"I don't have to take this," she said to herself. "I'm going home to Mother." But mother in America was really far away. From the window she saw the lights in the distance. "I know. I'll go home to André's mother." It was just to Cape Town. Catherine and André's mother connected with each other from Day 1. She knew she would get a listening ear and a place to stay.

It didn't take very long before André walked into the lounge, came up behind her and enfolded her in his arms. She turned and hugged him back.

Later on, they talked it through and André said he would try to change. Catherine stayed hopeful. She believed in his basic good heart, and at the same time she felt that change might not be so easy for him. What role had his manner played in this current conflict with the farm family? It made her worry that he had not changed all that much. But now, people were not taking it lying down.

As Catherine pondered what to do, other events, eerily like the present conflict, emerged in her thoughts. They also involved the issue of people arriving to live on this small farm. The number of people living in that small space was always changing; mainly increasing.

There was the baby incident. It happened shortly after they had moved to the farm. André had just come home from the office, and Catherine came out to the car to greet him as usual with a hug and a kiss. Then they heard a sound and he looked around, saying, "Where did that crying baby come from? I've heard it a lot in the past few days."

"Let's go have a look."

As they approached the *werf* of the cottage, they saw Laetitia walking with a baby on her shoulder, patting her. Catherine thanked Laetitia, who had cleaned the manor house that day and washed up what dishes there were, as she did once a week, in those early days.

Laetitia smiled at them. "We are raising her," she said.

"Whose baby is it?" André asked.

"That woman's, the one who was here a few weeks ago," informed Laetitia. The woman visiting was nine months pregnant and Laetitia had taken her in just to help her through the birth. The woman had left with the baby but now the baby was back.

"Where is the mother?" asked Catherine.

"*Daar onder*, somewhere, at another farm. But not to worry. We are raising this baby," repeated Laetitia. "No one was feeding the baby or changing her nappies and that isn't right."

Andréw's face grew redder by the second.

"This is fine for her but not fine for Bellezicht and all the people here already, in the small space there is. All depending on one job." He looked around for a second. "Come, Catherine. That baby must go back to its parents." He turned abruptly and strode back to the house. Laettia's smile became a scowl. Catherine's face showed confusion. But she said nothing and followed André reluctantly.

The small space there is, André said. But Laetitia had chosen the smaller quarters. Catherine remembered that when they first came to live there, Isaac and Laetitia had had a larger cottage at the bottom of the farm. Laetitia noticed the two small rooms built on to the back of the garage, which temporary workers had used at one time. Those rooms had running water, a toilet, and best of all, electricity.

"Ek is moeg daarvan om elke dag vuur te maak," she complained. She was tired of making a cooking fire at the larger cottage every day, despite plentiful branches to burn. The wind and rain were sometimes too much. The electricity called to Laetitia, and she chose to move her family to those two rooms. The living space was less but there was a *werf*, a yard where they could sit and enjoy it almost as a lounge. It was worth the move, she said. That cottage lower down the hill was later sold anyway with a long-planned subdivision of the farm.

Ten people had to find places to sleep in a two-room house. They were Isaac and Laetitia, their two sons Reuben and Tommy, and their two grown daughters Sheryl and Neela, who were still bearing children. At that early time Sheryl had just her first two children, Trina and Godwin, and Neela had her husband Henry and their son *Klein* Henry, or Henry Junior. Perhaps small children could find some space in a parent's bed. Bellezicht contributed bunk beds, but space was very tight.

And now, the baby.

Back at their house, André and Catherine just looked at each other. Another commitment, another place to find, more crowding, and long term. No discussion; just here she is. Finish and *klaar*.

"Can Laetitia just keep on taking people in? Does she see what pressure she is putting on her family who are already here?" André said. "Can we allow this continuous overcrowding in the small cottage?"

"Let alone more costs for us, higher water bills, more electricity for sure."

"Do you know what else? It is not nice to mention, but the farm has one septic tank, and the more the people, the faster it gets filled up. It's already overloaded. Who pays for maintaining it, for the truck to come and empty it? I do."

"Yes, and more trips to and from the clinic for this child, school expenses, greater needs as she gets older," agreed Catherine.

"You can bet on it that she will be a pregnant teenager. It's the farm way of life and no one tries to change it."

Catherine rolled her eyes. "If – when – she falls pregnant, that will be the end of her school life."

"So you tell me, Catherine; to what extent should we be culturally tolerant, especially when we have to foot so many of the bills? The child does have a mother and, somewhere, a father. The parents have to take responsibility for their child."

The next afternoon, a cold but bright-blue winter's day, there was Laetitia coming along the walk. André began to speak in his fluent Afrikaans and explained to Laetitia that the baby couldn't stay here to live.

Laetitia shouted defiance to all and sundry, her long arms reaching to the heavens. "*Die baba bly hier!* Here, and nowhere else! If not, then we will go too!" She glared at him. "Forget about my help in the kitchen – *ek is klaar met die kombuis!*" Finished with the kitchen. She smashed the house keys to the ground in front of him, and took long pounding strides back to the cottage.

Isaac emerged from the vineyard and followed his angry wife into the cottage. The other adults and children milled around and also flowed back into the cottage, to muffled sounds of unrest.

André and Catherine were taken aback but adamant. As the routine normalised in the next few days, they tried to talk to other family members. Their faces were sad but distant, noncommittal. Isaac obviously felt in the middle; he wanted to work, and he wanted to support his wife too, which meant keeping the baby.

He and André finally had a civil discussion. Isaac shook his head.

"*Baas,*" he looked away and then back, to look André right in the eye, something farmworkers did not easily do. "*Baas,* the baby is little. She doesn't take up much space." He looked away, then looked back. "The baby doesn't eat much."

André reported his response to Catherine. She looked long at André and said, "It's such a kind perspective, especially from the one person housing and feeding most of the others. But … ."

"Yes, but. He doesn't see the implications for the others, or the implications over the years. We can't give in."

Laetitia didn't like the situation one bit. Whenever she saw either of them, she threw her hands in the air and strode away. Isaac still worked in the vineyard. André and Catherine still went to their jobs, and Laetitia continued to tend the baby and to shout unclear angry words..

Meanwhile, the manor house got quite dusty. André and Catherine worked together to sweep and vacuum. They dealt with dishes, laundry and ironing. It got to be quite a lot of work. Two weeks went by, then another, then another. Catherine felt that Laetitia just needed more time. "We don't want to take away her job just because we are having a disagreement," she said.

André didn't argue but his vacuuming became less frequent, and pots and pans piled up in the kitchen sink. "Housework on top of jobs – this is getting to be too much, Catherine."

 So she urged him to talk to Laetitia again, to see if she had cooled off, to see if she wanted to come back to work. She waited while he walked back to the cottage. As he rounded the corner and Laetitia got a glimpse of him, she threw her arms up and began shouting. André turned and looked at Catherine with big round eyes: "You want to ask her?"

Shortly afterward they came home from work and found a letter shoved under the front door. It was from some housing authority saying no one can evict people without 30 days' notice. It was a shock. Catherine and André had never even thought of eviction. For the first time Catherine saw, underneath the defiance, something opaque and heavy; she saw their fear.

"André, I must admit, I'm rather shaken by this letter. I mean, people calling the law down on us and making us into bad people."

She didn't want an eviction fight on their hands, with high legal costs and deep uncharted waters. Farm evictions were a lot in the news. She could imagine the headlines: "Farmer evicts baby."

"Something new is going on," said André. "But now they've made a move. It's our turn."

The next day he invited them to come to the veranda, to talk things over. Snacks were ready. Isaac, Sheryl, Neela, Henry, and Isaac's two sons wandered near, with stubborn faces, but did not come up the steps. Laetitia was nowhere to be seen.

Desperation took over. Catherine stood on the veranda and spoke to the people milling between house and cottage, to whoever would listen.

"You are free; you can live where you will. If you want to move, we will use the bakkie and help you, if you wish. But you cannot keep taking people in. We know there are a lot of people who need help, and we want to help too. But there is a limit to what can be done in this living space. The baby has parents just down the road."

Hard faces, but less hard. Then Laetitia roared around to the front, ending any chance of talk. The family members drifted away to the back. André walked along and talked to each person individually, a word or two. The united front was weakening. "Do you really want to move?" No clear answers. They just didn't want to give back the baby. Catherine wondered if also they didn't want to cross Laetitia. There would surely be a big price.

Catherine found their resolve admirable. They were so torn. All they wanted to do was to help this little baby girl that they deemed uncared for. No money was involved for them. They were standing up to someone they considered powerful, and make no mistake, in their lives the farmer was very powerful. They were willing to bear the consequences. They had taken steps to get this letter to protect themselves, just in case. Torn but they didn't give in.

Her eyes found André's. He held her gaze for a long time. In his eyes she saw something that perhaps he usually tried to hide, something sympathetic, respectful even. Something in him had been moved; just as something in her felt different. At that point, Catherine knew what to say. She held his eyes again and said quietly, just to him: "Well, the baby doesn't eat much."

This baby wasn't the end. There was Koos, the gangling fellow of 17 with the size 12 feet. Laetitia and Isaac took him in shortly afterward.

Head to one side, he looked out from under bushy eyebrows as if he might run should anyone look at him sternly. Laetitia had told Catherine that Koos was an orphan and that he wanted to go to school. If there was any talk of education, Catherine knew she was like putty in people's hands.

Even from their little farm, she could see that there were not enough farm jobs for people who wanted them now, let alone for the next generation coming up. The younger ones needed better jobs as well. They would need education.

Isaac and Laetitia said that Koos could live with them and be bussed to the nearby high school, which served the area's farms. Catherine learned later that he had a stepfather living closer to town, but for some reason, he preferred living at Bellezicht. If that meant he had another chance at school, well, she thought that would help him in life. It would help the whole country, she argued, because then the education level would go up, however incrementally. She got André to agree. So then there were 12 people in the cottage.

Koos did all right at first, going to the high school, no matter that he was in only Grade 8 and was the oldest and biggest pupil in the class. He was getting a bit of pocket money from Bellezicht for weeding the flower gardens. Catherine bought his school uniforms and shoes and sports equipment and all the tools that he needed to succeed in his schoolwork. The difficult part was the shoes; they shopped hard to find size 12s.

A few months after Koos arrived, the farm owners noticed an elderly man was around too. He was short, sinewy and stooped. Deep folds lined his thin face; he had a toothless smile. He always wore a knitted cap and a brown too-large sports jacket, even in the summer. When Catherine asked Laetitia who he was, she said, *"Dis my pa."* Her father. They had never seen him nor heard talk of her parents and just assumed they had passed on. It seemed her mother had, and the father's partner had just died, so they took him in.

"It's even more overcrowding," said André. "He can't stay here. There are homes for elderly people. They will look after him well."

The next day Catherine ran into Laetitia and said, *"Laetitia, daar's nou baie mense hier.* Too many people for such a small space. There is a home right in Stellenbosch for elderly people, where he will be well cared for. It's the same home that Isaac's pa is in. You bring him here for holidays, and we can get both of them at holiday time. We want to help, but there is just no room in the cottage for another person."

Laetitia looked at Catherine as if she were a poor child who just didn't comprehend. Being a tall, big-boned woman, she could also look down, head tilted in sympathy for Catherine's limited understanding. With shining eyes, she said, *"Ons sal 'n plek maak.* We'll make room."

There was no question in her voice, in her attitude. For her the matter was finished. Catherine stood there speechless. Laetitia's eyes went somewhere far away. She turned and walked toward the cottage.

That evening before dinner, André and Catherine agreed to sit down and discuss the new arrival. Catherine knew that they would talk better over some wine. She got out a bottle from the small wine cellar, affordable ever-present chenin blanc. From the look on André's face, she changed her mind and chose instead a ten-year-old cabernet sauvignon.

They took the wine to the veranda. The light against the mountains was changing from peach to grey-blue, and the evening star shone steadily. Sitting side by side to face the view, they clinked glasses, took a sip, and Catherine began. "Well," she said to André, "here, the man has family. They obviously want him here. He is her father. Don't we all have to look after our parents?"

She thought of her own mother, who took in her elderly in-laws and cared for them for years, until they died. The feeling grew in her that taking in Laetitia's father was the right thing to do.

"Do you realise what this means? Another person with a set of needs. More food, a bed and a place to put it. We will be driving him and Laetitia to and from the clinic, the pension payout office, and who knows where else. Who's going to pay for that? Me."

André glared at the line of mountains against the sky. "And what about our time? We're professional people. Now, it would be driving them, waiting, meeting up somewhere, stopping for them to get groceries ... more groceries at that. We do this already and it isn't easy. Do you realise that?"

Catherine was silent.

"Another person," continued André, "a person with needs and with a huge number of rights. Rights! That's all we hear. Our farm is just too small for the whole world."

She sipped her wine, not looking at him.

"The old-age home will look after him. After all, it's a government place and we pay for that already through taxes." Catherine just listened, giving him a chance to express his feelings, giving him time.

When the time seemed right, she said, "André, we did the same thing. We cared for your own mother right here at Bellezicht." They had taken her in with love after her cancer had returned with a vengeance. "This is just what good people do."

André sat there and looked away.

Catherine just sat there beside him, both facing the mountains and watching the night lower itself gently in, letting the wine do its work of nudging them toward a decision they both could live with.

It took him two days to think past his own logic. The next Sunday André and Catherine made a point of walking together to the cottage, greeting "*Oupa*", Grandfather, as everyone called him. They each shook his hand. "*Oupa, jy is baie welkom hier by ons op die plaas. Ons hoop alles is gemaklik genoeg vir jou.* We hope you are happy here." Laetitia was wide-eyed. She had surely thought that all that was needed was her own decision. Now the farm owners showed, without discussion, that they had not consented before but were consenting now; that their consent mattered too.

After a few days André thought about offering the storeroom off the main house as a bedroom for Oupa. It had windows and electricity, and it could relieve pressure in the two-room cottage. Laetitia and Oupa accepted quickly.

As the days went on, Oupa actually got bored sitting around. He spontaneously began to help Isaac on the farm, weeding the rose beds, pulling long strands of grass out of the hedges, and eventually working beside Isaac pruning the vines. He began showing up beside Isaac on Friday night, wages time. Without any specific agreement or expectation, let alone discussion, surprise of surprises, André began paying him too. Everyone settled down.

So in those early days, there came to be a family of thirteen people living in the cottage: Isaac and Laetitia, their two grown daughters and two growing sons, son-in-law Henry, Trina and Godwin and *Klein* Henry, and Koos, Oupa and the baby. It was another potential claim on rights. Catherine wondered what legal position this situation put them in, because, well, she and André were allowing it.

Now, years later, she saw they were dealing with the same issue again. This time, however, it was with a new generation. They were dealing with the three tenuously connected visitors who just wouldn't leave, who were staying without the owners' consent and despite their opposition. If these people came from Robertson, as Esta once told her, couldn't they go back there? Couldn't they take steps to move themselves forward in life, either with education or training, or some kind of job? The girl was young, perhaps younger than her years; she walked around the cottage with a lollipop in her mouth, avoiding picking up orange peels from the floor, let alone picking up a broom. Did Esta and Neela and Godwin think they would wear the owners down, as was done in the past? Maybe now they were operating from collective memory.

With all the talk about rights, were there no rights for the other children in the cottage, Isaac's three grandchildren, who also needed nurturing and attention and space and caring? And let's not even talk about rights for the farmers.

To be fair, in the past the farmer had all the rights. Unfairly so, of course. Collective memory can collect injustices, so many historical injustices recounted over centuries by the farmworkers, injustices verified by the history books. She felt innocent of all that. But maybe not so innocent; wasn't she after all inadvertently benefiting from the injustices of the past?

She sighed long and deep, from some place within her that she hardly knew. The past was the past. Where do we go from here, she wondered. André would like to ignore what was happening, turn the clock back and be the unquestioned boss of everyone and everything on the farm. What could she do with that attitude? He felt like a stranger when he talked that way. It was putting a wedge in their relationship.

As she sat, deep in thought, Catherine's eyes moved around the lounge with its windows on three sides; its solid brick fireplace; its small worn rug. She stared at the photo of André's family, of the English grandfather who worked on the railroads, of the Afrikaans grandfather who had a dairy farm. Could she find even a glimmer of hope in her heart?

~ 7 Party ~

The cold nights of the Cape in winter did not always bring about an easy slumber. On one particular such night, the cold pinned Catherine deep in the bed, like Lilliputians pinning Gulliver to the ground. She turned slightly to view the red lighted digits on the clock. 03:37. Too early to get up, and too cold as well. She turned over toward André, who was lying on his side facing away. She lay again on her back and drew the duvet tightly under her chin.

How did she come to be on a farm in Africa? she asked herself. Where, exactly, is the start of anything? For her, a kind of start began years ago, when she first came to South Africa on a teacher exchange program. She'd always wanted to explore other places and cultures through travel but money forever being tight, she looked for ways to travel through work. Her background as a teacher of English in Pennsylvania led her into teaching English as a second language, and through this speciality she was recommended to teach in a program to help teachers in other countries to modernise and humanise their language teaching approaches. With language comes culture; yes, in this line of work, she was home. She'd accepted the invitation to work for some weeks in schools in Taipei, later in Khartoum, and then in Cape Town. Little did she know that a special someone seemed destined to make the delight she felt in other cultures become permanent: André.

She wasn't looking for anyone special in her time in South Africa. Her marriage of eight years had ended a few years before. Her ex had already been divorced with three children and did not want any more, and she had accepted it. What a fool she'd been; time marches on and now the possibility of children was diminishing fast. After he left she'd had some lonely times, true, but somehow the support of family and friends usually saw her through. Meaningful work helped. She had often enjoyed the attention of nice men, but no one motivated her enough to get involved again. Or if they did, they were unavailable.

So there she was, teaching at a private school in Cape Town on a two-month exchange, where she did her thing. Talk about languages, talk about cultures, feel enriched by the diversity of people. To Catherine, Cape Town was the real South African gold.

Then came an invitation through the mail, at the modest hotel in Cape Town where she stayed. Her colleague Rosalie invited her to a 30th birthday party she was giving for her husband. Catherine was over the moon. She wondered how a South African party would differ from an American one.

She was welcomed to the party of about 25 chatting guests by an enthusiastic host, who quickly put a glass of wine into her hand. Rosalie introduced her to a couple from Malawi who were working in Cape Town, and to a lawyer friend handling a current court case involving the unsettling effects on bystanders of protests and police action. She met other language colleagues of Rosalie as well as some colleagues of her husband, from the bank where he worked in the human relations department. Her eyes couldn't get enough of the mix of people of differing complexions, with differing accents, from different backgrounds and even different countries. Like her, but also not like her.

Still circulating, she found herself drawing near an older couple, pointed out earlier as the husband's parents. Elise, with her athletic figure, with her silver hair piled high, a warm smile on her face. Freddie, tall and well shouldered, a glint in his eye which tells a person he sees them. They both turned toward Catherine in greeting. There was someone else standing near talking with them. He stood a little removed, wine glass in hand, as if waiting.

"This is André," Elise said. Catherine nodded, and the group widened to four and resettled itself, with André across from her. He was of medium build, a gentle mesomorph, she noted. His shiny brown hair insisted on flowing over one side of his forehead. His cheeks were reddish, from the sun or from the wine, she wondered. He looked up from under the hair, head a little to one side, shyly. A certain light seemed to radiate from him, from his eyes. Soft light, yet brilliant. He nodded in greeting. Interesting, very interesting.

Elise and Freddie continued with their story to André, and now to Catherine as well, about their recent holiday trip to the Transvaal with their caravan parked in the dry river bed.

"Caravan?" she asked, immediately intrigued. Images flooded into her head of camels trudging in line across sand dunes, the sun a red ball behind them.

"Americans call it a trailer," said André, smiling. "I was also puzzled about that on my first trip to the States."

Elise addressed Catherine. "We had a bit of bubbly under the stars, millions of stars, which are so clear when you are far from city lights. When Freddie finally tore himself away from his star-gazing and came into the caravan, he crawled into the bed, and then the whole caravan tipped to that end! I was pinned against the wall, the bubbly and the glasses went flying … ."

"No, Elise, it wasn't like that. It was like this … ." His hands swept away her version, and a sour dialogue ensued. It stirred up in her some old familiar feelings, bad ones from her divorce, feelings she realised with a start that she had still not succeeded in forgetting.

She turned slightly while acknowledging the group, but only André noticed. He nodded in response, and she slowly backed away, taking her eyes to the other party guests. Once out of range, she glanced back and saw Freddie and Elise still going at each other, hands up and down, flinging themselves back into the dry river bed.

Looking over those angry hands stood André, face tilted upward, bright eyes following her, eyes meeting hers for a long split second. An unfamiliar feeling sprang up. Her hand shook from some life of its own, making her so nervous that she almost dropped her glass. She felt her cheeks getting hot. She knew that that split second was a bit too long but she felt frozen in time, unable to move. Easy, she cautioned herself. His wife is probably here too. Cool down with a sip of wine. Then she let herself be swept along by the couple from Malawi, telling her about their studies, their plans to stay in South Africa as long as possible.

Careful. Be careful of those stirrings in the heart.

Before the evening was over, André found her again for a brief chat; no wife, he was divorced too. He invited her to lunch where he worked, in Stellenbosch.

She wasn't so sure about starting a new friendship just days before she was due to return to the States and to her life there. She was busy closing down her exchange work, and there were reports, goodbyes, final shopping. But somehow, despite her pragmatic, practical self, she accepted.

That lunch at a very good Italian restaurant in Stellenbosch was about getting-to-know-you. André and some friends had just bought a small wine farm, where they had set up offices.

André held the door for her as they left the restaurant. "Come stop by the new farm. It's on your way back to Cape Town." He brushed aside his thick brown hair. But he didn't take his gaze away from her. She felt herself again warming to his light-emitting smile. More than warming; more like stirring, stirring up, whirring to his presence.

Well, there was a bit of time. She drove her little rented Volksie behind André up the winding dirt road, up the hill, and turned into the farm at the sign "Bellezicht" swinging noisily from a tall wooden post. They drove in between the rows of grapevines, the gravel on the entrance path crunching under the tyres. As she stepped from her car into the yard, she caught her breath in wonder.

The luminous grey sky, soft with layers of white light, was just clearing above the mountains across the valley. How close those mountains! The jagged, textured peaks went on and on, up and down and sideways. Their softer mountain feet were edged by the green and brown patchwork of farm after farm. She looked down at the round hills in the valley between those blue stone mountains and the farm where she stood, high on the slope of the hill. The winter rain had stopped for the moment but the moisture carried a fresh green scent, calling up primal feelings about, what, the goodness of life?

André was beaming now, his heartlight shining out past his jacket and tie, as he showed her through the house. A few offices. Desks and bookcases and files and a few computers, even a photocopier. But oh! The view from every window was like one French impressionist painting after another. Rows of grapevines bare in their winter rest. Rows of blue-flowered crops, cover crops, explained André, to put nutrients back into the soil. From another window, hills. More mountains from an opposite window. The town of Stellenbosch in the distance, nestled just before the mountain pass. Peaks behind, peaks beside one another, each one unique.

"How can anyone work here?" she said, overwhelmed. "I'd be sitting by one window after another, all day, watching the show!" André's cheeks flushed with pride.

They strolled around outside the single-storey house, noting its large rich-wooded windows, all with louvred shutters. "The wood is teak. From West Africa," said André, half-smug that his durable shutters had come from that bit of teak grown on his African continent.

There were two outbuildings nearby, a garage on one side, and a solidly built sheep pen on the other, with no sheep but lots of ducks. "To eat the snails," explained André. "It's a natural way to keep down the number of snails that feed on the vines." Well, she thought, someone is thinking.

They strolled past a small garden. A short, sturdy worker emerged and stood there smiling at André. "This is Isaac Jacobs. He tends the vines for us." Isaac took off his floppy khaki-coloured hat. His curly grey hair contrasted with his brown complexion. André introduced her.

Isaac nodded. Catherine noticed that his smile was toothless but that didn't seem to bother him. André continued, "Now that the vines are in their winter mode, Isaac has time for some gardening." Then he repeated it in Afrikaans, so that Isaac could understand. "He is wonderful with the vines. He has, as we say, green fingers."

"*Groen vingers*," Isaac translated, as he held up his hands. His smile broadened.

"Do you live on the farm?" she asked Isaac. He looked to André for the answer.

"Yes, he and his family, extended family at that, stay in the cottage down there, near the entrance to the property. You drove past it as you came off the tar road." André moved on and Isaac returned to his weeding, still smiling.

One side of the house had a wide veranda with a full view of the whole mountain range. Just off the veranda grew a tall hibiscus bush, in full bloom, giving out sudden, pinkish bugle-shaped flowers.

"Not the kind of bush you see in Pennsylvania," she said. She opened her camera bag and photographed it. Up to now she'd been so stirred by the large beauty of the farm, and of the whole mountainous Stellenbosch area, that taking photos had been the last thing on her mind.

"Look," he said. "There's a chameleon right there, behind this bloom." Catherine put her face close up to the hibiscus bush and focused on the little lizard inside, its large round eyes moving each in a different direction, its slender body motionless as it clung to the small branch. Another thing you don't see in Pennsylvania. The camera took her attention far into the bush, into the space behind the leaves, and after a few clicks, she stayed there, examining the little universe inside.

A small spider web to the right. Some ants lining their way up another branch. Drops of water glistening here and there. The underside of leaves. Everything not motionless at all, but moving, moving, ever so slightly. The chameleon very slowly removed one long-toed foot and placed it higher, curling its toes carefully around the twig, as if making a deeply thoughtful decision. The food chain writ small. All, everything, right here, within a glance. A second. A moment of contemplation. A slip into another reality.

She had to slowly step back into the world of sky and rain, of people and events, of mountains and politics. The world of people who want to live according to their highest principles, yet with human needs. Wants and needs.

André watched from a small distance. She felt that he was honouring her, not interfering, somehow sensing that she was experiencing many feelings all at the same time.

As she manouevred her big Nikon camera, she became quite self-conscious as she saw that, again, he didn't take his eyes off of her. She dropped the lens cap and fumbled with the tangled-up camera strap. She felt a warm glow spreading. Though a bit embarrassed, secretly she was pleased.

"Let me get a nice shot of you, André," she smiled. He smiled as well, directly into the camera's eye, which was her eye too. She took some care with this photograph. He stood framed by tree branches overhead, a few leaves adding a lacy effect against the mountains and the mist. That brightness about him – again she felt that stirring. Little did she know that this photo would carry her through the next year and more.

It would carry her through letters and phone calls and another exchange assignment in South Africa, this time in Soweto, Johannesburg, along with some days as a guest of André's family, the Steenkamps, in Cape Town. That photo drew her bits of courage together like a magnet, enough courage to leave America – actually leave America! – and little did she suspect as she snapped it, that photo would bring her back to Stellenbosch, to the little church in the green centre of town for her wedding.

Ultimately it would bring her back to this very farm, no longer as visitor but as co-owner of Bellezicht. It would bring her back to become a wife, now lying in bed with André.

Getting to that point had taken two years. It had demanded that they bridge two hemispheres, two oceans, and seven time zones. There were cultures to cross too, and political systems, one in permanent crisis. All this, in the days before the ease of the Internet.

Getting to know André even a little was a blip of good fortune that had come her way, as Catherine recalled. However, she'd had to be realistic about wanting more. How to follow up? South Africa was just too far away from home, and she was then on track to get back to her real life, her life back in the States.

But André had seemed to ignore these obvious obstacles. Although he was quite the cool fellow on the surface, he'd phoned her the very next day following their lunch. The memory of it made her snuggle herself under the duvet with a wide smile in the dark.

"There's a great Greek restaurant in Cape Town and I'd like to take you there. Tuesday evening?"

"Sounds nice but I have to leave on Friday, back to the States, back to my life. I still have to finish my report, buy more presents, pack … ."

"But you will have to have dinner anyway. Let me pick you up at seven." No negotiating.

What he didn't know, she thought, was that I already had a date for Tuesday, just a friendly one, with a Scottish businessman who was also staying at this hotel. She knew which date interested her more. She left the Scot a message.

André came for her in his old, rusted-out bakkie. The lock on the passenger door worked only from the inside, and gallant André went to great lengths to hold the door for her. He insisted that she stand there and wait while he went around the back of the bakkie to open the door on the passenger side. Once she was settled inside, he went around and leaned over her to lock the door. As they arrived at the restaurant, he leaned over her again to open the lock, and made her sit there while he ran around the bakkie and opened the door for her, then ran back into the bakkie to lock the door from inside. Whew.

"André, it's so easy for me just to get out of the bakkie by myself." Her American independence asserted itself.

"No, no! I'll do it." He kept insisting and finally she accepted his chivalry, and then was charmed by it. He was determined to treat her right.

She caught the scent of his freshly-washed hair, his male body, or was it his pheromones. Whatever, she knew she liked it.

More getting to know each other. His family didn't sound so different from her own: middle class, working people, late father had held the status of a bank manager, mother had been a bookseller. Sister a secretary, brother a teacher.

At her insistence he dropped her off at her hotel, seeing there was no place to park. He'd insisted on seeing her off at the airport on Friday, despite the Scot wanting to come by (she held him off), despite the local

American Center staff, whose job it was to facilitate her travel. He stayed to the end, helped her with some misplaced luggage, and then, time to go.

They faced each other. She took his face in her hands and gave him a light kiss, their first kiss. It would have been a brother-sister kiss except for her hands holding his face. She then had to slip around a barrier and disappear, but once at the barrier, she looked back, just like at the party. She saw him looking at her, just like at the party. Feelings welled up within her. She heard a small voice within, saying "This can't be the end."

After the whirlwind of re-entry into America, she found a bit of time to reflect. "Take a chance," she told herself. "What have you got to lose?"

The letter to André was brief. After a few customary remarks, she said it all.

"I've figured out a few things along the way of my life. One of them is that most of my regrets are not things that I've done, although I can find a few of those. Most of my regrets are things I haven't done, things I haven't said, time I've let slip away. So I'm telling you now: of all the experiences I had in South Africa, meeting you was the most interesting. I'm not sure where to go from here. Just wanted you to know."

Three weeks later, Catherine brushed the snow from the mailbox at her house in Pennsylvania and drew out the 17-page letter from South Africa, along with a photo of André, plus an article entitled "Sexual chemistry." Incredible.

More letters. The impossible was happening. She got herself sent back to South Africa on another exchange. His mother took to her, saying, "The more I know you, Catherine, the more I like you."

Catherine's mother took to André too, as did her friends, when he went over to the States later that year. She had always intuited that she would be the one to move, and that's what happened. First she took a leave of absence from her job and later resigned. She sold her car. She rented out her house for a while and then sold that too. The wedding was in Stellenbosch. Luckily she found work and two years later, Bellezicht became theirs. All she had was now invested in South Africa, in André, in their little farm. There was no going back.

She was so hopeful, so idealistic then. She and André weren't rich but they scraped enough together for a deposit and managed, not easily, to obtain a big mortgage. They would both work, they would keep the vineyard going and help the people on the farm to better their lives. Maybe, just maybe, they could start a family. That at least was her dream and she believed André would go along with it. She couldn't see any other way to live in such a magnificent place as Bellezicht. But now, the shouting. In all their 16 years living on the farm, she never anticipated farmworker aggression. Was their dream dying?

~ 8 Morning ~

H is tongue flicked the top of Catherine's ear feather-like and led his lips to the soft fleshy earlobe. Warm feelings like a cat purring stirred from somewhere in the middle of her chest.

She turned in bed to face him. His trim torso was softening a bit but there was still no middle-age *boep* for him. Solid shoulders, smoothly muscled arms, chest hair that narrowed as it went down. His body curved cat-like, tense and focussed. His eyes streamed light.

She reached out her hand and caressed his face. He moved to take her waist in both hands, a touch he knew she especially liked.

She snuffled in his scent, his own special body signature, as one noses a wine. Winespeak for André. His scent offered a fleeting dash of lemon, a hint of guava and the light biscuit of a good champagne. She had revelled in it from the start. After she went back to the States from her second visit, André mailed her one of the shirts he had worn, the red plaid one. He included a little note saying "smelling of André." She'd kept this scented shirt close to her in bed until he came across the oceans to explore whether anything might lie ahead for them, crazy as it all seemed. His scent, scent of a dream, a prayer. Scent embracing her from the inside.

Gently, she and André began asking the universe to grant them the eventual grace of those trance-like moments preceding joy, those transcendent moments, giving up control for ecstasy.

"Bacon and eggs. And coffee. Fantastic!" Catherine scrambled to sit up in bed and receive the tray. André smiled, light all around him as he slid into bed beside her, balancing his tray with one hand. The day joined them through the windows, cold and sunny, a good Cape winter day.

She'd slipped on a jersey, large and old with a muted pink and grey pattern. He was happy in just his grey pajamas of many years. "We match well," she laughed, finger-combing her touseled hair. Clothes were not a priority. She knew that André didn't like change, but in this case it suited her well that he was quite happy to wear the same things every winter.

She finished her last bite of toast. Then, putting the tray aside, she leaned back against the soft headboard, drew up her knees, and still under the covers, turned to look at him. "Well, we have to face it."

He gathered their trays and set them aside. He knew what was coming.

"We agreed to discuss the farm at the weekend and here we are. My issue is, how long can we wait before something else happens? Maybe something worse."

His glossy hair, usually so neat, went this way and that, with a few greying strands standing up at the crown. He leaned against the headboard and turned to look at her. She saw the frown appear above his green-brown eyes as the farm upheaval came rushing back into his mind, an unwanted memory.

"I don't know,' he said.

"We can't just ignore the situation. If we do nothing, then don't we consent by silence?"

"It can't be. It was never that way before."

"Well, I've heard that's the way it is now," she noted. "But if the visitors stay, then they might acquire residence rights ... there are lots of new laws. Who knows what a mess we could get ourselves into. I've heard that you can't make people leave if they have slept even one night at your farm."

"But we don't know if that's true," said André. "How do we know about these things?"

"I've asked around whenever I've gotten a chance, but our farming neighbours don't seem to know any more than we do about the new laws. They tell me a few things here and there, but with both of us working, there isn't a lot of time in the day to ferret out information."

"We've lost our own lawyer ... ."

The mood turned sombre as they remembered what happened recently to their lawyer of several years. A hiker had found his body by the river. He had shot himself. He was a smoker and they had found the area around him littered with his cigarette butts, a poignant detail not lost on Catherine.

André resumed the discussion. "We can't afford thousands of rands per hour right now, just to find another lawyer who may or may not understand our needs. It would cost a lot just to pay for their time in getting to know our situation."

Catherine nodded slowly. She knew cash was tight, with a newly planted vineyard eating up resources and still two years from yielding a harvest.

"Besides, this whole situation is nonsense. It will blow over. We just have to wait until they get tired of it."

"André, it's unsettling. And hard on the emotions."

He gave a little laugh. "On your emotions. Not on mine."

She wasn't sure she believed him, but decided to move on.

"They really started this fight," she said. "It's become like a little game. They win if the visitors stay. They lose if the visitors leave. The poor visitors have become pawns. So my guess is, the visitors are strongly encouraged to stay put."

"Well, why should they leave? They've got it nice here, and all for free."

"That's for sure. Even electricity is free for them to take, and they take it freely. You and I use it too but we consider the cost and try to keep it down."

Some weeks earlier, before all the trouble, Neela had complained about a leak in the roof of one of the bedrooms. The next day around noon Catherine went to the back to have a look. There in the bedroom were the three visitors, tucked into Godwin's bed, watching something on Godwin's large TV. They were dressed in summer clothes, although it was cold outside, and they had an electric heater on, going full blast. André had seen the bill shoot up and then he knew at least one additional reason that money was draining away. The visitors had enough clothes to dress warmly. They just didn't bother. Those young visitors were not working, not looking for work, saying they will study but making no effort in that direction.

Outside, a cloud rolled in from nowhere and stopped the sun streaming in. André crossed his arms and lowered his head, going deep into thought. She shifted her position and reached for the farm notebook, where she tried to journal events and decisions, noting the people, time and date. Part of it was just to remember what was decided, and part of it was to have a paper trail, if things ever went to court. With more and more laws being made, mostly in favour of "the worker", where an employer stood got increasingly difficult to know. How these new laws might apply to a specific situation was unclear.

"I wonder if fighting puts Esta on an emotional high. It's as if she lets all her feelings out, everything, without even a thought for the consequences. Just lets rip."

"It's a tough position for Godwin, though," said André, in a rare moment of empathy. "He's got to feel trapped, with everyone now depending on him for a place to live."

Catherine made a note in the margin. "That's nine people now living in the cottage, and twelve if you count the visitors. All riding on one job."

"Well, what choice do we have?" Another question-statement from André. "If our worker leaves, we have to have the cottage to house his replacement. We can't keep people from his family here forever, just because they were related to Isaac. Let alone all the hangers-on."

Catherine pictured in her mind's eye all the relatives: Isaac's two sons, Sheryl and Neela with their children around them; Oupa and Koos; the adult Godwin with Esta; and now her family planting themselves here too, like runner beans extending shoots and branches all over the farm.

"Well, it's what they expect, it seems."

"Poor Isaac, dead now almost two years." She recalled the day he approached her and André, tears in his eyes, saying he just couldn't go on any more. So he and Laetitia stayed on in the cottage at full pay. He spent several years there in retirement. Godwin was just not interested in vines. André found a neighbour willing to take over the vineyard care and bring his workers and his tractor. But it still didn't work well for

Bellezicht. The harvest tonnage went way down until replanting seemed the only option.

"Really, André, I don't know why you tolerated that."

André's eyes narrowed. "What was I supposed to do? Godwin was the only option."

"Well, yes … ." She didn't want to fight about Godwin, not now; she knew André would get defensive. There were bigger issues at the moment. She also knew she was touching a sore spot, managing other people. He knew he wasn't good at it.

"Isaac. You were very good to him, André, to let his job morph into a part-time gardener's job, just to give him something to do in retirement. But the vineyard is suffering. How does it all end?"

He didn't answer. His gaze was out in the vineyard, dimly visible. The sunny day was giving in to swirling mist with threats of serious rain. The furrow between his eyes told her things she didn't want to know.

PART TWO

~ 9 The walk ~

The night of the shouting stayed with them for weeks. There was no way to go back, for them or for the people on the farm. At the same time, daily life had to resume. André went to his office in the town as usual, and Catherine taught the children in her English classes, as usual. The children in the farm family went to the government school as usual. Godwin cut the grass, trimmed the hedges and edged the flower beds cheerfully as usual. The women made a job of sitting in the sun as usual. Groceries in, garbage out, as usual. The adults at the cottage totally ignored André and Catherine. That was not usual. But still.

"Come, Lola! He-e-e-y Jonty!" When in the evenings André called the dogs, the ridgeback and the terrier, they bounded to the *werf*, tails up and mouths panting for their daily walk up the hill. When the farm children heard that call, the two older boys materialised immediately. The younger ones came out half walking, half running, struggling with eager effort into boots and jackets, not wanting to be left behind. Even the lanky farm dog Ringo came bounding. The ranting of the adults had made no difference to them. Quickly the daily walk resumed, as usual.

The little party of seven people and three dogs always started out the driveway between the vines. As it turned right at the dirt road leading up the hill, it streamed out like a procession. Dogs ran in front, criss-crossing as they snuffled at this and that. The small children, 5, 6 and 7 years old, ran ahead of the others in order to hide in the long roadside grass and be spied out with great fanfare. "Where's Jannie? Where is Jannie? *Het julle Jannie gesien?* Jannie, Jannie!" Out would pop Jannie, face ecstatic. "Oh, there he is!"

The two older boys had become too teenage cool to run and play. They walked slightly ahead of Catherine. Then came André at the end, walking stick in hand, striding along with the solemnity of a bishop.

As they started up the hill, the cottage at Bellezicht was visible between a few shorter rows of vines. It sat near the main house, both buildings in the centre of the farm. That first day when the walks resumed, shortly after the shouting, there at the cottage stood the smallest little boy, the child with the visitors who never left. He stood there crying to join the walk. Esta stood nearby, ready to help him into his boots and jacket. She looked over at the group slowly streaming out. He was her grandchild, after all. Or was he? Was the relationship just another "story", a creation to get someone out of a jam? Whatever, the group was walking on.

Catherine kept her gaze straight ahead, then looked over a second time. The little devil sitting on one of her shoulders told her, "Just keep going. The little boy will hold up the whole walk, it's getting dark, the dogs are already out of sight, maybe the neighbour's Rottweilers are just behind those trees, you have to think of the other children. Serves the farm people right after all that ranting. Let them deal with that crying kid."

The little angel on her other shoulder said to her, "Take it easy, will you. Esta and the adults are one thing, but this child had no say in things. Nothing is his fault. It will be petty of you not to wait for him. He will cry even harder at being left behind. Maybe he'll remember it all his life. Maybe even hold it against you forever. Against you and your kin. This is just a walk, after all."

Catherine stopped walking and stood there, vines all around, facing the cottage squatting at the end of the rows. André passed her, frowning his disapproval. The little boy broke free of Esta, jacket only half on. He ran through the vineyard between rows of vines. His determined will to join impelled him in anxious labouring steps over the tilled earth and turned-up stones, over the mesh of sticks fallen from pruners' shears.

As he neared the road, Catherine lifted him by the shoulders to help him jump onto the road over a piece of loose vineyard wire. She looked up at Esta and hesitated, then waved. Esta hesitated, and waved back.

Had something changed? Maybe, maybe not. It was just a minute's occurrence. A good feeling flooded her chest. Maybe.

"André, wait for us!" she called. The little tyke forged on ahead, eager to be part of the action.

The lengthening group now of eight plus the dogs, all in a pack, flowed around the first turn, then down the slope with lots more hide-and-seek games so dear to children. The bottom of the path spread out into a large mud puddle, catching rain water from the farm above. The little boy hesitated. It must have looked to him like Lake Victoria. One of the older boys wordlessly crouched down, the little boy climbed onto his back and all were through.

André did a quick check, no, no vicious Rottweilers, and raised his arm to signal forward. The pack flowed down the embankment onto a larger, firmer boundary road.

André seemed happy and more at peace when he went walking up the hill. The farm roads outlining the neighbouring farms, the cultivated earth, the mountains, the sky, all seemed to nourish his soul. There was no aggressiveness or defensiveness in him now; only harmony.

They continued on and up under a crisp sky. The earth smelled fresh after the rain. In the mid-distance, among rows and rows of arrow-straight vines, they could see neighbouring manor houses and clusters of neighbouring farmworkers' cottages.

André always sighed when they reached that high on the hill. "The place is getting so built up. It's not like it was when we first came here." Catherine just smiled. She knew that all of them, including Bellezicht, meant encroaching development. Despite tight regulation, it was probably just a matter of time.

At one point Catherine said, "André, where is Quinton?" Sheryl's teenage son was not with them anymore.

"Don't worry, he's probably taking a leak." André laughed. "This is farm country, Cath!"

Catherine wasn't so sure. For a boy just to disappear without saying where or why was just not done. Quinton had been sought out by a worker on a neighbouring farm for stealing a cell phone, and somehow the neighbour had gotten it back from Quinton and that was the end of the story, at the time. There was something crafty about him. Having left their supervision, what was he doing? Was he up to no good?

André kept walking. At one point he bent over and indicated a pair of bokkie tracks in the soft earth beside the road. "From a mama and her baby," he said. The older children also bent over to look and nodded sagely. Two pied crows squawked as they flew overhead.

The group approached the small tin structure of convoluted pipes housing the neighbour's irrigation control system. "Be careful," André warned. "This is where we saw the snake." A year ago, a Cape cobra there had been surprised by the dogs and it raised itself to face them as a cobra does, its body arched, its flat hood extended. Lola was barking herself inside out, head extended, the ridge on her back standing straight up. When André and Catherine saw the snake poised to strike, they shouted the dogs back in a high-pitched note of fear, an unusual call. The dogs turned their heads as if to verify, and the cobra took the gap and flipped away into the undergrowth with just a flash of tail. Everyone gave that place a wide berth.

"We're coming up to the Big Rock. Let's make that our about-turn for the day."

"No, no, we're not tired!" Going for a walk was special; it was not in farmworker routines. "Not now. Please, up to the High Road." The High Road was really an overgrown path but it sat high on the hill.

The Big Rock nestled next to a clump of bushes and a small tree. "I wonder if that yellow cat is still around," said Catherine. The small tree hadn't hidden the cat from the dogs. A few months before, the larger dog Lola had grabbed the cat before it reached the tree and gave it one powerful shake. As she shook the cat up into the air, the cat released an arc of urine golden against the evening sun. André shouted at Lola, who probably was surprised and then loosened her grip. The cat twisted free and made it to the top of that little tree, which offered scant safety. But it was enough against the frenzied barking and jumping, until Jonty and Lola and Ringo lost interest and moved on with the pack.

So it was up to the High Road before André called, "About turn!" It took about 40 minutes to walk back. There was a calm good feeling as they approached the farm.

As the children re-entered the farm, they ran this way and that. Suddenly André slammed his walking stick near a raised row of small aloe plants, where little Jannie was balancing his way back. Jannie jumped down with a shocked look on his face. André's face turned scarlet.

"What's going on?" cried Catherine, reaching out her arms to enfold the frightened child.

"He's trampling on the aloes! I just had them put in," said André.

"Well, you didn't mark them off, so how could the child see that?" she responded. Jannie bravely held back tears. "You can't treat a child like that, just out of the blue!" She hugged him.

"The aloes are still fragile," said André.

"And so is this child," she said. She knew to stop now and discuss it later, when André's temper had cooled.

They walked back to the house in silence, past the oak trees, past the rose garden, around the hibiscus bush and the hedges. The other children hadn't seen the incident. They were grouped around the front door waiting for their treat, usually bananas or apples; but today it was a whole sack of oranges, affordable in season. All but Quinton.

André probably knew that Catherine would remonstrate with him later. So he took Jannie aside and apologised to him and even shook his hand. The little fellow nodded, still brave, and picked up a few oranges.

~ 10 Missing ~

The visitors in the worker's cottage stayed far away from Catherine and André. During the day they sat in the sun with the women or watched Godwin's television, while André and Catherine went off to work. They had just been melted in, without consultation or permission of André or Catherine. The issue was principle, not personal. The situation was still in stalemate.

One morning Catherine received a call at work from André. He had left the windows open by mistake, and he had noticed her cell phone at home. They agreed that the farm people were there so no one could enter the farm undetected, and thus the house would be safe enough.

When they got home after work, they both looked around thoroughly for her phone. It was nowhere in the house. So they approached the cottage, behind the house, to ask. In the mellow afternoon, Neela's husband Henry was wheeling his bicycle up the road, coming home from his painting job. Neela, Esta, and the visitors were sitting on the *werf* in the sun, with the little ones playing around them with homemade toys. Sheryl and a few others came out of the cottage, leaving a pot of stew bubbling on the stove. The cottage dog Ringo wagged lazily but the adults stiffened, remembering they weren't speaking to the farm owners.

André spoke gently. "*My aarde, Catherine se selfoon is weg.* (My heavens, her cell phone is gone.) It's a silver sliding phone. We just want to ask, did anyone see a stranger around today, someone who could have taken Catherine's phone?"

There was no hesitation. Their eyes all turned toward Quinton and the message was clear. Not "a" suspect, but "the" suspect, right here on the farm.

This was a different issue altogether than the fight about who could live in the cottage. The adults gathered in a circle to include Quinton. The other children melted back into the cottage. He tried to melt too but his mother Sheryl caught him by the arm and marched him back. Quinton stood there, his wiry body in a too-large red T-shirt and shorts that he had been wearing all week. They peppered him with questions.

"*Nee, nee, ek het nie daai selfoon gesteel nie.* I didn't take it. No, not me. I didn't do it. I didn't steal it."

He shifted from one foot to the other, head and eyes down, a set to the mouth. One thin arm held the other, behind his back, so typical of an eleven-year-old boy.

"No, I don't know anything about it. No, I didn't see anyone strange around. No, I don't know where it is. No. No. No."

Then, silence to the repeated questions. He moved one bare foot back and forth in the dust.

His mother Sheryl stooped down in front of him and said, "Stand up straight, look at me and say you didn't take it."

"Nee, Ma, ek het nie die selfoon gevat nie." (No, Mama, I didn't take the cell phone.)

The quizzing went on. Obviously his own family didn't believe him. Not even his own mother. It began to seem quite possible that he had climbed in through one of the open windows and taken the phone. There was a small light deep to one side of his eyes, as if he knew something more.

Sheryl stooped down to talk to him again. *"Het jy die foon gevat?* Where is it? Admit it and ask forgiveness. Nothing will happen to you if you tell the truth. Give the phone back and everything will be right again."

He just stood there.

She went on. "I clean the windows in the house, and I see the Missus's diamonds and I never take anything. We should not take things. But if you did, tell us the truth."

He just stood there, eyes in the dust.

The interrogation went on, from his family members, from the farm owners. Catherine tried to be kind, to be non-threatening. She kept her voice soft. The vibe seemed to be in ebb and flow: asking Quinton, trying to get at least some information from him, losing steam, then starting the cycle again.

"We aren't getting anywhere," said André finally. He also began to shift his weight from one foot to the other.

"Exasperating," Catherine agreed quietly. "But that part about the diamonds – you know I don't have any diamonds. I'd rather put the money against the bond."

André smiled. "Yes, ever the practical woman."

Day was dissolving into evening. Like the energy of everyone except Quinton.

"André, it's no use." She shook her head.

André addressed the group that was left. "We know that you are honest people. This is the first time that anyone has stolen anything from our house. It is serious. We have trusted one another for many years. But if we can no longer trust our own people, then everything will change. *Diefstal verander alles.*" Everyone just stood there.

"Come, Catherine." They reluctantly stepped away, turned and walked toward the house. "I guess this means that we have given up on getting to the truth."

She looked at him. "But not without big losses. More than a phone. Losses on all sides."

"Catherine. I think we need a big glass of Scotch on the rocks. What a day." They settled down in the lounge, in front of the fireplace that was never used.

She opened the subject. "So what do you make of it all?"

"The kid is guilty as hell. He's just good at stonewalling."

"The poor kid doesn't have a father. Never really had one."

It was ironic that, being the third of Sheryl's four children, Quinton was the only one born while she was married, however briefly, to the biological father. That was before he deserted them to go live on the street and die there.

Catherine paused to sip her drink. She recalled an earlier incident with Quinton. Sheryl had come pounding at the door, her eyes not flirty now but determined, shouting "Call the police!" In the *werf* stood a woman and three other people, farmworker people, from a neighbouring farm, Rozenvlei. The woman wanted her phone back, saying Quinton had been visiting and he'd actually handled her phone. Then – it was gone. She'd just bought it at Edgar's and she had even brought the receipt, R500.

At first Sheryl had defended her son. "Why does everyone think it's Quinton all the time? He didn't take it! Go away! We will get the police to stop your empty accusations."

Catherine knew that getting the police there, then, for that reason, was like getting snowballs to survive in hell. She had test papers to mark against a deadline, and she definitely did not want to stand on the stoep and take part in that confrontation. But such things went with farming, it seemed.

Neela had come out to see what the fuss was about. Everyone stood around in a circle. Quinton denied taking the phone. Lots more accusations. At one point, Quinton said quietly that he'd had it in his hand; and then he threw it over the fence. But he would not admit it again, nor repeat it loud enough, nor say which fence, where, how to retrieve the phone.

Neela said, "Quinton, make it simple. Just go get the phone. It's somewhere on this farm. Where did you hide it?" But he wouldn't.

On that occasion, Sheryl seemed to accept defeat. And responsibility. She asked Catherine for a loan of R500 for the woman and said she would work it off, washing windows.

Later, Catherine had asked her privately, like a fellow conspirator, what she really thought. Had Quinton taken that phone? Sheryl had looked away and then said, "I don't know."

André drained his glass. "Yes, I can see why Sheryl didn't defend him today. She's seen this movie before."

"Neela was ready for him a year ago. But really, what could they do?"

"Give him a few good hidings, I'd say."

"André! Teach him a lesson? No. It will just make him angrier. I think he is already an angry little boy."

As she sat there, another memory of Quinton popped up, the day she went to the local hospital to bring him home. He was just six years old then and had been quite ill. Sheryl had asked Catherine to meet her there but she herself had not shown up. The hospital staff were reluctant to release the boy to someone not his parent. Catherine had to talk fast, to persuade them she was legit, to tell them where she lived and where she taught, and the staff verified what they could from the boy. Dressed in just a child's hospital gown and a diaper, this wisp of a boy held Catherine's hand as they walked through the corridors, past stares from everyone at this unlikely duo. Quinton strode alongside, engulfed in his own black thundercloud.

Catherine had wondered about the effect of hospitalisation on Quinton, about what illness and separation could do to a child. Angry this boy was, definitely.

The next morning, as Catherine was leaving without her silver cell phone, she ran into Neela, who had come to the refrigerator in the garage. Neela, despite her anger, raised her head and looked at Catherine, opening her droopy eyes wide. Catherine stopped and waited.

"Missus," she said quietly, *"Quinton steel altyd ook in ons huis.* He took his grandfather's watch. He took his grandmother's watch. He steals from all of us in the house and we have to be always on our guard."

Catherine's eyes widened. Neela went on. "That's why we wear the keys to our rooms around our necks." Then she turned her back and went about her business.

Catherine went back into the house to tell André. "For one brief moment, it was us, just us, not us and them."

André had just made himself a cup of coffee. "Here," he offered her his cup. "Have some coffee before you rush off. Sit down for a few minutes."

She sat with him at the kitchen bar as the tentative spring sun threw in some early beams.

"That's a shift in attitude," he said.

"And very welcome. But then, about a week ago, Sheryl brought an unhappy Quinton to the door and asked for money to take him to the clinic. He lifted his shirt and I saw spots all over his small chest. '*Puisies*,' Sheryl said. 'Is it chicken pox?' I asked. 'No, just spots.'

"Of course, I gave her the money and some for a snack afterward. When I got home after work, I went back to the cottage to hear the diagnosis. I saw Neela and Esta and despite their stony faces, I asked, 'Is it chicken pox?' 'Yes,' they said.

"Just then, Sheryl came out of the cottage. I said, 'So it's chicken pox.'

'*Nie, Missus*; it's allergies.'

'Allergies? To what?'

'To bread, *Missus.*'

'What? To bread?' I was quite surprised. 'Then what can the poor child eat?'

'He can eat butternut, *Missus.*'

'Butternut?'

'*Ja, Missus*. Allergies. It's what the doctor said, Missus.'

'But those *puisies*. They look so much like chicken pox.'

'The doctor said, *Missus*. And he's the doctor.' She turned to go inside.

"I looked at Esta and Neela standing there with little smiles on their faces and caught their eye; Sheryl didn't see. They knew they had told me chicken pox, and they could see that Sheryl was playing a game with me.

"I said to Sheryl's back, 'Well, he's the doctor.' Two can play this game. Again I caught their eye. Some contradictory things had been said, but everybody knew the truth. Later I left a large butternut on their stoep."

André sighed. "Why can't they be straightforward? What's the problem in acknowledging that it was chicken pox?"

"I'm not sure, but knowledge is power and maybe they just don't want us to know too much."

"Hide – one way to resist."

"Sheryl likes to thumb her nose at us. Even when things are going well." She thought for a moment. "I get miffed when I can't get a hold on the reality, on what is really going on."

"You let them make a fool out of you. You do it all the time."

"What?" She turned to face him.

"They get you running around, doing this and that, driving them here and there, paying right and left … ."

"You don't care about helping them?"

"There are better ways. They just exploit you as much as they can."

"André, we have responsibilities here. They live on our farm. We have to go the extra mile."

"Sometimes, yes, but not as a norm. We can't live their lives for them. We can't fix up everything in their lives. They make choices. Then they take the consequences."

"But André, we can do something. We should try." Her face grew grim.

"Well, you do try. Way too hard. Get rid of your white guilt. You didn't put them where they are. You can't just take them out of their situation, just like that."

She could feel her anger rising. "I don't like your tone, André."

They sat there for a while in silence.

"Anyway,' she said, "the only theft we've had was from Quinton, and nobody else."

"Well, there was Koos … ."

"Oh *ja,* yes." She thought for a minute. "The piece of cheese."

Koos had sneaked in through a window, a very small one at that. He went to the fridge but the only thing he found was a piece of cheddar. He took a bite and then threw it aside. The cheese even showed the small space between his front teeth. Then he ran off the farm. He later admitted it and apologised.

"In his case," André said, "I think it was just a young fellow testing the limits."

"I've often imagined how he felt, after seeing all the nice food we serve ... and then, once inside, he could only find some cheese."

She pictured the typical Bellezicht braai they gave for their friends, usually on a Sunday. Lamb chops marinated overnight using André's special recipe; preparing the meat for the braai was a man thing. He cooked the chops over a wood fire on the special built-in braai place on the veranda. She made little potatoes and a salad and a dessert. Her family in America sometimes had a barbecue but it is not the same thing. The barbeque typically uses briquettes, it does not last so long and it's mostly about the food, not the social event. The braai offers lots of starters for when guests arrive, but most of all it has lots of wine, and it allows plenty of time to savour the wine and socialise before the chops even go onto the fire. The aroma of the wood smoke blends with the roasting chops and it's all part of the party. Not to mention the stunning Bellezicht view, the envy of all their friends.

"Poor Koos."

"He wasn't a bad person. Just too old and too grown up for school. He was basically alone, except for the stepfather, who in the end killed him with a hammer." They went silent.

The next school day, to try to retrieve the phone, Catherine stopped by to see the principal of the primary school where the farm children went. She and Mrs Hendricks had worked well together for several years, trying to see why Godwin wasn't achieving, trying to keep an errant Quinton in school, supporting fund raisers and field trips. Mrs Hendricks said she would ask Quinton's teacher, a former detective, to follow up. She told Catherine that earlier it had been reported to her that Quinton had thrown a puppy off the bridge.

"Cruelty to animals. That shows us we may be dealing with more than a boy testing the limits."

"Disturbing." She told Mrs Hendricks of André's birthday braai, during which Quinton had set fire to the vineyards. Luckily Henry saw it and got the garden hose to put it out. That year was very dry and fires all over the mountains endangered everyone, vines and animals and people alike. The police came in due course, ready to take a charge of arson and send Quinton away. Sheryl and Quinton pleaded with tears in their eyes and promised it would not happen again, so Catherine and André dropped the case.

Very early the following day, Mrs Hendricks phoned back. "The teacher just asked the class: 'Has anyone done anything wrong?' and wonder of wonders, Quinton stood up! He told the class that he had stolen a cell phone. She praised his honesty and just now brought him to the office."

"Amazing!"

"Can you come to the school, now? Bring his mother too. I think we can retrieve the phone. We know the fellow he gave it to, living at a farm just up the road."

Catherine turned to André. "We're in luck. I'll phone and ask to come in late today. Let's drive down. I'll get Sheryl."

At the school, Mrs Hendricks had Quinton in her car. Sheryl climbed in too. Then Mrs Hendricks came over to André and Catherine and said, "The fellow with the phone, Lewis; his mother told me he has just gone to visit a girlfriend at Vredelust farm. Just follow me."

André laughed as they drove out. "So the convoy sets out down the Lynedoch Road ... there will be a standoff ... at the OK Corral! Let's see who survives!"

Mrs Hendricks and Sheryl knew their way around the farm community. Through a maze of cottages they found the right one, separated from the others only by a few strands of wire fencing. An older man came out.

"Kan ons asseblief met Lewis praat? Can we please speak to Lewis?" asked Mrs Hendricks, a model of politeness.

Some shuffling and out came a nice-looking young fellow. "Cell phone? I don't have any cell phones."

Quinton spoke up. With surprising energy, he lifted his whole arm and pointed directly at Lewis. "He's lying. I threw the cell phone over the fence to him."

Lewis played for time and showed his ID. He was just 18. Everyone waited. Finally Lewis went back inside and brought out an old Nokia.

"No, that's not my phone," Catherine said.

"I don't know what phone you had, I don't have any phones, you won't get phones here ... ."

Then of all people, Sheryl spoke up. She gritted her teeth and flamed her eyes and spat out the words, "Just go get the phone." And he did. Just like that. The silver sliding Samsung.

Victory! Sheryl and Mrs Hendricks turned to leave. But Catherine hadn't yet finished. "Lewis, you are 18 now, an adult. You are leading this boy into crime. I think that in itself may be a crime."

But support was dwindling. Mrs Hendricks wanted to get back to her school, taking Quinton with her. André wanted to get to his office. Sheryl and Quinton turned to leave. She had no choice but to walk back to the cars too.

The question remained what to do with Quinton. Praise him for coming forward? Punish him for stealing? Should he just go back to school, to his classes? He came through as a star, and as a star witness. But how should they get him not to steal in the first place? Neither Catherine nor Mrs Hendricks could find easy answers.

Catherine wasn't happy. She drove into town to the Stellenbosch Police Station to follow up about how to stop adults from leading kids into crime.

"You got your cell phone back," said the constable. "All you lost was the SIM card. What does that cost, R35? Not much."

"Do you think I'm here about the phone card?" Catherine was incredulous. "There must be a law against corrupting a minor. I want us to act against Lewis."

The officer sighed, shook his head and turned away. What could she do, especially as she wasn't sure about the law on this matter. You asshole, she thought – but enough for one day. She resolved to do her homework on laws about corrupting a juvenile and get back to his supervisor.

A few weeks later, she saw on the calendar that Quinton's birthday was coming up. She always tried to get something decent for each birthday child, to make them feel special; something active, such as a cricket set or jump ropes or paddle balls. Later that day she saw Quinton walking up the farm road from school.

"Quinton, what would you like for your birthday?"

Without hesitating, he looked her straight in the eye. "A cell phone."

~ 11 Happy anniversary ~

The *maître de* opened the panelled door very wide, with a smile to match. He seated Catherine and André at the reserved table for two. Despite the conflict on the farm, the calendar marched on and showed the anniversary of their wedding.

White tablecloths always pleased André. But that evening, he commented only on the *maître de*. "He obviously expects a good tip."

The wine list seemed to demand his full attention. "Red?"

She nodded. He ordered a pinotage-shiraz blend produced at a nearby wine farm.

He raised his glass. "To our first sixteen years." Her eyes softened and she smiled. "May the next sixteen be easier." They each took a sip.

"Easier? What is that supposed to mean?"

"Well, we've come a long way from anniversaries where we used to just walk around Cape Town like tourists and have a light lunch. Now here we are at a top restaurant."

"Yes, it costs money. But I got paid yesterday for a commissioned study."

"That's part of what I mean, easier to afford at least a few of the finer things. At a special time."

They smiled at each other and took another sip. The wine was a real winner, dark and dense and well-wooded.

"Most of my income goes right into that blood-sucking farm. The bond, the running expenses, the wages. Office rental, monthly parking in Stellenbosch. Maintaining the vehicles; not to mention the rising cost of petrol. At least you get to drive the big car and I make do with the bakkie … ."

"Well, my income just disappears too. Do you know what it costs these days to run a household? Catherine looked at him. "Maybe it will get harder, not easier, in the next sixteen."

"Sy kla met witbrood onder die arm." She knew what he meant; she complains while carrying a loaf of white bread, complaining in the midst of luxuries. She forced a rueful smile.

They sat for a while savouring the wine, and then ordered a moderate entrée, moderate for this restaurant.

"Well, André," she said. "No starters, no desserts, no coffees. We agree on that. It's more than enough to eat."

"True."

"And more than enough to drink," she said. "I'll have just one glass, so that I'll be able to drive, okay?" He smiled at her offer and poured himself more wine. Drivers suspected of having drunk too much could possibly be arrested on the spot. Not a pretty place, the jail cells with iron bars and cement. Catherine had seen them when she had taken the teenage boys at the farm to visit the police station, to try to motivate them to think about a future career. And to stay out of jail.

As they left the restaurant, he handed her the key to the 4x4. "Don't put the wipers on; remember that the spray doesn't work and with the dew they'll just smear the windscreen with mud."

With the bill had come a few peppermints. He suggested they give the sweets to the guard at the gate, and as she pulled out of the parking area, she was busy telling André where to find them in her handbag.

Then he shouted, "Stop! Stop! Stop!" She hit the brakes hard.

"Do you know what you almost did?" He half-screamed, half-shouted at her. His face screwed into a knot. Two shock waves rolled over her, one for the stopping and one for the shouting.

"You almost hit those bricks! You almost did serious damage to the car! How could you!"

Her mouth fell open in disbelief. The guard at the gate came to her window. "Is there a problem?"

André kept shouting. "This is a big car! You have to learn to drive it! You almost put a big dent in my door! Back up! Now!"

She checked in the mirror and saw that, luckily, no car was behind them. As she shifted into reverse, André kept up his tirade. Shouting. Was he taking lessons from the farm people? It was as if someone else was sitting there beside her, not her dear André. Someone from close to Hades.

"Why did you cut it so close? You have to take it wide, with this big car! Didn't you see those bricks? You could have put a major dent along the whole side of the vehicle! What's the matter with you!"

She backed the car at a wide safe angle, out of the path to the exit, and they sat there for a few moments, engine still running. She tried to look for what was getting André so excited.

"Do you know what it would cost to get something like that fixed? A lot of money, that's what. But you don't care. You don't take care; that's the problem!" On and on.

She just sat there, stunned. Absolutely stunned.

Then the *coup de grâce:* "Let me drive!"

She knew he had quaffed most of the wine and she knew it was not wise for many reasons to let him drive. However, the anger that welled up in her – hell with logic. Propelled by anger she jumped out wordlessly and handed him the key.

As he drove through the exit gate, he pointed out the stubby pillar of bricks. They looked just like the bricks paved in the driveway. From the passenger side, and being right beside it, she could now see it clearly. It was there for the extended arm of the driveway boom to rest on. Bushes had grown out beside it so that it was not easily visible as one drove out. It was too short to be seen over the bonnet of the vehicle, from the driver's seat. That height is a well-known problem with 4x4s. And it was night. Never mind the dirty windscreen.

But she didn't get the chance to admit her error of judgement, to explain how she had been negotiating the exit as well as explaining about the sweets, to apologise, to thank him for stopping her in time.

"Why weren't you more careful? You were mere inches away. This is a big car. It's 12 years old and it would cost a fortune to replace! Don't you realise that!"

Finally she spoke. "Why are you shouting at me like this? You could speak civilly. I don't like this. I don't like it at all."

"So what's your problem!" He shot back.

"Why are you shouting at me like this? I don't think it is called for." She paused for a moment and raised her voice a notch higher, "I won't have it!"

"You've been under stress," he barked.

"What! Don't you patronise me!" She was seriously shouting back now. "Are you shouting at me because I'm under stress?"

She heard her own voice go up a few more decibels, and this time she pounded her fists on the dashboard. "No! I won't have it!"

"Watch out or you will release those air bags."

Another deflection. She pounded the dashboard even harder. Exploding air bags were the least of her worries right now.

"How can you shout at me? I don't understand it! It's abuse! Verbal abuse! This has not been in our relationship and I won't have it now." More pounding. "I just (pound) won't (pound) have it!"

Dimly she heard her own shouting; she felt the sound waves rising up out of her. Something strange evolved out of her. She became aware that she was shouting back at him. A little message from inside her reminded her not to reply in kind, but the anger couldn't think and made her ignore it.

He got silent.

He pulled into a Shell service station. "I need to get the windscreen washed." The attendant smiled at the R20 tip, when R5 would have been enough.

On the road again, for the 30 minutes to home. Her fury curled her up in the seat facing away from him. She closed her eyes. Withdraw; a woman's best weapon. She identified every bump and turn. It was a long, silent half hour. In the end it was a merciful half hour. There was not much traffic. He drove slowly. Tempers softened.

She silently did a few chores and got ready for bed. He walked around the house a bit and then came up behind her and reached to take her in his arms. She did not warm to it.

"I'm very sorry for the way I treated you tonight. After that lovely dinner. And then … ."

For the first time, her tears began; they spurted out, and then came the sobs, one after another, as she gasped for breath. "You don't know the damage you did, the damage your shouting did," she sobbed, her breath catching. "You never waited for me to give my point of view, what I was aiming at to get the car out of the restaurant grounds, even the fact that I never saw that square of bricks. You just ran me into the ground!"

Holding her still from the back, he put his face against her neck. "I'm very sorry." His tone was mournful.

"I know it's my fault for not seeing those bricks," she sobbed. "I was the driver. But it was an error of judgement, not a deliberate act."

He held her, just held her. Gradually she moved. She turned toward him and forced her arms around him. She was not one to hold grudges but tonight's episode was something out of the blue. It was primal. Who is this André? It wasn't him, yet it was him.

"I'm so sorry, so sorry," he repeated, again putting his face against her neck. They stood there a long time.

She took deep choking breaths. Soon her sobs got less. "Will this happen again?" she whispered, wiping away tears still flowing.

"Definitely not. No, definitely not." He gave her a strong hug. She just couldn't look at him, at his face. "My darling. I'm just so sorry." She kept her eyes away from him but heard a convincing sadness in his voice.

She wanted to believe him. It was such an uncharacteristic episode. Somehow they both had fallen into deep uncharted waters, and she didn't know which way to the surface.

92

They stood there, arms encircling each other.

They lay down beside each other. After all, it was their anniversary. But there was no excitement, no anticipation, no joy; just the residue of sorrow that comes after struggling with a heavy weight, or after surviving a rockfall. Another time there may have been sex, but not tonight. There was just the shared sense of a great, great loss. The way one feels after someone close has died.

~ 12 The farm ~

The days stretched into weeks and still no movement from either side. The waiting game weighed heavily on Catherine. How long could this impasse go on? Something had to change, but how? The seasons were changing; winter was easing off into spring. What about the people? Couldn't people change too? Couldn't we all learn from the seasons and ease off?

She pondered these questions on a quiet Saturday afternoon, as she sat curled up in the big worn-leather chair in the lounge. She could view the mountains from there, while being protected from any cool wind.

Through the French doors, she watched the big cumulus clouds puffing their way across the steel-blue sky. This particular piece of land had been used as a farm for over 300 years, starting with the European settlers. Actually, history pointed to people living on this very slope over half a million years ago, thanks to the stone tools found on it. Chippers, scrapers, even hand axes had been found throughout the area and had recently been authenticated at a neighbouring farm. Similar stones had been found at Bellezicht too. They were brought to the surface by such things as deep plowing, wind, rain and irrigation runoff. Catherine looked through the doors at the ones she and André had discovered, displayed on the veranda wall.

This farm had felt the plow, the hooves of horses and donkeys and cattle and sheep, as well as the feet of many people as they herded, planted, harvested, bought and sold over the centuries. She and André had hiked up to the top of the hill above their farm one crisp Sunday, and they discovered an old cannon still in place.

That cannon in the old days wasn't used for fighting; it was used for communication. She asked herself, is there a lesson here? Why must we fight when we can communicate? When a ship came into Table Bay, relays of cannons stretching eastward were fired, one after the other, to let the farmers in the hinterland know to bring their produce to Cape Town for sale. After all, the Cape was founded to be a rest and supply stop as ships sailed to India for spices. André and Catherine often joked about the importance of pepper in their lives, as it was the quest for spices, among other things, that spurred the great exploratory journeys of old and ultimately brought them, and the rest of the world, together.

However, it was only in the last 100 years that these few hectares, and other pieces of land like them, were chopped off of large tracts claimed by the settlers and sold with their own title deeds. The main house, the cottage, the garage, and the sheep pen were built and Bellezicht came into being. The children of workers on other farms grew up and found jobs on these new small farms. The jobs gave a small sum of wages and most importantly, a place to live.

A place to live. On the bookcase under the window she could see the two volumes of documents that André had had bound, showing the vast amount of paperwork required for their purchase of this small farm. Two heavy red volumes.

Not everyone needed paperwork for a place to live. The previous owner told Catherine and André something that showed the importance of a place to live. One morning he had opened the front door and there stood a gnome of a man, knitted cap and all, his brown skin lined from his years. His blue work shirt and Wellington boots identified him as a farmworker. He hadn't knocked; he'd just appeared there and waited until someone noticed him.

He had seen the old empty cottage lower down the hill and asked if he could live there. Luckily the new owner needed a worker and Isaac Jacobs nodded and grinned his toothless grin. The owner said he needed a few days to fumigate that cottage against the spiders and flies there but that didn't worry Isaac. He moved his family in that afternoon and that was that.

Recalling the story, it seemed a bit strange to Catherine that Isaac had not asked for a job, but just for a place to live. Only a lot later did it come to light that Isaac was receiving disability payments due to an injury from the previous job and was not really supposed to work. That was why he didn't have a place to live. But his previous employer had accepted the situation at face value, as did André in his turn, and only years later did the full story come out. Despite his ethic of honesty, there was Isaac, double-dipping from the state. Nothing personal. Anyway, he had a big family with his four children Sheryl and Neela and Reuben and Tommy still at that time with their parents, plus a few grandchildren, and he needed the money.

But now? Isaac had passed away, as had Laetitia. The next generation who were his grown children and all of them parents now themselves, were lining up behind the visitors. The sons had left to make their own way at other farms in the area. Now Neela, along with Esta, had led the shouting and threats. There seemed to be no clear way out.

Actually, Neela was quite a good and peaceful woman. She loved her family and took good care of her small son and even kept her husband Henry with her, despite his love for the night life. She was straightforward and even risked standing up to André when she felt it was right. Catherine felt that eventually she would become the heart of the family. But now, under Esta's influence, another side to her came out.

Catherine asked herself if she and André really wanted to stay there, if things could get this bad. How would it be if they had to live a life of constant enmity with the people staying a few metres from them, who were also their neighbours, and an employee? She had a sense that life would never be the same again, that there was no going back. She tried to shine a light into that dim, less defined place inside herself where her own wants lived. She did not look there often enough. She asked herself, what does this farm mean to me?

"*Dis net 'n lappie aarde,*" writes a famous South African writer of his own farm; just a little patch of earth. His description fits Bellezicht too. Its boundaries are surveyor's lines on the map in a rough rectangle, but geography makes its own boundaries. The northern border is just on the far side of a gully, a donga. Because the farm is in a small, exceptional part of South Africa, it has the Mediterranean climate of the Western Cape. That means long dry summers and cold wet winters. The donga, dry most the year, sometimes after winter rain gets very full and floods the lower part of the farm. André even joked that in some years he needs a rubber duck to get around.

Being a language teacher, Catherine looked for the origin of the word donga. The dictionary says it comes from the Nguni language family. It probably made it into English through Zulu, after its prefixes were cut off. So donga is indigenous to South Africa. It's another contribution to the vocabulary of the world, Catherine noted, along with *boer, veld, rooibos, apartheid*.

Apartheid – even the word shouts division. The policy is long gone but a word, as the poet says, has long boots. It is another Afrikaans word that has migrated into English. It connotes memories, attitudes, remnants of beliefs and behaviours that still dog people, no matter how hard they try to be colour-blind. The slight turn of the head away from the other; a defocusing of eyes so slight yet perceptible; a mother pulling her child closer as if to protect the child from danger, the assumed danger of "them." Beware. Stay safe; stay apart.

But now the Bellezicht conflict was not based on racial divisions, although the situation stemmed from those roots. The conflict would have been the same if she and André and the younger generation on the farm now, Godwin and Neela and Esta and the others, all were white or all were black or all were so-called coloured. The issue was about who could live where, about who had the final say in new people arriving and settling in to call Bellezicht home.

When push came to shove, Catherine knew in her heart that she and André, being owners, had a strong say in the matter. But it was a right that sickened her. She just did not want to go there. Just like in her professional work, she had the right to use her institutional authority, but the moment she has to use it, even though she may win at the moment, there is something lost.

As she sat quietly and pondered these things, the loud chuffing of a tractor came in through the French doors. She walked outside, down the steps, and waved to the driver who was helping out. He was dragging a many-bladed implement through the vineyard row by row. It turned over the soil and at the same time deftly turned the weeds under, there to rot and fertilise.

Catherine walked over to the first row of vines and stooped down to look closely at those poor weeds; how she hated and loved them at the same time. She hated them cluttering up the vineyard and absorbing irrigation water intended for the vines. But, being organic, the farm was not allowed to use herbicides so they grew freely.

But she loved the weeds too for their beauty. They showed up in early spring in thick patches of bright golden flowers. There were purple weeds too, thousands of them, with fuzzy stems and small flowers. The patches of yellow and patches of purple made a random flowing design in and around the vines. They lined the dirt road that marked the southern boundary.

Catherine appreciated how the vines stand together in their rows. Each vine has one main stem with two horizontal branches reaching along the supporting trellis wires to touch the next vine. Like brothers and sisters of all the people in the world, in solidarity. With a common purpose, to bear fruit.

In October, small shoots come out of what looks like a dead, gnarled stem.The vines sprout fragile, transparent leaves, yellowish and light green. The vines then look like ostriches standing on one leg, in a row, each with a rounded back full of fluffy yellow-green feathers. Their ostrich wings stretch out tip to tip.

In November the vines give out tiny white blossoms as small as the head of a pin. They become the grapes. Catherine had actually not seen them for years, until she learned to look carefully.

There are lots of sprouts on each vine, as if it is taking every chance to be alive. Too many of these sprouts will only divert its energy. Are they like all the hangers-on, visitors who come, sit, and draw your energy away?

What does this farm mean to me? Catherine asked herself again, caught up in this new cycle of vineyard life. I'm only a small blip, she thought, hardly a speck of dust on this little piece of earth. I know I'm privileged to be part of this cycle of farm life, of human life. I will be gone but the land will remain. We exist in the present. The present is what we have to worry about. Catherine felt a sudden prayer rise from a deep somewhere. "I believe, oh how I believe, that on this farm we can cause vines and people to become a little better, here and now, if we try. I want to try. Please, God, please, help me to try."

~ 13 Anna ~

Anna Solomons came every Friday to help in the house. She was aptly named: she was short and full of power. She was a positive force for good, a force for change from not-so-clean to very clean. She was what they call a *stywe vrou* – not fat but a solidly built woman. She wore her hair close cropped, a fitting frame for her coffee-cream complexion. The small curls were developing silver threads.

She was a definite personality. With her clear set of principles, she did not suffer fools gladly. She had a strong faith in the Lord, but experience had made her wary of her fellow human beings, especially the churchy ones. She went to church on Sundays and gave the rest of Sunday to her family. Thus she was never available to help out for a Bellezicht Sunday braai. Besides, for André to drive her home all the way across town after enjoying wine with friends was never a good idea.

She took full responsibility for the care of Bellezicht's house and everything in it. Catherine knew it was too much work for her to accomplish in just one short day, especially to her exacting standards. "Just leave it if you don't get to it, no problem." That was not good enough for Anna. Things had to be right.

"Time to go, Anna."

"Okay, but I just wanna finish this."

Not only did she dust and sweep and mop; she washed and ironed and cooked. She could make food for two or two hundred, typical Cape dishes that kept you wanting more. She was a genius with food. Not only that – she cooked a pot of stew while she multitasked, while she was running back and forth to the washer, repositioning the clothes outside on the line and using the vacuum.

Catherine tried to get her some help from the farm family. Sheryl had done housework for other people, but Sheryl had her own ways of doing housework, rebel that she was; taking direction did not work well with her. Catherine realised that they were both too strong to work together smoothly, so she tried Godwin.

When Anna couldn't lift the floor polisher, she asked the young Godwin to help and then he took over that job from her every week, plus washing some windows, plus sweeping and vacuuming and shining copper pots and polishing the two silver trays, gifts from friends. He didn't mind her exacting standards and gained some skills in the process. In fact, he grew to love her.

The farm family respected Anna greatly. They addressed her as "Tannie," auntie, showing their deference. Not only did she live in town and not on a farm, a step up of course, but she and her husband owned their own home.

Anna and her family had made the move into the first world. There was not a lot of money, but the life style was there. She had a digital TV and a microwave. Her husband held a decent job in building maintenance at the University with medical benefits and a retirement plan. The educational level of the children was catching up, with two of her four children, all sons, finishing high school and holding decent jobs.

André drove to fetch her on Fridays, just after the traffic. Catherine usually arranged to take her home, with a stop at Pick n Pay. The drive allowed good chatting time.

"How are you, Anna?"

Quiet.

"Anna?"

"Miss Catherine, I don't wanna complain, but … ." Then it would come tumbling out, the son who was in trouble with the law; the nephew who fell out of the back of a bakkie and died under its wheels; the daughter-in-law who nagged Anna's son day and night. Then her own health problems; vertebrae that required not just one but a series of operations; a leg with sores; acid reflux. There was a breast exam for which Catherine took her to Paarl and stayed by her side for the entire day.

There were doctor bills that went beyond the coverage of the University's medical aid plan. When Anna couldn't stretch the money any more, she knew she could ask for a loan. But the steep fees of private doctors went beyond what could possibly be paid back. Catherine insisted on picking up the slack. Anna just wanted better medical care than the usual clinic provided, as competent as it was, and Catherine supported her without hesitating.

When Catherine went to the shop weekly for herself and for the farm family, Anna would ask for a few items too and then pay Catherine later. That was a difference from the farm people. When Catherine and André lent money to them, they knew that it would never all come back. Ah, there was a trip to the clinic. Ah, an auntie passed away and money was needed to go to the funeral. Ah, the son was in jail and they had to go visit him, and the taxis are so expensive … . Extend the payments – next week, next month, until some other crisis would appear and the farmer would say all right, forget about the rest. But Anna – no. Anna always repaid, and repaid in full.

The shopping list was quite indicative. Catherine would buy a 500 gram packet of butter for home. She would buy a 500 gram packet of margarine, the cheapest as requested by the farm family, and they would reimburse her for it on payday from Isaac's wages, and for whatever else they asked for on their weekly list, such as sugar, coffee, matches, tobacco, bread and coffee. She would buy a 500 gram packet of high-quality margarine as requested by Anna, but not butter and not cheap, also to be reimbursed. The same with brands of coffee. The shopping cart told the story. Anna and her purchases stood in the middle.

Anna was a go-between in many ways. She understood both worlds, the world of her employers and the world of the farm family. One day, one of many, that Catherine heard loud noises at the cottage, she went back to investigate, thinking that there was *huismoles,* domestic violence. She saw just Neela and Esta dancing around and shouting. They had been ignoring her and André after the shouting on that late August night. Here might be a chance to get them to say clearly what they found so wrong and maybe how to get talks going. She asked Anna if she would kindly go and to listen. Anna came back into the house with a pained expression.

"Miss Catherine, oh my. It's about you and *Meneer.*" She paused, then continued reluctantly. "They are not happy that you are telling them to leave the farm."

"Anna, we are not telling them to leave. We are telling their visitors to leave."

"Esta wants Godwin to leave with her, and the rest of the people should stay at Bellezicht."

"And no one to work on the farm? Not even to do some gardening?"

Anna was silent.

"Anna, that won't work. Godwin is the worker. If he goes, we will have to get someone in his place. We will need the cottage for housing. So how can the other people just hang on? Housing on the farms is linked to a job."

"Miss Catherine, you have to understand. Where can they go? They are so afraid."

"Anna, what are they afraid of? Don't people move house sometimes?"

"They've been here many years now, and they don't have money. How will they manage?"

"Can't Godwin get a job on another farm, with housing benefits?"

Anna shook her head. "I hear it from some of my family. Jobs on farms are very hard to get these days. Godwin has a lot of people with him; not easy to take all of them along. Besides, where will they find someone to treat them as well as you and *Meneer* treat them?"

"Thank you, Anna. But now, what do we do about the shouting, about the bad relationship developing so close to us? Everything is changing, and fast."

"I don't know. But I don't think they mean you any harm. Maybe they feel pushed into a corner and they are coming out fighting. If they have to leave ... it is life-changing for them. I don't know ... they just have to get their heads right."

"Can you get them to talk to us?"

"I don't know." They stood together in silence.

Neither Anna nor Catherine could bear the disorganised living style, especially the dirt, in and around the cottage. Never mind the health risks.

"Miss Catherine, how can they live like that, not to pick up the trash, the empty plastic bags right outside their doors? The garbage lying around."

"I know. I wrote '*Was my*,' wash me, on the windows with my finger two days ago and the windows still haven't been washed."

"That bad smell – they don't clean, they smoke inside, they don't open the windows … . They don't even cover the garbage bin." She was merciless.

"Well, they can't say they don't have a broom, a mop, buckets, Handy Andy or Doom," Catherine said. "Anything they want. There is hot and cold running water in the kitchen and the bathroom. They don't have to pay for cleaning materials. All they have to do is put it on the shopping list."

"It hasn't made any difference," sniffed Anna.

The farm family complained once that their TV stopped working. André took it to a repair shop in Kuils River. Two days later it was fixed. The problem? *Kakkerlakke* – cockroaches inside! When they heard this, to their credit, they gasped.

A strip of fly paper hung from the ceiling. However, there was no space left on it for new flies to land. Not to mention the presence of mice – lots of them. Surely their droppings, just left in place because furniture was rarely moved out, didn't help.

To Catherine, the problem was obvious. The place had to be cleaned regularly and kept clean. Her background made that clear to her. The Pennsylvania Dutch have a saying that puts cleanliness right up there next to godliness.

She had asked Laetitia, gently, if she'd like Anna to show her a few tricks, a few things about how to keep the place cleaner. Laetitia was quite agreeable.

So Anna showed her some things to do, from time to time. Anna even washed and dried the occasional blanket or jacket, using the house facilities, *skelmpies,* on the quiet. Just a little conspiracy to help out.

Catherine supported her. "I'm glad to hear this, Anna. Help them all you can."

Obviously it wasn't enough. But it made Catherine realise that a more direct approach was needed. Anna and Laetitia agreed on a date, and Anna arrived for a day of housework dedicated to the cottage.

She organised Laetitia, Sheryl and Neela to work with her, the general marshalling her troops for battle. She had them move out the furniture and clean behind it. She had them wash the dirty fingerprints off the walls. Wash the windows and open them daily for fresh air. Wash the cooking pots after using them. Wash the dishes. Wipe up crumbs. Make sure the lids fit properly on the trash cans. Scour the sinks. Brush out the toilets. Mop the floors. Clean the corners. Use new fly paper. Use Doom.

For a week or so afterward, the cottage looked good and it smelled fresh. By the third week, fingerprints and window dirt reappeared, plastic chips bags popped up, banana peels drew flies; back to the way things were.

Anna shook her head.

~ 14 April 1994 ~

Trying to make things better was not something foreign to Catherine. It was part of her being, from childhood on. It was not surprising that she consistently found opportunities to keep trying to help people make the most of their lives including and especially the farm family. But it was not always a straight path, and people often did not see matters the same way. Like the time in the early 1990s, when Mr Nelson Mandela came out of prison to mould the new South Africa. Voting for all would surely follow.

Laetitia shook her head. *"Verkiesings? Nooit nie. Dis net moeilikheid. Nee, Missus, ons gaan nie kies nie."* (Voting? Never; it's just trouble. We are not going to vote.) Isaac turned away with her. As they started walking to the cottage, she added, *"Verder wil ons niks daarvan hoor nie."* (Further, we don't want to hear any more of this matter.) End of discussion.

Distress settled over Catherine like morning fog in the valley below Bellezicht. How could it be that finally, finally, freedom came knocking at the door and they wouldn't open it? The tide was turning toward full democracy. But now, what to do with Laetitia's attitude? Catherine would have to confer with André. She could not just accept Laetitia's decision without question.

She went into her kitchen and made herself some coffee, the decaf instant kind, to afford some time to think. The majority of people in South Africa had never been allowed to vote for their country's leaders. Her own feelings for democracy ran deep. Growing up in the USA, she had witnessed her parents going to vote. The idea that everyone can have a say was taught in school through elections of student leaders and through civics classes, boring as they often were to adolescents whose minds were focused more on one another. Still, something had taken. She had had problems all along about the lack of full democracy in South Africa. This lack had led her to think a lot about whether or not she could morally go to live in such a country.

It was outrageous that the excluding factor was prejudice against people because of their so-called race. Ironically, it was a black friend of hers in the States who encouraged her to go to South Africa and marry André. "We need to fight injustice everywhere," he had told her. "You are a teacher. Change will come, and that country will need an educated population. Go."

So she went. She joined projects for upliftment and knew that was the right direction. When Mr Mandela left Victor Verster Prison after 26 years of incarceration, she was over the moon. He set the tone for building a just and diverse land. But the farm family, unexpectedly, didn't feel that way.

She approached Anna. Anna herself was not so sure that these changes were all good, but she did open her thoughts to Catherine.

"Apartheid – it is bad. First it was everyday things, like black people, all of us coloureds and Indians too, having to step aside for white people. If there was a conflict, the black people lost. They wouldn't educate us much because we were supposed to stay servants, doing slave work. They believed we were not able to think because of our race."

Catherine nodded, admiring Anna for being so articulate.

"Then they passed the Group Areas Act," said Anna. "It made people live in certain places according to race. If we travelled out of 'our' area, somebody white had to be with us, or we had to show a pass or face arrest. If people didn't move out, bulldozers came in and levelled their homes and forced them to go. Forced removals, all over the country."

"Bulldozers," said Catherine. She had first learned about those bulldozers when attending a play called "District Six." The setting was a district in Cape Town where thousands of coloured people lived in a poor but vibrant way. The play told their story. The sound of the bulldozers even on the stage had shocked Catherine. It was unbelievable that this was "the law." But in those days the whites had the power. All the power.

"Of course there was always resistance," said Anna. "A lot of it came at election time, elections of white people by white people. Only white people. Elections just ignored most of us."

She described how resisters would block the roads with burning tyres. They would march and face police, police with their whips and batons, their tear gas and bullets. Rubber bullets and real ones. Best to stay away, far away.

"So, Miss Catherine, it's no wonder they don't want to go and vote. It could cost us our lives."

"So, Anna, do you feel that way too? What are you going to do?"

"I don't know." She looked distraught. "But I will see, closer to the time."

Well, vote or not, Catherie saw one thing she could do to nudge them in that direction, even if they chose not to go the full way. Not many people on the farms had their ID book, and without that unique personal identification document, one could not hope to vote. It was not easy to get. The officials at the Home Affairs Offices remained legendary in how they obstructed people, of how they tied them up in bureaucracy, of how they themselves were tied up in bureaucracy.

André affirmed it. "It is easier for the officials to say no. If they say yes, it means they have taken some responsibility and could be held accountable. It's safer to say no."

Catherine asked Laetitia if they had IDs; no, not one person of the 12 people on the farm. Did they want ID books? Definitely; but it had seemed impossible. Just the preliminaries of paperwork and transport were daunting.

But not for Catherine. She set to work.

First, get the application forms. The date and place of birth were clear for the younger people, but they turned out to be big problems for the older people, Laetitia and Isaac and Oupa. Another form was needed before the ID forms, to establish a birth date.

Isaac did not know when or where he was born. Nor did Oupa. At least Laetitia had a paper she had used to apply for public housing, but it was long out of date. How can you determine your date of birth, when you could not read or write, when you had no documents, when the state had no record of you being born? How in the world had they all gotten clinic folders, Catherine wondered. But when you are ill, they have to help you regardless.

André had some ideas. He sat down around the dining room table with Isaac, Oupa and Laetitia to ask them about their earliest memories. Catherine took notes.

Isaac spoke first. *"Ja, Baas, ek was een jaar by die skool, net een jaar."* One day in his first and only year of school, the teachers took all the children out and lined them up along the road. *"Ja, Baas, hierdie pad, net hier."* This school, right down this very road. The school gave the children little flags to wave. Eventually a motorcade came along the road, very slowly. The children waved the flags and cheered at the top of their lungs, especially to the family in the big open car. He recalled that it was an important man and woman and two young girls. Then the teachers took them back to the school for cake and sweets.

André knew; it was the visit of the Royal Family of England, in 1947. So how old could Isaac have been? About six or seven? They agreed that 1940 was his most probable year of birth. What date? No information. Isaac said, "I'll take the same day as the *Baas*." And so it happened.

Laetitia was younger but by how much? Laetitia had a date, 12 May, but no year. André suggested that 1948 or 1950 would make her more youthful. "Well, André," said Catherine, "she mustn't wait too long before she can retire." After some discussion, everyone agreed on 1945.

Oupa was not so easy. His earliest memory was of a very big war going on somewhere. "World War II," said André. More discussion, and he too found a date.

"Think it over for a few days," cautioned Catherine. "Maybe you will remember something else." After a week they made it final and these, they agreed, would remain their official dates of birth, to be used on all documents to come.

The next step was to get the late-registration-of-birth documents and submit to Home Affairs. Catherine worked with the others to find and copy their own birth information and submit it to Home Affairs.

She found out that in the new political climate, Home Affairs would actually come to the farms, take fingerprints and fill out all the forms needed for the ID. She organised a date with them and invited neighbouring farms to have their workers and anyone else applying for an ID to join in.

Photos too would be needed. The ladies made an extra effort to look their best and Catherine drove everyone to the photo place and sponsored all the photos. On the right date three officials with their files and fingerprint pads showed up at Bellezicht and got everyone's application in place. It took several hours but it was done.

They waited for the ID books. None were arriving even after two months. Catherine called Home Affairs. Oops, they had lost the documentation. They had to come again for a repeat round of documents, photos and fingerprints. Then two more months. When books finally began to arrive, whose joy was greater, farmers or workers, was hard to say.

However, the process was not over for Laetitia. Instead of her ID book she had received a paper requesting more paperwork. It seemed that Home Affairs did have some record of her, and that record showed that she had been born in 1947, not 1945. "Well, we were close," quipped André.

That wasn't all. She had given her birth date as 12 May. Home Affairs had another surprise for her, for Catherine too. Home Affairs had Laetitia's birthday on 28 August. Ironically and just short of astounding, it was the very same day as Catherine's birthday. Paperwork was adjusted accordingly and from then on, every year brought double birthday celebrations.

Meanwhile, resistance to voting dwindled like rain in the Cape summer, but there was still unease. Catherine found a civic organisation which had developed a programme to educate people on the voting process, Lawyers for Human Rights. They also worked with overseas donors and the local Rural Foundation. They were willing to come to farms, and even more, the training was free. They used pictures to explain and they even set up sample polling stations and showed how to mark a ballot. The training ballot itself, like the eventual real one, used pictures. The trainers emphasised "Your vote is your secret."

A neighbouring farm volunteered the use of a wine shed for training. Workers from several farms gathered, listened, and went through a mock election.

"Seeing the other farmworkers participating probably helped them to feel easier about it," Catherine explained to André.

The actual voting day came, 27 April 1994. For Catherine it was a dream come true. For this very first election, you could vote at any polling place. André agreed to drive the very old Peugeot. Its broad bench seats could fit three people in the front and three in the back. Laetitia, Isaac, Oupa and Sheryl could be accommodated. Except at the last minute, Oupa decided he just didn't want any part of making his x; so he stayed home. Sheryl and the others preferred to make their own way to the local polls.

As the day dawned, the air buzzed with election energy. Catherine was part of this extraordinary day, this day of the first vote of the people on the farm and of most people in the country. The last outpost in the world withholding human rights was about to fall. The day was proclaimed a public holiday so that one's job was no excuse for not voting. You could smell the fresh aroma of democracy.

What to expect? To be prepared for a long wait at the polling station, Catherine packed a basket with a flask of hot coffee, sandwiches, juices and lots of water. She was ready for the queue at the local community centre, however long it might take. Neighbours would certainly be there. The officials were to mark your thumbnail and a bit of skin with a dark ink that would prevent you voting more than once. She could visualise them there among the neighbours and workers, greeting and smiling, equal in voice. Ah, this was what the struggle was about, centuries of struggle, everyone being recognised, having a say in the direction of one's own country. She felt proud to be a kind of midwife to the birth of this new phase in the country's history. This was justice; now there could be peace.

There was no suspense regarding the outcome; the party of Nelson Mandela expected a majority of at least 70 percent. The outcome of the other 20 or so parties was the real question. Who would be the official opposition? It didn't really seem to matter that much anyway.

André drove out. Instead of turning into the local polling station, he kept going. He didn't say a word.

"André, what are you doing? This is our community. We need to vote here."

André was silent. He kept driving. Where was he taking them?

"The longer we drive around, the longer we have to wait in the queue, André." Her frown deepened. There had been early news reports that morning of polling places running out of ballots.

He kept his gaze straight ahead. They passed the wood factory, the agricultural quarantine station, the dam with the water birds circling. Into Stellenbosch he drove, then turned to take another road, this one toward the sea. Without a word to her or the farm passengers, who remained stoical.

Inside she was fuming. What was happening to her plans, simple and straightforward as they were, of voting on this first day? Everyone alike, farmworker and farm owner, men and women, rich and poor, making their crosses. And worst of all, why wasn't he talking to her?

Finally, finally, he pulled into an area where there was a high school used as a polling place. Why did he choose this place? Why was she overlooked and ignored? Wordlessly they joined the queue, a serious queue that snaked from the entrance door, down the long driveway, out of the school gates and into the tar road.

The queue was orderly and patient; typical of South Africa, with its fine ability to organise.

Catherine had to fight against the angry words roiling inside her cheeks. Slowly she looked around. Well, these were not the people who lived right around them, but they were neighbours in the larger town. Laetitia and Isaac queued in front of them and the Bellezicht party inched forward, for about one and a half hours. Officious local election officers darted in and out of the building. The snacks stayed behind, no longer that important. She began to chat a bit with Laetitia and eventually relaxed, but did not find anything to say to André. He just stood there also in the queue with uncharacteristic patience. Maybe he was drawing upon the culture of his mother's English forebears.

They eventually entered the hall. Catherine went first as if to lead the way. She stopped to present her ID book, then to get the ink mark on her thumb, then to get her ballot, then to stand at the little private booth to mark it, then insert it into the ballot box. Laetitia followed suit, and as they both exited the hall, Laetitia turned to lean against the door frame, weak in the knees. She put her hand to her chest, looked at Catherine and exclaimed, *"Ek was so op my senuwees!"* (I was so nervous!)

Then Catherine knew that the first voting day had been a success.

Despite its ups and downs, it was a day like no other in the history of the country. Where there had been disruption, there was now peace. When Catherine and André switched on the TV for the evening news, they saw pictures of long queues everywhere. Interestingly enough, it was a day with virtually no crime. It seems that even the criminals were too busy voting.

That day marked a new beginning for South Africa. Mr Mandela's inauguration was still to come, but his words there reflected the spirit of 27 April 1994: "Never, never and never again shall it be that this beautiful land will again experience the oppression of one by another."

~ 15 Sheryl's wedding ~

"*Missus*, this is Reggie." Sheryl presented him proudly. "Reggie Syster. We're going to get married."

Sheryl, the free-spirited elder daughter of Isaac and Laetitia, mother of two, getting married? Amazing. It was just a few years after that first voting day, so at least she had her ID book and a legal marriage was possible.

She tilted her head to maximise her snappy brown eyes. She smiled shyly, but Catherine knew that shy smile. It was just a front for her strong personality. Godwin was 12 at the time, doing well in his special education classes at school. Her daughter Trina, nearly 18, was on her own; well, kind of, with her boyfriend and the child of two years.

Sheryl had been making her own way in the world for many years, dropping her children on the doorstep to be raised by their grandparents Isaac and Laetitia. Catherine knew a little of Sheryl's adventures – she'd once had to go to Cape Town to get Sheryl out of Pollsmoor Prison. Sheryl had spent a few days there charged with stealing bicycles. The police couldn't catch the boyfriend, who probably had stolen the bikes, but they caught her. Somehow Catherine knew that Sheryl wasn't that sort of person. She'd never stolen anything on the farm and Lord knows, there was plenty of opportunity.

After the police dropped the charges, Sheryl spent a few weeks at the farm, going up and down to and from the tar road, fighting with her sister Neela, disappearing from time to time for a few hours or a few days. Catherine found a bit of cleaning work she could have Sheryl do; the copper pots always needed attention, as did windows, and a few throw rugs at the doors catching mud and dust needed washing. It was a way to let her earn money and Catherine paid her very well. It fitted with Catherine's principles, as a way for people to earn.

Did it also assuage Catherine's conscience? She felt sad at the disparity of income between the family in the house and the family in the cottage. Was this white guilt at living in such an unequal society? She had felt that way while still in America, which still had numerous poor people.

But there, with 95% employment, one could always find some sort of a job. Not in South Africa, and definitely not on the farms.

With Anna in charge of the house, it was her territory; not much chance arose for Sheryl to have a regular job there.

Catherine tried to help Sheryl find steady work somewhere else. Sheryl said she wanted to clean houses. She had dropped out of school long ago in Grade 6. Catherine found a company called Marvelous Maids in Stellenbosch. She and Sheryl eked out a one-page CV.

Yes, Sheryl knew where it was. The next day, Catherine took her and her CV into town and dropped her at their office. But Sheryl never went in. Why not?

"Missus, hulle betaal min. What they pay isn't money." So something had spoiled her. Was it Catherine, paying her too well?

Sheryl went back to sitting in the sun, with frequent trips to the tar road, frequent disappearances. There were whispers that she was making money using her womanly talents, especially around the end of the month at payday time.

What she didn't do was spend time with her two children, in school and living at Bellezicht. She never took them anywhere or did anything with them. She left all that to Laetitia. Eventually she disappeared to move in with a boyfriend on a farm on the other side of town. But the poor boyfriend fell ill and died. So Sheryl came back to Bellezicht for a while.

In a few months Sheryl went to visit relatives in Tulbagh, a farming area about two hours' drive. Then she was back. But not alone. Enter Reggie.

Reggie was about 10 years older, barely taller than she was, and showing quite a few grey hairs. His smile, though toothless, was quick and he connected nicely through his eyes. It was remarkable – or was it? – how much he seemed to be like Sheryl's father, Isaac.

So after a few more months and several plans and many phone calls from the Bellezicht phone, the wedding was set for a Saturday in the Pentecostal Church in nearby Kuils River. Sheryl and her mother arranged for the preacher, Brother Stander, who often gave an evening service on the farm, complete with electronic guitar and doof-doof speakers. On such evenings, it was interesting that Isaac, ever the dedicated worker, seemed to find urgent things to do in the vineyard.

André and Catherine agreed that such a wedding, blessed by both church and state, would give a good example to the children. Maybe it would inspire some of the little girls to wait for a lovely wedding of their own, rather than become teenage single mothers. Only much later did Catherine realise the ways of farm culture and how strongly they are stacked against middle-class ways. Wait until marriage? With dreams of happily-ever-after? Was she crazy?

The wedding began to take shape. One afternoon as Catherine drove in from work, Sheryl stopped her. "Missus must find a wedding dress for me, and let me know how much it costs to rent."

Visions of countless hours of shopping on top of job bombarded Catherine's brain. Catherine could take her when going into Stellenbosch, but she could just as well do her own shopping. Besides, how could she know her size, and tastes, and finances? What kind of wedding did she want? What could they afford? Bellezicht hadn't yet had a farm wedding, so there was no common point of reference.

Actually, Catherine was willing to give her support, but first she needed some options. She was reluctant to impose ideas on Sheryl. People in farm culture were so used to being powerless, often saying "Yes" to avoid disagreeing but then not following through on the yes. Catherine felt she was constantly working to empower people to take charge of their own lives, and out of principle she resisted their efforts to put her in charge. She wasn't keen to be Sheryl's Wedding Planner. Also, there seemed to be an unwritten rule that those who made the decisions must pay the bills. She wanted to help, but not do it all.

When she drove Laetitia and Isaac to get his pension every month, it was easy to chat naturally on the way, with Laetitia sitting in the front seat beside her. Oupa and anyone else who wanted to come squeezed into the back seat.

"Laetitia, who are the people coming to the wedding?"

"*Nee, Missus, ek weet nie.*" (I don't know.)

"Well, who will be in the wedding besides Sheryl and Reggie?"

"*Nee, Missus, ek weet nie.*"

"Food for afterward? What kind of food?"

"*Ek weet nie.*"

"How many people do you expect to come to the wedding?"

"*Ek weet nie.*"

"Will people come back to the farm afterward?"

Laetitia just shook her head.

"Well," Catherine said, "Let's see what develops."

Some days later, Catherine was busy in the kitchen, making a favourite dish of hers, stuffed peppers. André was pouring them each a glass of red wine.

"André, Sheryl asked if we could pick them up from the church after the wedding, around 4:00."

He stopped pouring. "Well … I guess we could do that. As long as I have time on Saturday morning to lie in bed and read."

Catherine smiled as she stirred under the peppers to prevent burning. André continued.

"Just don't ask me to drive any wedding car. People get hyper, they tell you different things to do, and it's frustrating. Leave me out of that."

Her smile inverted to a frown. "André, they don't have a lot of resources, compared to us. We have to do what we can."

"They can organise rides when they need to. Let them ask Brother Stander."

Resources, thought Catherine. The farm family have some resources, it's true. With lots of claims on them.

Competing claims, increased geometrically by keeping on taking people in. At least they hadn't taken in anyone since the baby, now seven years old. Laetitia did try to take in a girl from an orphanage but André wouldn't sign, so that didn't happen. They saw only the need, bless them. Catherine felt that she and André did try to share their resources, without taking away people's own pride, dignity, or self-sufficiency. But there was a limit on this small farm, in this small space. There were other ways to help people who came across their paths pulling a wagon full of needs.

She knew however not to press André further. He was already coming to the party and that was very good indeed.

Sheryl needed a wedding dress and eventually she took the ball and ran with it, so to speak. She found a dress she liked, that fit, that she could afford. It cost a week's wages to rent, but what could you do. She came up with a fourth of the cost, Catherine contributed half, and she borrowed the remaining fourth from André (which he later forgave).

At some unspoken level of awareness, Catherine knew that she and André could not escape involvement in this wedding. The dress, picking them up after church … they were already involved. How would they get to the church in the first place? It was as if Sheryl was waiting for them to connect the dots to get their help without directly asking for it. They still had a lot to do and to pay for, it seemed.

Weddings were female territory. André seemed quite willing to look the other way, but not Catherine. This must be as proper a wedding as now could be done.

The Thursday before the wedding was the next pension day, and Catherine tried again to get specifics from Laetitia, but no luck. She couldn't even get enthusiasm for the wedding cake. What to do with what she saw as this lack of planning and arranging? Were they bypassing Catherine's efforts? She couldn't figure it out. So she made the decision. "We'll get the cake and you can do the rest." Laetitia agreed and said thank you. As usual.

That decision put Catherine into the role of Caterer. She phoned Anna on Thursday evening, Anna whose advice in such matters was always spot on. Anna volunteered to make not one but two fruit cakes, as is the South African tradition, and they'd be ready for Saturday morning. Catherine hadn't even known what to ask her, and she'd solved the problem.

"Make a list of what you need," said Catherine. "Better still, let's go to the Pick n Pay together. I'll pick you up Friday after school, around 3:00." They got the goodies.

Lacking specifics, Catherine played with the idea of getting sandwiches as well, or maybe even sausage and rolls, but she couldn't get enthusiasm from Laetitia or Sheryl. Or André.

Catherine envisioned lots of farmworkers and their families coming to the cottage, and music on their *werf*, and maybe beer and wine, and as far as she was concerned, they could party as they liked. Just no trouble, no "*moeilikheid*" with people getting drunk and smashing up the place, or fighting, or waking up André to call the police.

"Now things are working out well," Catherine boasted to André. "I'll get the cakes from Anna on Saturday morning. After picking up the wedding party from the church and taking photos, we will be finished and can get on with our weekend." André just nodded, although with a wary eye.

Coming home on the Friday before the wedding, after school and after shopping with Anna, Catherine was stopped on the short walk from car to house by Sheryl carrying two big green garbage bags, but containing the opposite of garbage: her wedding outfit. Catherine invited her in.

In the dining room Sheryl opened the bags delicately. She fanned out the dress to show the white satin with pearls and sequins on the veil and on the front, with the skirt flaring from the hips, the dress with long wedding-dress sleeves. Definitely the real thing. Sheryl had had it taken in at the shoulders to fit.

"Let's hang it up in the highest place, on the rack in the laundry room." It looked so good.

"Has Missus got the pink ribbons for the car?" Asked Sheryl. "And the pink balloons? And the confetti?" And one more thing, R200 rand for Monday for her to finish paying off the dress rental.

"Was I supposed to get these things?" Sheryl had mentioned those things but by way of sharing her plans, so Catherine had thought.

"I know Missus is very busy," she said.

"Well, yes," Catherine replied, liking this appreciation of her work. "But Sheryl, I had time earlier today but I didn't know you wanted me to get them. We all have to plan. It's too late now to run back into Stellenbosch."

"*Ja, Missus.*" She agreed with everything, end of story. She just waited.

"I guess I can try tomorrow morning. The wedding's not until 3:00." Okay, Sheryl won. Catherine made a list for when she went back to town to pick up the cakes.

"We want to be the only ones in the old Peugeot," Sheryl said. "*Net ons*; no one else."

"The Peugeot!" The classic car from 1961, parked at Bellezicht by Uncle Johannes, who had bought it for his wife when she gave birth to their daughter. It had been the wedding car for Catherine and André, and for a few neighbours too.

"Of course, but why didn't you say anything sooner? We have to be sure it is running. And that it has enough petrol, and that it's clean." She asked André and to her surprise, he didn't give her uphill. She didn't ask him directly, but they both knew that he was the only one who could drive it well. So against his desires, he was being sucked into this wedding as Driver of the Wedding Car. Uh-oh, Catherine thought – not good. But there was no discussion. *Fait accompli.*

That left Catherine as Driver of the main car. How else could Sheryl's family get to the church?

"*Ja, Missus.*"

The Big Day dawned mild but overcast, a good photo day. This was one thing that Sheryl had set up well in advance. Catherine had purchased lots of film and extra camera batteries, in the days before digital, ready for her role as Wedding Photographer. The farm family didn't have a camera but they always appreciated photos. Catherine knew the value of photographs in her own family history, and indeed, in her life. Although she took photos only as a hobby, she looked forward to what she could do for Sheryl on her wedding day. Photos also made a unique wedding gift.

Catherine made sure she took good care of her husband early that day. She was getting the sense that some surprises were waiting and she didn't want André to feel deprived before the day even got started. She made him eggs Benedict accompanied by yogurt, melon and coffee.

Anna had the cakes ready, two high, heavy squares, nicely iced and decorated with silver beads and pink roses. She had made other cakes too. Little squares with red moist sides and coconut. Other squares with ground peanuts on top and sides, with more fruit on top. Two large jam rolls. Another chocolate layer cake. Small lady locks with cream inside. *Koeksisters*, an Afrikaans speciality like a donut twist crusted with syrup. With significant quantities of each one.

"All the cakes are for you," she said with a proud smile.

"I can't believe it. You just baked all these cakes out of the goodness of your heart?"

Out of empathy for a woman trying to have a proper wedding, and out of empathy for Catherine not knowing quite how to help.

On to the shops. Catherine strode into a convenient one, no time to lose, and bled the shop dry of everything pink: ribbons, confetti, balloons, serviettes with pink hearts, even a bouquet of fresh pink flowers.

As she pulled in to the farm's driveway, she saw André, still in his short summer pajamas, overseeing two boys playfully washing the cars with him, with Jonty and Lola and Ringo catching the hosepipe, chasing one another around. No leisurely lie-in for him today. She smiled at him broadly. He gave her a rueful look. One thing she could say for him, he knew when he was beaten.

They all helped to carry in the cakes, after a scary moment when their dear but thieving ridgeback nearly scrambled into the back seat where the cakes were. It would have been curtains for those cakes. As they found places for the goodies in the kitchen, high out of Lola's reach, Catherine noted that the kitchen was still untidy from the morning's breakfast and last evening's burnt pot, a casualty of her attempt at making *stywe pap,* an African corn meal staple.

Sheryl knocked. "Time to get dressed," she announced.

Catherine showed her and the dress the guest bedroom and closed the door.

It seemed that the wedding was now at 2:00. Brother Stander wanted the wedding party to meet him at the traffic lights by the wood factory and everyone could then arrive at the church together. André somehow finished with the cars and he showered quickly. He didn't want to keep the preacher waiting. He even donned his best grey suit and wore his red tie and matching handkerchief.

Sheryl called. The elastic on her stiff petticoat had snapped and there was a little too much of her for a pin. By some miracle Catherine found elastic and they threaded it into the waistband. When her dress was on, they moved into the main bedroom, where there was a big mirror. André had installed it for a friend's bride some years ago. The two women fitted on the veil and headband. Sheryl viewed herself in satin and sequins and lace and she glowed.

Catherine said, "I have now become the Mother of the Bride." Sheryl smiled.

"Lipstick?" "Mother" asked. She was really getting into it. Sheryl declined, even though Catherine knew she liked it. Did the church frown on lipstick? Maybe. But communication was too difficult across languages and cultures, especially when time was short.

"Jewellery?" Catherine asked. No, Sheryl didn't have any. Catherine held out her grandmother's pearls. Sheryl took the necklace and chose the dangly earrings.

She was ready. She walked with stately grace down the passage and out to the cottage. As she rounded the corner, the elders turned to stare and the youngsters stopped their soccer game. Then they all burst into applause.

Someone ran for a chair from the stoep and set it on the thick grass. The bride nestled regally in her satin and lace, a white gardenia on the green lawn.

Brother Stander was waiting at the traffic light, car full of people including, it turned out, the best man and the maid of honour. People on the road, seeing the classic car with its ribbons and balloons, waved and hooted, to the great pleasure of the bride and her groom. In the second car, with Catherine as driver, sat Laetitia and three children from the farm, including Godwin. Isaac was nowhere to be seen, nor were sisters or sisters-in-law or even Trina. There was room for more people but they didn't come along.

At the Pentecostal church, despite the scheduled wedding, work was still in progress for the new addition. A man was varnishing the door, two workers were filling a wheelbarrow with rubble, and young fellows were digging with spades in the sandy yard.

"I hope you will finish soon," Brother Stander asked with a worried look.

"*Ja*, soon," replied one, tossing pieces of brick into the wheelbarrow.

Brother Stander, backed by his tall, well-dressed wife Sheila, turned to the wedding party and said in his calm, kind way, "They say they won't be long. Besides, we have to wait for Reverend Appollis to do the wedding. We must just be patient."

There was nowhere to sit, and luckily shade was not needed on this overcast day. But protection from the legendary Cape wind was another story. The wind picked up some sand and lifted Sheryl's veil and ruffled the bridal dress. It plastered clothing against bodies and stung faces. But no one complained. Catherine, now the Wedding Photographer, took photo after photo to pass the time. André ushered the bride back into the car for refuge.

As the bride was resplendent, so was the groom dapper, in a well-fitting dark green double-breasted suit and wide green tie. Sheryl had shown off his suit some weeks before. You could see your reflection in his polished black shoes. He smiled with calm dignity throughout the day, raising his head ever so slightly, looking directly at you, always keeping his lips together.

Finally the newly-varnished doors opened and people from Brother Stander's car filtered inside. A combi drove up smartly and about 12 more people passed the wedding party and entered the hall. It seemed that the church community had come to help celebrate this momentous occasion.

The church doubled as a community centre with a stage sporting a vase of artificial flowers and a set of drums. Ah, music, thought Catherine. But there was no organ and no one approached the drums. There was not even a tape player. Finally a cloud of dust approached and up drove Rev. Appollis.

Brother Stander coached the entrance. Reggie must go inside. The bride will be brought in by her mother, seeing that her father didn't come to the church (was he already "celebrating", Catherine wondered).

"Take her arm," said Brother Stander. Obediently, Laetitia grabbed Sheryl's arm, but above the elbow as you might a child's. They walked in like that. As they entered, the hall filled with melody, as the church people burst into song with full, clear harmonies. Ah, the music.

Reggie had positioned himself near the stage. He then took his bride stiffly by her other arm. Laetitia probably didn't realise she was supposed to let go, and the three of them, followed by the maid of honour and the best man, walked in solemn procession to the centre and the waiting Reverend.

Catherine and her camera found a good vantage point behind the artificial flowers, where she could pop out and flash as needed. Rev. Appollis preached a lengthy but appropriate sermon drawing on biblical stories and offering marriage advice. So loud was his voice for the few assembled faithful, André later observed, that had the Lord wanted to take a nap that afternoon, He would have found it quite impossible.

Then came the exchange of vows, a ring for the bride, and the dramatic bridal kiss.

Catherine slipped out quickly, supplied the boys with baskets of confetti and a few seconds of instruction, and captured some action photos.

As the excitement died down, the bride asked her for some cash for the minister. Catherine had now become the Financier. But she had given out the last of her cash for the cakes of that morning and André came to the rescue.

They rode back to the farm in slow triumphal procession under the ribbons and balloons floating from the bridal car, followed by Catherine with the family and then Brother Stander. All three cars made as much noise as they could, hooting long and loud. People in passing cars turned to see, smiling and laughing and waving and hooting back. The bride thrilled to it all, to her fifteen minutes of fame.

Catherine had left instructions for Neela to set up for the party in their yard in front of the cottage, borrowing the table and chairs from the veranda. Catherine expected that she would just bring out the goodies and *voilá,* their job was over and the family would party on.

But no – nothing had been done. So, as everyone got out of the cars, the church people kind of flowed toward Bellezicht's veranda, joined by the family who had stayed behind. There was no doubt about where the party would be.

André quickly put out the cushions for the white chairs. Catherine's best tablecloth, luckily pink, went onto the table. People sat down. Children ran to the grass to play. In the blink of an eye André and Catherine had become Host and Hostess.

Despite his grumpiness about becoming involved, André's inherent graciousness won out. "Where are the drinks?" he asked Laetitia.

"*Nee, baas,* the person who was supposed to bring them hasn't turned up."

André knew this was just a "story." There obviously had been no planning for drinks. Though Sheryl had said that her mother was making something, there was no food either. Catherine wondered again whether this was a strategy of farm people, to throw themselves on the mercy of the farmer, who in their eyes can – and will – give them everything if only he decides to. Or could it be a subtle, unwritten expectation from the start that the farm owners should provide, but they didn't want to ask?

So back to Caterer role. André helped Catherine to scour the pantry for anything and everything wet, everything munchable. Luckily there was extra orange and lime and raspberry mix on hand, bought for workers on weekends, plus a big bottle of Fanta and one of diet Coke. André mixed, Catherine put glasses on trays and found plastic cups for the children.

They would have offered the adults wine; but they knew without discussion that if the church frowned on lipstick, wine was out of the question.

Sheila offered to help. She arranged Anna's cakes and the myriad goodies on trays, Catherine grabbed farm roses from the dining room, and abracadabra, they created a respectable wedding table.

Sheryl wanted more photos "by the flowers", in front of the deep pink bougainvilleas on the side of the house. She sat on the grass and Catherine swirled the gown and train around her. Look this way, turn your head so. She was so happy.

The church people chatted in a mix of Afrikaans and English. Laetitia had given everyone to understand she was expecting more church people. They got the message and left a lot of the cakes.

In the kitchen, Catherine observed, "André, how can these good people leave so many cakes? In America, they would have eaten them all, and too bad for anyone who didn't get there soon enough. Even the children didn't keep taking."

André nodded. "That's our Afrikaans culture. Mothers warn their children never to finish up the food."

She shook her head in admiration. Then she commented, "André, I feel a bit embarrassed by our lack of readiness. They surely see it."

"Neither Sheryl nor Laetitia were clear to us about what they wanted. They just didn't plan."

"Maybe there are more things going on, cultural expectations, who knows. Were we just supposed to know?"

"Well, Catherine, we are doing our best at the moment. Besides, we can't be blaming the bride."

She nodded, pleased that he didn't blame anyone, including her. They both carried more drinks to the veranda.

The bride settled strategically near the cakes. Despite Catherine's suggestion that she walk around and greet the guests, she stayed put.

At one point Sheryl's father Isaac, her brother Tommy, and Oupa, her grandfather – three generations of menfolk – filed slowly up the steps to join the party. All three were glassy-eyed but mobile. Urged by the guests, Isaac made it over to kiss the bride. Catherine ran for the camera but in the minute before she came back, the three had gone, back to a different kind of party.

Camera in hand, Catherine waited until the moment seemed right for the bride and groom to cut the wedding cake. The night before she had polished the special silver knife that she and André had used at their own wedding, not so long ago. She showed them how to cut the cake together, both of them holding the knife, explaining to them and to the whole group in her basic Afrikaans that it meant that married people have to do things together, care for each other, give each other food, see to each other's needs. She could see that this cake-cutting business was news to them, but they liked it. They posed for the photo like professionals.

She heard later that Sheryl recounted the cutting of the cake to a friend with much excitement. Catherine felt glad that she had made a contribution, kind of; but was it really necessary, she wondered, to do things the way she herself would have done them? Did she have a right to change them, to move them into her ways? Her unease niggled at her.

Presently the church people got to their feet and several hymns broke out, followed by a few sprays of deeply felt hallelujas. The goodbyes started. The ladies all helped to carry in the food from the stoep and they washed up the dishes. Catherine controlled her nervousness over the messy kitchen and that soaking burned pot.

A final leave-taking and the church people drove off along the driveway through the vineyard, chased for thrills by the dogs. André seized the chance to slip into old clothes for taking the dogs on their daily walk up the hill behind the farm.

The red sun seemed rather to be walking down the hill, the bride was showing fatigue, and Laetitia and Neela and Catherine packed up the remaining goodies. They started to carry them back to the cottage and just then, up drove a combi with another group of church people. André, being a clever man, smiled broadly and strode away, canines prancing around him.

The scene was like a film running in reverse. The three women just turned around and carried the goodies back onto the veranda. Catherine could feel the bride's disappointment with having to give out the cakes which could have been seriously indulged in privately. Out came the blue cushions and the small benches which quickly filled. The cold drinks were gone, so Catherine offered tea, which people preferred anyway. These ladies also helped, and in no time everyone had tea and cake and contented smiles. More small talk. The bride became even more fatigued. Evening loomed.

One of the men, dressed in a three-piece suit, went to the combi for a guitar and there were more hymns and more hallelujas. Cups and plates got washed up and then, just as people prepared to drive off, back came André. He and Catherine and the bride and groom stood there on the brick paving and waved the guests off, the combi again chased happily by the dogs. As in a well-rehearsed play, Laetitia and Neela silently carried away the final box of goodies and André and Catherine went inside and closed the door.

Catherine couldn't face the kitchen again still with its stack of breakfast dishes and burnt pot, fading flowers and spotty pink tablecloth. The idea of cooking dinner was daunting. She wanted to stay with the warm feelings inside. Her role of Maid could wait. By a series of small miracles, it seemed, and despite themselves and despite lack of planning, they had helped Sheryl to have her proper wedding.

"I'm so proud of you, André. You rose to the occasion nobly. You didn't complain even once. Let's go out quickly for a late dinner. My treat."

When they got back, they saw some well-worn cars in the *werf* and heard voices and a loud *doef-doef* coming from the cottage. Another party had arrived. But this time, they gathered their two dogs and managed to escape inside. People could carry on until the next day if they wished.

The next day brought yet another surprise. As Catherine opened the front door, she saw a package there. No, two packages, two big green bags. She lifted one to move it and found it very light. There in the bags on the front stoep lay the dress of satin and lace, the dress of triumph, with all its extras. One bag sported a big pink ribbon, and the other, a pink balloon. Saying a wordless thank-you for a once-in-a-lifetime wedding that Sheryl, along with Catherine and André, would never forget.

~ 16 More weekends ~

The arrival of the baby in those early years did not change things much. Catherine had hoped that the baby's presence would be a softening influence. She'd hoped it would reduce the rough edges of drinking to excess, of secretive drug use, of family violence. But it was not to be.

One of the worst times was yet to come. It was another Saturday. Why always a Saturday? Because wages were paid Friday night and weekends were free and farmworkers could do whatever they wanted. Starting Friday night and ending Monday morning.

That awful Saturday, Isaac was again beyond any reasoning. Worse, so were his two sons. Tommy was running to the front stoep at the dining room window, wearing a red band around his head, shouting unintelligible complaints about the others in the cottage, and then running to the back again. André went to the window. Reuben was stalking around the vineyard, but not so innocently. He had a ferocious expression on his face and, like father like son, he held a huge panga raised in his hand, a shining one. The women were screaming.

Reuben's girlfriend suddenly was at the dining room window, a fearful expression on her face. Catherine opened the door, let her in, and quickly closed it.

The girl just said, "*Missus.*" She lifted her long blouse and showed the blood on her skirt.

"Who did this, Susanna?"

"Reuben," she said, near tears but remaining stoic. "With the panga."

André felt it was his duty to protect the women and children. He got his pistol from the safe, carried it in his right hand with his arm straight down, never pointing it, and walked out toward the vines. When Laetitia saw that, her eyes got a panic-stricken look and her loyalties reversed – she saw that her son there was in danger and she took his part against André. So did Catherine.

"André! Please, please come back! Put the pistol away!" Catherine begged. "Let the police deal with Reuben. He's so dangerous now and you can't solve things. You could get into worse trouble. He's not hurting the others. Please!"

André turned around and looked. Reuben ran off into the donga. André shook his head but walked back toward the house.

Catherine took Susanna into the bathroom and closed the door. Susanna lifted her skirt to reveal a big gash on her hip. It was wide but Catherine assessed it as not so deep, not needing stitches, not needing a trip to the emergency room. She'd heard stories of how farms had to do a lot of their own doctoring, being far away, and now here it was, her turn. She got a washcloth, soapy water, disinfectant, and bandages. So Reuben had already drawn blood. Again. From his own girlfriend.

Still outside, André observed as best he could and decided it was time for the police. He phoned and everyone settled down to wait. Catherine made Susanna a cup of tea, and brought her to sit and wait with André on the veranda. From there, they could see the road and the yellow police van en route to Bellezicht.

Then Sheryl appeared in front of the veranda, with Reuben running heavily after her. The children materialised on the veranda steps. André went to get a stick or something to fight him off if needed. Susanna and Catherine jumped up and pulled the kids into the house, turned the large key to lock the double doors with their many small panes of glass, and threw the curtains shut.

Sheryl ran up to the locked door, with Reuben after her. Catherine was wide-eyed, fearing the worst. But amazingly, Sheryl somehow slipped away from him at the door and ran off. Catherine peeked out through the small space between the window frame and the side of the curtains. He looked like something from a horror movie, face contorted, eyes flaming, drool down the side of his mouth. He stood there fuming and snorting, staring at the door, trying to work out his next move.

Inside, Catherine moved back and tried to shield the children huddling behind her. One powerful swipe and there would go window panes, curtains and all. Glass in people's eyes, a panga at their throats. She peeked again. Reuben kept looking, kept trying to focus his eyes. Could he not see her? Just centimetres away, just on the other side of old window panes. A long, long moment. Then he lumbered down the steps and disappeared.

Eventually two young police officers arrived. They'd seen this story before. One officer gave chase but did not catch the two sons, who dissolved into the vines and into the trees by the donga. But they had Isaac, and they took him in.

An hour or so later, the two brothers wandered back, exhausted, no longer threatening. The women came for the children. The same procedure as last time, as every time. Police phoned Sunday morning to come get Isaac, who had slept it off but was left with a massive headache. There was the usual meeting Monday after work, with a contrite Isaac and the women, but not the two sons. Laetitia told André that Reuben asked pardon; he had been hallucinating and he had thought the people he saw were big bugs to be killed and that's why he had tried to kill them.

Not quite the little paradise that guests saw when they came for a Sunday braai.

Shortly after that event, again on a Saturday, Laetitia came to ask for help. Reuben again; this time he was attacking his father with a big stick. André walked to the back. Both father and son were under the influence of who knows what. Reuben then half-ran out to the road.

It was not the first time Reuben had attacked his own father. Once in the vineyard, he threw a stone at his father; the next time, he hit his father with a vineyard pole. This was the third time. Someone had to act. But how?

They had asked some of their neighbours how they dealt with these issues with their workers. Surely it was not that different. But situations on farms seemed to vary a lot. Farms being farms, people were physically separated from neighbours. Contact had to be deliberately arranged, and time was always a problem. Unlike a small farm the size of Bellezicht, the larger farms had clusters of worker houses at some distance from the manor house, and those farmers did not concern themselves much by what went on in the cottage areas over the weekends or any other time.

André asked one neighbour, an elderly experienced farmer, how he maintained discipline on his farm.

"Discipline?" he replied. "There's no discipline on this farm. The workers' families do what they like and there is not much we can do about it." That was no help.

Another farmer said, "My wife gets involved with them, but not me. I make them so miserable that they just leave."

Definitely not our style, thought Catherine.

Neither in those early years, nor as time went on, could they find clear solutions. Eventually, when a long weekend was coming up, André suggested a visit to his cousin Mostert Muller, who owned a large farm in the Little Karoo.

"Mostert – he's the big fellow with the big hands, right?"

André laughed. "Right! And lots of white hair. Remember when you first shook his hand?"

Catherine smiled. "It was so broad that even my long fingers couldn't grasp it." She thought for a moment. "It will be good to compare notes on farming matters."

"He's so capable. He can make a success of just about anything."

~ 17 Mostert ~

Two donkeys stood underneath the sign that indicated "Ladismith", heads down, as if waiting for an appointment long past the agreed time. André slowed as he turned the bakkie off the asphalt road. It was slow enough for Catherine to snap a photo of the resigned donkeys.

"What in the world are they doing here? No farm or owner in sight, no halter or lead on the donkeys, just standing in the sun."

"Still around. Amazing. " said André. "My Afrikaans grandfather drove a donkey cart in his younger days, before they could afford a bakkie."

"Your *oupa*. Not so long ago. Farming people don't use donkey transport these days, do they?"

"Actually, they do, especially the older generation. You might still see them on the farm roads."

"Donkeys; even in Biblical times," she mused. "The pregnant Virgin Mary rode into Bethlehem on a donkey."

"And Jesus rode into Jerusalem on a donkey. A special one, at that." André knew his Bible. "There is even a monument to the donkey, in Upington, in the Northern Cape."

As they negotiated the gravel roads, André explained that, about ten years ago, Mostert had decided to go back from Cape Town to his family roots, their family roots, and take up farming. To the livid consternation of his Cape Town wife, Mostert bought a farm and moved the family there. But it wasn't a wine farm; the dry terrain limited him to sheep and goats. His farm seemed small by Karoo standards – it was only 5 000 hectares.

Catherine was impressed. "Compare that to our five hectares."

"Well, yes," agreed André. "But it's semi-desert, open and not inhabited. It's a bit like Arizona in your country. It's even got tumbleweeds."

She'd noticed how the landscape had changed once they got over and away from the mountains near Cape Town. Parts of it looked like moonscape, barren and rocky.

André went on. "The only places where things grow here are near rivers, small as they are, or where people can collect water in a dam on their farm."

"That makes me feel lucky to be in the Winelands, even with its winter rain. When I was growing up in Pennsylvania, there was so much rain that you hated it. It spoiled your fun."

"Not so in Africa. In some African languages, the words for rain and blessing are the same."

As they drove up to the farm, Marianna, Mostert's wife, came to the car. "Welcome, welcome," she smiled, warmth in her eyes. They lived deep in the mountains on this tucked-away farm, yet she looked like she'd just stepped out of a fashion magazine. She wore a flowered dress with a lacy open back, a silver pendant on a silver chain, dangle earrings set with lapis lazuli. A silver comb caught up her hair, allowing a few artful strands to trail along her neck.

Mostert, wearing a blue shirt, shorts, and solid outdoor shoes, grabbed André's hand and pulled it in jest, while looking directly at Catherine. "Hello, Yankee!"

The Mosterts' two teenage sons greeted the visitors, carried up luggage and wine and the fresh vegetables not easy to find in remote areas, and went back to their video games.

What a unique house it is, thought Catherine. Built in a cleft in the mountain, it had one wall just mountainside, beautiful natural rock, still in its million-year natural place. The other walls were glass, with several huge glass sliding doors, so that the people inside could always view the opposite side of the cleft and watch its mountain buck, the klipspringers and their young ones, and the plump squirrel-like dassies living in the rocky hillside.

Catherine couldn't stop gazing around. "With all this glass, it's as if you live right in the mountain."

Everyone smiled. Mostert especially.

Sitting in the lounge, they could view the distant mountain tops of Ladismith with its signature peaks, blue against an even bluer sky. This formation sported two tall rounded peaks with a smaller, sharper peak between them.

"They call it the Witch's Tit," said Marianna. "It's in all the sketches of our little town." Her silver bracelets clinked as she lifted her drink to share in the welcoming toast.

Mostert explained to Catherine how he was able to farm with sheep and goats that were foraging in the veld. He had installed nine kilometres of black pipe to take the water from the spring behind the house to where his flocks were. He had the help of two workers who lived in cottages not close but not too far from his house.

"So you have to manage other people, with their families too," Catherine said.

"Yes," said Marianna. "The difficult part is when they get drunk and don't know what they are doing."

She recounted the story of a recent Christmas, the day the dam was empty, despite the flowing water. Mostert and their sons spent the whole day out on the farm trying to find the leak in all those kilometres of pipe.

Then one of the boys found the problem. It seems that each worker had his own small vegetable garden, which they watered every evening. They used water from the dam that Mostert had built to catch the spring water flowing down the mountain. On Christmas Eve, it seemed that Lukas had already been "celebrating" with whatever he drank and after watering the garden, he had not turned off the tap to his plot. So all the dam's water had flowed away during the night and there was nothing left for the animals.

Christmas morning activities were of less importance than water to the flocks. Mostert was furious but at least they had found the problem. It would still take about two days for the dam to fill up enough to pipe water to the sheep and goats, not to mention to the household as well.

"So did you fire Lukas?" asked André.

"*Nee, wat*," said Mostert. "Better the devil you know. At least his wife said sorry."

Lukas gave them another problem, this one from a visitor. One Sunday Lukas's little girl had run up to the house, saying they had an accident. Mostert went down and found Lukas with a knife sticking out of his arm, his right arm. When Mostert pulled out the knife, he noted that the blood flow did not indicate that a vein or artery had been severed. Getting him to the hospital on Sunday night would not have helped; he would still have to wait until the doctor showed up on Monday. So Mostert bandaged up the arm and very early the next morning Marianna took Lukas into Ladismith where the doctor treated the wound.

So the wife and daughter still maintained it had been an accident, but Mostert knew what happened. First, Lukas was right-handed and he would not have put the knife into his right arm. Second, they had had a visitor, a known troublemaker in the area. Maybe the men had been drinking and something went wrong and the visitor had stabbed Lukas. No one in Lukas's cottage would say for sure.

Mostert knew and he did not want that visitor on the farm again. But the visitor came back. Then Mostert laid a charge with the police, of trespassing. It was not a heavy crime but it was something, and then it would give the troublemaker a criminal record which would not be in his favour the next time he would cause bad things.

"Your turn," said Marianna, as she raised her glass. "Isn't there a saying about the duty of visitors to bring stories?"

"Rather it's a most pleasant privilege," laughed André. He spoke about Bellezicht and the irrigation pipes and the lack of a decent harvest for this year, as well as the violence on so many weekends.

"The men are bad enough when they are drunk, but the episode with Reuben and the drugs and the panga – and the effect on the children – that was the worst," Catherine said.

"Let alone beating up the women, even drawing blood," added André. "Reuben doesn't live at Bellezicht any more. He stays with his girlfriend on another farm. But weekends, he comes home to his ma."

"There is something you can do about him," said Mostert. "Isn't it obvious?"

André and Catherine looked at each other.

André spoke. "Neither Reuben's ma or pa or his girlfriend will press charges. We've tried to get them to do it, but they won't. Not against one of their own, no matter what they do."

"It's not as formal as pressing charges," said Mostert.

Catherine sat forward, listening closely.

Mostert looked directly at André. "You trespass him. You forbid him to come onto your property. If he does come, then you get the police to arrest him."

Catherine looked at André. "We've had discussions with our neighbours – a few, anyway – but no one said that they'd used formal trespassing as a management tool."

"No," agreed André. "Usually they just commiserated with us on how difficult it was to live with them. Or shared outrageous stories, not good ones. Like domestic violence or incest, or problem kids that stole, or druggies, you get the idea."

"Well," said Catherine, "tell us. How does it work to trespass someone?"

Mostert sat back and stroked his greying beard. "Don't worry; he'll know about it. First, talk to him. Show him the boundaries of the farm that he mustn't cross. Point them out clearly. Even walk him around the farm."

"As in, tell him that the boundaries are the dirt road from x to y, the row of vines at the top of the property, the neighbour's diamond fence, and the wall with the bougainvilleas." Catherine was catching on.

"That's the idea," said Mostert. "Then tell him clearly that, if he does come onto the farm, you will call the police."

"Really?" She couldn't believe it. "Will the police come out from town to the farm, just for something as small as trespassing?"

"It's really not a small matter," said Marianna. "That man can be dangerous."

Catherine's mind leapt from her imagined scene of police loading Reuben into their van, to another imagined scene of police loading the three unwelcome visitors and driving off, and she felt sick. Reuben was already a druggie and he would get over being arrested, having been arrested many times before. But maybe not that young couple, let alone the child. It would traumatise them, and maybe the others too. There would be little hope of future reconciliation.

Marianna went on. "You know the saying, A Man's Home is His Castle. It's stated in sexist terms, but you know what it means; that you are the boss of your property. If you don't want someone on your own legal property, then they are trespassing."

"And that's against the law."

Catherine sighed and made a face. "A pity. No place of his own to go to. No modest little castle."

Marianna agreed. "But he does have a place to live, on another farm. So it's not as if he's got nowhere to go."

André turned to Catherine. "That's something to think about. Reuben has been violent before on Bellezicht. On weekends he comes to his parents, and that's when the trouble happens."

"You might give him just one more chance," said Mostert. "Then don't fool around. You know he'll still get drunk and take drugs and still cut people up. You have to act."

André looked at Catherine. "I'm not sure the trespass would work for us, but it's something to try." She nodded.

And try it they did. The next time Reuben brought trouble to the farm, André trespassed him. He was too drunk to understand at the moment, but his mother understood very well. Catherine lobbed in from the sidelines, "Trespassed for five years."

"What's the big deal about five years, Catherine?" André asked her later.

"Because you never know; he might change. Maybe the trespass will give him a reason to change. He wants to visit. Remember, he's a mama's boy."

André just shook his head. "He's been a troublemaker for years. And you think he just might change. I can't believe you are still so naïve."

She stopped making the salad for lunch and went to her study. Why did he always put her down, when she was just trying to be a decent person?

About a week afterward, she called André to come see. There was Reuben back on Bellezicht, flaunting his presence right outside the kitchen window.

They looked at each other. André reached for the phone. She could see the "I told you so" look in his eye.

The police came and took him off the farm with a warning. After that, he would come to visit but would stay on the farm road boundary. His mother would walk out to talk to him.

After three years, she came to ask if the boss would reconsider. In the meantime, he'd become a father for the second time, had given up drugs and even drinking, and had become a hard-working family man, even taking on a Sunday gardening job nearby. Perhaps the strong action had motivated him to change; maybe at least it helped.

So they lifted the trespass. Reuben's wife, the girl he'd once sliced up, sometimes had him bring a huge bouquet of wild arum lilies to leave on Bellezicht's doorstep.

That story had a happy ending, then. What about now? Did they really want to trespass the visitors? Would they then have to follow through? She couldn't imagine the police taking the young couple away, let alone the child. Couldn't they find another way?

~ 18 Another kind of weekend ~

As they rose from their bed in a corner of the bedroom, the big brown dog and the small white one began their morning routine, Saturdays and every day, yawning and stretching, then wagging while slurping over anyone's hand, begging to go out. Catherine knew it was easier to get up than to clean up after them, assuming they had waited as long as they could. While she struggled getting the key into the old-fashioned lock in the veranda door and turning it stiffly, the dogs thumped against the door – hurry, can't wait. Duty first, however, as they sniffed all around the veranda to see who or what had been there during the night. The worker's dog Ringo? A lost mole? A mongoose, perhaps? Field mice? Any frogs? No, all clear; then they ran down the steps to the grass and sniffed out a comfort place.

One particular Saturday morning was warm and dusky but cloudless, with still a long while before the sun would throw a few tentative streaks, javelin-like, from behind the low places in the mountain crags. If the dogs couldn't wait long, neither could the birds. One could think they were calling the sun to get up, get up quickly. Catherine stood on the veranda listening with an inward smile. Guinea fowl with their blue heads, wild geese, hadedas, roosters and even a distant peacock. The cacophony sounded to her like a sunrise symphony.

Many Saturday mornings offered children too.

"Jannie! Quinton and *Klein* Henry and little Godwin and your big sister Trina too. Would you like a story?" They came running. As people came and went in the cottage, there were often more children joining in and Catherine welcomed them all.

She led them to the veranda, then situated everyone including herself on cushions on the steps, and opened the story book written in Afrikaans. She loved language and she spent her workdays teaching English to other children; reading in Afrikaans was for her a language learning experience.

"Look at the pictures. What do you see?" The first thing was to extract information from the cover to get the mind ready for what is coming.

The cover showed mice. "*Waar bly daai muis*? (Where does that mouse live?) What are the mice wearing?" The kids were learning to compare and contrast in the classic story, "The country mouse and the city mouse." They acted out coughing and sneezing, "*hoes*" and "*nies*", and could recognise the words on the page. They got so excited about it.

They loved it when she spoke a bit of English and asked them, "How do you say this in Afrikaans?" because then they became the teachers. After the story and discussion, they taught each other songs. "*Vader Jakob, Vader Jakob, slaap jy nog*?" to the same tune as "Are you sleeping, Brother John?" "*Baa baa swart skaap*," have you any wool? Poems like Humpty Dumpty: "*Hompie Kadompie sit op die wal. Hompie Kadompie het afgeval … .*" Great fun.

After snacks, she led them back to the cottage where they could resume playing. Often then, Catherine would go inside the house and take out her gardening tools. That was their cue for more fun and the children would quickly reappear.

"*Missus,* can't we help you in the garden?" She nodded and instantly they were with her among the roses. They dug out weeds with great concentration. Catherine organised turns in using the simple weeding tools, which they found fascinating. Everyone picked leaves off the rose bushes that had black spot and put them into the garbage drum so that they would not spread the disease. Little Jannie's style was first to stuff the black-spotted leaves into his pockets. Where there are roses, there are bees. Catherine tried to model calm respect for bees rather than swatting at them and no one ever got stung.

When they saw Catherine putting on gardening gloves, they all wanted gardening gloves and she found at least one glove for everyone. They observed the ladybirds and little green spiders and aphids and once, a small snake. They saw it as fearsome even though it was little and harmless. Catherine held it and got the older boys to hold it before she put it in a jar for later release in a far corner of the vineyard. Farmworker ethics dictated that the only good snake was a dead snake, but no, harmless snakes had their place on a farm, especially mole snakes. Those were long and dark and they kept down the mole population.

The scent of newly dug earth on such a Saturday morning remained a great pleasure of farm life, in garden and vineyard. Breathing plant-cleaned air. Feeling the sun, most of the time weak enough in the morning. Glancing at the mountains, far and yet near. The feeling of working in a team, of accomplishing to clear a few metres of garden. She lavished on each child attention and praise. These children did not seem to tire of garden work and it took time to get them to quit. The younger ones found it fun and, like children everywhere, also played in the dirt.

Eventually it was enough; the children couldn't go on without supervision. Catherine made sandwiches and something to drink and offered lots of fruit. Then came the best time: wages. The older boys who did the heavier work got more. She tried to instil the principle of working for your money before you spend, and saving some as well.

"Take half and save half," she said. With their parents' approval, she kept a ledger of each child's earnings. They could have it when their mother said so.

André the economist approved. "You are teaching them wealth creation," he said.

"You've already given me that lesson," she responded.

"Yes," he said. "If you don't spend, you don't consume, and then you have something. That's how people get wealth. How do you think we ended up getting this farm?"

Catherine wondered what money-equivalent value she was contributing on such a Saturday regarding child care. From the smiles of the mothers she inferred it was significant.

One Saturday just the two older boys were available for Saturday gardening. Afterward Catherine produced two plates of hot food, mainly leftovers: potatoes with onions and nutmeg, broccoli with cheese, some beef burgundy, sesame chicken. She knew that American children can be picky eaters. She sat the two boys on the veranda and said, "If there is anything you don't like, that is okay; not everyone likes everything."

One boy looked at his plate, looked at her, waved his hand in a circle over the plate, and said emphatically in a clear, just-breaking voice,

"*Missus, alles.*" The other one nodded and repeated in English, "We like everything." When she came back for the plates, not a scrap was left.

One such Saturday brought a serious event. André was away at his office in Stellenbosch, working on a report for his clients. Catherine had just finished the Afrikaans reading followed by the gardening. She took a cup of coffee with her to the bedroom and was about to lie down for some much-needed rest when there was a knock at the bedroom window. Somehow, the farm people always knew just where the owners were inside the house.

She was so tired that she ignored it at first; after all, she'd just spent hours with the farm children. Only after another few knocks, insistent knocks, did she get up and answer the door.

Neela and Sheryl stood there, surrounded by the children, all looking anxious. Neela spoke urgently in behalf of her husband. "Henry slipped and fell in the vineyard, and cut himself on a piece of glass."

"Where is he now? Catherine asked. Neela stepped aside. "*Daarso.*"

She stepped out and he was sitting right there on the steps at the front door. He was bent over, holding a large bath towel to his side. The left side of his shirt was bloodied, and the towel was still soaking up large patches of fresh bright red blood. What could she do? She threw on her jeans and got him into the car, blood still seeping out into the towel and into the fabric of the seat. She raced him to the hospital's emergency room and helped him in, passing two long rows of tired, ill people waiting for emergency treatment. They stood back.

A nurse and a security guard shuffled him into the treatment room. Catherine busied herself with the paperwork and then sat to wait on those hard benches. The doctor stopped the bleeding and, he said, put in lots of stitches. They released him wearing a hospital gown that covered the large white dressing over his side. There was no use taking back the ragged shirt and the bloodied towel.

When finally they got settled at Bellezicht, Catherine wanted to see the piece of glass and where was it, exactly, that he had slipped and fallen?

"It's certainly a safety issue," she said to Isaac.

"We threw the piece of glass away," said Isaac. He wouldn't produce it. Where can one throw it away on the farm on a Saturday afternoon, where it could not be retrieved?

"Well, then, where did Henry slip and fall?"

"Somewhere up there," he answered with a broad wave of his hand. Some indeterminate place.

By then, she knew there was no falling on a piece of glass. It was a knife wound. The knife had severed a vein or an artery. The family rescued him and covered for him. Neither Catherine nor André could ever get the blood stain out of the passenger seat of the car. But Henry's life was saved.

PART THREE

~ 19 Need ~

A ndré drove into the *werf* to the usual flurry of three barking dogs running up to the car, in a frenzy of wiggles, competing to kiss his hand. He unloaded his briefcase along with a packet full of the week's mail. Godwin waited to brief him on the day's happenings at the farm. There was an air of normality, as if there had been no shouting past midnight, as if farm relationships were going along just fine, as if things were not brewing seriously beneath the quiet surface.

"*Naand, Meneer*. The fertilizer man was here with his team. They sprayed CopStar on all the vines. They were here from around nine to three o'clock. They left me this." He handed their invoice to André. "The security bakkie came around this afternoon, on patrol. No problems. They have a new officer with them, Pieter."

"Good."

"The handle came off the spade. Something broke there and I can't fix it."

"Just put it in the quad, by the back door. I'll get someone to fix it."

Two farm children stood behind Godwin. "*Baas*, there is a fundraiser at the school." The children addressed André as *Baas*, as the older people did. They had not yet learned its connotations of dominance, not yet learned to use the modern term *Meneer*, sir. The children thrust papers from all four school-goers into his hands and stood there smiling in hope. André received the news and the papers with stolid patience. He thanked them and moved toward the door.

"Are we going walking with the dogs?" asked six-year-old Jannie, face upturned, a smudge across one wide cheek.

"Of course," replied André, as he replied every day, "as soon as I have my tea." The children nodded and turned back to the cottage to wait.

Catherine greeted him with the usual hug and kiss and pot of rooibos and tin of rusks. "I like it when you are here before me, to welcome me home," he said. She gave a thin smile.

He sensed something. "Are you all right?"

"Am I all right? No. Definitely not." She shook her head and he saw her eyebrows come together. "This standoff is getting to me. André, I'm getting that stress rash on my back. I'm feeling physically sick at times, like I want to throw up."

André said, "Well, maybe you should see your doctor."

"Maybe. But I don't think it's a little germ. I think it's this whole thing, this whole trouble on the farm." She shook her head and her eyes went down.

"I told you before, Catherine. It's a waiting game. We just have to wait them out and then things will get back to normal."

"But it's like a dual existence. For months now."

He looked at her, trying to puzzle out what her problem was.

She gave a deep sigh. "The children go on as normal, but under the surface things are not normal. Surely the teenage boys can sense it. Godwin goes on as normal, but he is party to whatever the women say. And they are still furious."

"So what?"

"So what! Is that all you can say?" Her tears began to flow. He just stood there and crossed his arms. Putting up his wall.

"André, there's something else." She stepped around him to get a tissue. "Shortly before you came home, about an hour ago, the dogs started barking like crazy. I went out as usual to have a look. Godwin was nowhere to be seen. The others stayed at the back, which was okay, but then I saw three men walking down the road on our southern border. Three of them, walking abreast."

"So? Farmworkers are always up and down that road. There are three or four farms above us that they could be coming from." He thought for a minute. "Even though it's a private road … ."

"Those men weren't wearing farm boots, nor farm overalls. They weren't faces I recognised. Farmworkers don't walk three abreast. It all struck me as very strange."

"You said they were walking down, toward the tar road?"

"*Ja.* More like strolling; not like farmworkers with an aim in mind, say, to get home. Looking all around."

"So they must have walked up at some point. Even along another road, maybe. But what's the problem with that, Catherine?"

"Don't you see? I feel it's a threat. They could be who Neela and Esta called 'our people.' They could be studying our farm, with plans in mind. They could bring other people here, maybe to toyi-toyi. Maybe to burn tyres – do something to intimidate us. Our people would probably join them. And then, anything could happen here." Her eyebrows went up into a pleading look. "André, we've got to get some kind of resolution. I just don't know what."

His lips went taut.

"André, we try to be good people. But Neela and Esta and Sheryl and Godwin, all of them, are making us out to be the bad people. Oppressors. Dictators. People who, on a whim, want to kick them out on the street. But we're not like that."

"So you want them to like you, all the time, no matter what?" His tone was not friendly. "You need their constant approval?"

"Well … ." Her voice quavered. "André, I can't help feeling that it's meant to be intimidating."

"Catherine, take it easy. Those men could have been anybody. Maybe looking for work. Don't get so worked up over nothing."

"Over nothing? Nothing? You say it's nothing?"

"I'm sure it's nothing. But you are making a big deal out of it."

She looked incredulous.

He saw that he'd struck a nerve. "This is about you, about Catherine. I know you are unhappy about things, but really. Is your image of yourself challenged? Good, kind, caring Catherine, now unable to please the farm people? You try to please everybody, no matter what."

"So? I do try."

"When they don't act pleased, your world falls apart? You see threats everywhere?"

She gave him a look through narrowed eyes. "They are more than displeased. Their fury hasn't let up since that horrible meeting. And yes, I do feel threatened. Is this trouble only the tip of the iceberg? Have they always felt so deeply angry with us? Do they really hate us? I don't want to believe it. It's like there are cracks, big cracks, in what I thought was a solid foundation."

"No ... I don't know. We are here, they are there, and that's that. We just wait until they come right again. They aren't threatening us. Relax."

He took a different tack. "We didn't ask to be born privileged. We didn't ask to be born as a 'have.' It just happened that way."

He went on. "It just happened that they were born into a less-wealthy farm family. There's a famous Afrikaans poet, I think it was Adam Small, who wrote about the identity of the brown man, the so-called coloured people in South Africa. *"Die Here het geskommel en die dice het verkeerd geval vi(r) ons daai's maar al. So dis allright, pêllie, dis allright."* Let me translate: "The Lord rolled the dice and they just didn't fall in our favour. So let's make the best of it."

She looked away and crossed her arms.

He continued. "'It's how the dice fall. That's all.' We're just coming from different worlds. Who's to blame for that?"

She strode around the kitchen, hands to her head, rambling on. "That's hard enough. But what's happened to our years of talking things out? Is this how the have-nots stand up to the haves?" She was building up steam. "Is Neela really such a have-not? Granted, she and Henry do not own a house or a car. Granted, they are dependent for transport living way out here on a farm, and their room is small. But really. Neela has a husband, a family structure where she fits in nicely as the second of four children, of two stable parents. Her husband has a job, they have two boys and a grandchild, they live in a safe and beautiful place, they pay nothing. And we're NOT pressuring them to leave."

He shook his head, as if to figure out how to respond to her argument, actually several arguments in one. He started with the first part. "You told me that your family didn't own a house until you'd grown up and left. You didn't always have a car. My family too. We were fine but fell on hard times when my dad died. I was still in school. We had to cope. And we did."

She looked at him, assessing the truth of his words. "Well, I can't argue with your history. I guess that not owning a house or a car does not make you a have-not. But, André, I don't know … there is something else going on here."

But now André was getting into it. He quoted his father's brother, Oom Johannes, a successful businessman. "Oom Johannes always said that the coloured community is a generation behind the white community when it comes to development. They will get there. It takes time, and it takes education. The opportunities are now in place. They just have to use them."

"Opportunities. They seem irrelevant to this farm family."

"Catherine, that's another discussion. The opportunities start in the schools, schools that are quite accessible to our farm. You're the teacher; you know that better than I do. But these people don't persist. You know what they do? The youngsters fall pregnant and then they drop out. How much can we do about that?"

"Well, it's their culture's permissive attitude toward sex at any age."

"Yes," said André. "Neela and her little family have a good place to live all right, safe and beautiful surroundings as you say. They are right there with their extended family. They have a security service. Lawn care. Free rent. All utilities paid, including electricity. They have a home where they are comfortable and well-treated, especially by you with all your talk of treating everyone with dignity and respect. So well treated that, in the end, she thinks she owns the place."

He went on. "She even said that. She said her father gave her that house and it is her house. So how can we make her move? She believes she has a right."

She gave him an angry look. "So what do we do with that? André, we need to resolve this thing, this us and them."

"I don't think we need a resolution. If they want to make a big fuss, then let them. We are not making anyone move away. Except, of course, the three visitors. As I always say, we need people here for security."

"But what if they themselves become our security threat? This breakdown could be used by outside forces and then we will have bigger problems on our hands." She hesitated. "That's what I realised today."

"Don't go making a catastrophe out of it. I've had about enough of them and their attitudes. We are making do with the farming without them. I've been paying our neighbour to come and farm for us, at huge cost. All because Godwin can't take working with the vines. Despite his love for plants, despite all he learned from the grandfather who loved him and taught him."

"André, I go to work every day and my salary, modest as it is, goes right into this farm. So I pay too, not just you. I know cash is tight. But somehow, we need to put an end to this trouble."

He slammed his cup into the sink. "They can toyi-toyi all they want. We can just ignore them. If they bring their political people in, we will deal with it then. We are in the right. There is no need for all this fuss. No need for change. We must just get back to the way it was before that awful meeting. The meeting they called."

He stomped back to the bedroom to get his walking shoes, and continued stomping out the door and up the hill. The dogs all leapt for joy. The children flowed out behind him, then ran in front of him, skipped, dashed and hid, seemingly unshaken by events in the rarified atmosphere of adults.

André came back into the house after the walk, and found the fruit Catherine had set out for the children. The exercise in the open air had cooled his temper, which was always close to the surface. He joined her in the kitchen as she was making a tomato bredie for dinner, just the way Anna had taught her.

"Catherine, I have a solution. Why didn't we think of this before? All we have to do is trespass the visitors. That was Mostert's advice and it worked."

"Trespass. Hmm." She thought for a moment. " The way we did for Reuben? But that was years ago."

"So? We are making a big deal out of these visitors who never go. It can be so easy. Once we have trespassed them, we just call the police."

She stirred the pot and then put down the big spoon and turned toward him.

"What will the police do with them? Handcuff them? Take them to jail?"

"I don't know. That's not our problem. It's our farm and we have a right to say who can be here and who not."

"Those rights are changing all the time, it seems." She thought for a minute. "Trespass? What did the visitors do wrong? Were they violent? Did they bring drugs? Did they threaten us? Are we just removing them on a whim?"

"No, but they use the resources of the farm and we have to draw the line somewhere."

"Hmm." She looked out the window toward the cottage. "The police might have a problem with that. The visitors aren't being accused of any crime. They aren't disturbing the peace, at least in usual ways. They might see our problem as trivial and hesitate or even refuse to take the visitors away. Remember there is a child involved. Then what will we do?"

"Come on, Catherine. That's their job to enforce the law, and the law is on our side."

"Are we so sure about the law? New laws are popping up all the time."

He turned away in disgust.

"So André, we use force, you say. Those three people go and nine people still live here, right here. Have you thought ahead?"

She continued. "Whatever positive attitudes those nine people might, just might, still have for us now – that vestige of good will be gone forever. Can you imagine the police taking a child out of the cottage? Probably a crying child. Everyone will cry. There will be threats. There will be shouting past midnight. They might call in their people, those three men, whoever they are, and there might even be violence. What if they made a big scene? What if they burned a tire in our *werf*?"

"So? At least the visitors will be gone."

"André, André. At what price?"

He pointed his chin in a pout.

She shook her head. "Getting the police in – that's an authoritarian solution. That only makes things worse. That's not a human solution."

His voice went up a notch. "So – back to your perfect, kind world where you just cruise along and everybody loves you."

"That's not fair and you know it. André, I want something to happen, some solution to this deadlock. I'm afraid that if we don't act, we leave a gap and things could spin out in ways we don't expect. We have to do something. But not a trespass. Not with police. Not like that."

"I've had just about enough of your bleeding heart. What about us and this farm? You don't like my solution? Then come up with a better one, if it bothers you so much." He went back to his stomping down the passage. She heard the bedroom door slam. She stirred the stew but lost her appetite for it, lost her desire even to finish cooking it.

~ 20 Freight train ~

"I hear that train a-comin' Comin' round the bend

I ain't seen no sunlight since ... I don't know when

Stuck in Folsom Prison ... I hang my head and cry." – Johnny Cash

It felt to Catherine as if that train, heavy with freight and disdainful of passengers, were rushing down the Bellezicht hill, aiming for the farm and everyone on it, bringing a doom from which there was no escape, no way out for "them" or for "us."

Something had to change, but what?

So despite the stalemate, one evening Catherine went back to the worker's cottage, in her hands a big plate of fish left over from dinner. Even though the worker's family members were not speaking to Catherine or André, food is food and must not be wasted. Would they accept it?

She could not leave it in a Pick n Pay bag by the doorway to the *agterplaas*, where she often had left many things they no longer used, things such as old newspapers to wrap garbage in, clothes being sent on, functional coffee mugs whose pictures had dimmed. The dogs on the farm were no fools when it came to unguarded edibles, so Catherine had to deliver this plate by hand. At the door she knocked and asked for Neela, the mother figure in the house of 12 people. Catherine stepped back to respect their privacy.

Neela appeared at the door in the waning day, the cottage lights silhouetting her ample figure. She angled her body away. Her mouth was turned down.

"Neela, *net 'n bietjie vis*. (Just a bit of fish.) It was too much for us." Catherine handed her the plate heaped with pieces of fried snoek. She used both hands to offer, in the African way.

Neela's mouth twisted in conflict, but she stepped forward and took it, also with both hands. *"Dankie, Missus."*

A little boy was playing with a toy car made of wire and wood. His "brrr-brrr" seemed to propel the car around him in a circle. Catherine noted that he was one of the "visitors" unwelcome by her and André, used by the farm family as pawns, to see what they were going to do about it. Just a little boy playing with a toy. He got up, came over and gave her a hug at her knees. She bent down and patted his shoulder.

But could she just say nothing, just go along as normal? Though they had left "normal" some time ago. Didn't silence mean consent? The two teenage boys glided out of the cottage and shadowed Neela, all eyes and ears.

"He is so very sweet. *Maar … hy moet nie hier wees nie.* But … he shouldn't be here." She tried to say the last few words softly, kindly. It wasn't the little boy's fault. She tilted her head and forced a wry smile. Her eyes pleaded with Neela's.

Another adult and a child appeared silently at an opposing door. Dusk deepened. There was a stillness. She stood there, not knowing what to say next. Strange for one so loving of words. Should she say, "That's okay, he is sweet enough to stay," and undermine the principle of no new people living here? Should she say, "When is he going?" and wait for an answer she knew would be shouting and swearing? How she wanted to reach out and say, "Let's talk." But they had decided not to talk, advised by some secret shadowy figures, maybe politicos panting for a fight – whoever they were, they would eventually come to light. But for now, Neela and her sister and her friend followed their advice: "Don't talk to the farmers and don't sign anything."

It got darker. The seconds drew out. Neela faced her silently, feet planted, hair standing up in unplanned spikes, maybe also trying to figure out her next word. The little boy stopped playing. The other figures seemed frozen.

Catherine took a hesitant step backward. She nodded, and took another step. She turned and melted back into the big house. She could hear that train a-coming.

~ 21 Marina ~

Like the flowering of grass at night, Marina was easy to miss. Short, softly rounded and shy, she was the only youngster of all Isaac's grandchildren who had not dropped out of high school. She was always there in the background when the extended family assembled at Bellezicht, with her straightened hair combed stylishly over her brow. She was there when André and Catherine drove the family to their annual Saturday at the beach. She was always there the day that Catherine took the mothers and children to Pep Stores in Stellenbosch, at the start of every year, to buy school clothes. The little ones first. Marina's turn would come later.

"Missus, here's Jannie's list." Sheryl just handed over her son's slip of paper from the primary school Grade 2 down the road. "The school says he needs a white shirt with short sleeves, a white shirt with long sleeves, short trousers and long trousers, a pullover, a rain jacket, plus long and short socks to go with the uniform."

Catherine read through it. "And a white T-shirt and white shorts for Physical Education."

"And shoes, Missus. Shoes for the class and shoes for sport."

With enough socks for all the shoes and enough underwear for a reasonable change, Catherine knew. "All right."

Jannie himself thrust another school-issued list into Catherine's hand. "*Die lysie vir potlode en penne.*" The list for pencils and pens in specific colours; scissors, glue, book covers, notebooks for each subject. And a backpack to hold everything.

Same for Quinton. Same for all the boys. Same for the girls; just exchange short trousers for a skirt and regulation underpants. The girls also needed long trousers especially for winter. Bellezicht bought the school clothes and classroom tools for the job for all of Isaac's grandchildren, including the ones living at another farm in the area, Arendsvlug, the flight of the eagle. It was well named; it rested high up on one of the hills in the area.

At the shop, each child carried his or her own Pep Store basket and filled it with his or her own right-sized items as the mothers and Catherine and the saleswoman moved from shirts to trousers to shoes to backpacks. Catherine had learned the hard way. She ruled out any running back and forth to exchange items for size. Get it right the first time.

Two more mothers for the afternoon's shopping, four more children, bigger children.

"Missus, here's my basket." Marina's choices differed a bit from those of the boys and the little girl. She held up two bras and two pairs of underwear. Then, with her head to one side and a shy smile, she held up a pair of red hot panties.

"What! For school?" Catherine looked at Marina standing there holding the panties and resisting her own shyness. Her round face was flushed but she stood firm. A thought struck Catherine. "How old are you, Marina?"

The response came in a small, quiet voice. "20, Missus."

Catherine studied her for a moment. "Still in high school." She'll be 22 when she finishes Grade 12. She probably needs to feel feminine, womanly. With a smile, Catherine said, "Okay. But for you, not for the boys."

"No, no, just for me, not for the boys," she promised.

She looked at Marina thoughtfully. "Marina, one big request – please, please, don't fall pregnant now. First develop yourself, find the right man for you, and then have your babies. Just be patient; it will come."

Marina nodded slowly, eyes wide.

This girl had quietly gotten herself to Grade 11 before Catherine realised it. When she did find out, Catherine decided to try to see what she could do for her. Maybe even help Marina go for further education. There still seemed to be a chance for her to graduate. What did she need? Definitely more than red underwear.

The situation at Bellezicht had settled back into waiting mode. There seemed to be no way that the farmworker's family would even consider discussing things with the farm owners. Marina's family, though relatives, stayed out of the battle, at least on the surface. Who knew what they really thought.

First Catherine spoke to Marina's mother. "Susanna, *ek is so bly,* so happy that Marina is this far. I'd like to see what we could do to help her finish high school, and I'd like your permission and your involvement."

A wary look from Susanna, then a nod. *"Ja, Missus. Dis okay."* There seemed something strange about her response, Catherine observed. Why did she seem reluctant?

Where to start? "Have you got her school report from last year?" Susanna promised to send it along, and she did. The marks from Grade 10 were low and some subjects were failed miserably.

Catherine contacted one of the teachers at the school who functioned in career guidance. She tried to make an appointment to include Susanna, but Susanna declined. "Missus must just go on."

Tutoring was not the answer, the counsellor said. "She also must go to ask each teacher what she needs to do in that class. She needs to make a weekly schedule of her hours and manage her time." He gave the tasks that his subject demanded, Life Orientation (LO).

Catherine worked with Marina nearly every weekend. Marina could walk to Bellezicht. Paved roads connected Arendsvlug with Bellezicht indirectly by car, with winding, potholed dirt roads up to each farm, but the back pathways over the hills were more direct, taking Marina about 20 minutes. They sat down at the dining room table and addressed the main task in LO, job shadowing with a written report, all in Afrikaans.

Marina wanted to be a hairdresser. So Catherine arranged with her own hairdresser's business on Saturdays, for Marina to observe and interview the owner, the other hairdressers and the assistants. Usually Catherine stopped at a coffee shop for them to finish off that day's work with tea and cakes.

On other Saturdays they moved on to other subjects. English was not easy for Marina, with assigned essays and the reading of short stories and poems. History was her worst subject. She showed Catherine all the class notes, which she copied from the board without understanding.

Discussion helped but time and ability to stay focused were limited. They decided to focus on language and numbers.

To Catherine's surprise, mathematics seemed manageable for Marina. The problem was word problems and all in Afrikaans. Catherine had no choice but to cajole an Afrikaans-speaking maths-teacher friend, who gave up a few weekend days. He said there was so much that Marina lacked in the basic skills that underlie word problems, which in the end are real-life problems. Marina's maths teacher was delighted. The friend did what he could but the impact was small.

Catherine identified a program of study in hairdressing at a training college and took Susanna and Marina there for a visit, to hear requirements, to see the facility, to think about getting there and back for two years after high school. It would cost some money but Catherine was sure she would find a way. Maybe even establish a study fund for Marina and canvass her family and friends in America for dollars.

Grade 12 came, more of same. The exam results at the end were disappointing. Even with passing Grade 11 marks, just the required 50% for all of them, Marina was not accepted for hairdressing. "If she barely squeezes by in high school," the admissions officer said, "she won't be able to pass the courses here in college. Besides, we have over 100 applicants for 20 seats. We admit learners with the highest marks." The school advised her to get a job.

Catherine realised only later that Marina's passing marks did not represent her achievement. She was just too old to be staying behind and the school was forced to move her up to the next level. It had been just a social pass. The college knew that but, typically, Catherine had to learn it the hard way. As did Marina.

It was toward the end of Marina's Grade 12 that light came to Catherine through Marina. Another Saturday, after tutoring Marina in English for two hours, Catherine was driving her home to Arendsvlug. At the turn off the tar road up to Arendsvlug stood several substantial women weighed down by packages.

"Missus, it's my ma. Also others from our farm." Catherine knew that was a request to give them a lift. She was happy to be of help, as long as the people were local and known. The road was long and uphill all the way.

"Dankie, Missus. Whew, these potatoes are heavy." Susanna stood at the car door, sweating from the sun even though the air was cool. She had put on some weight after becoming a mother and wife. Catherine coached Marina to hold open the front passenger door for her and help her settle in with all the packets. Marina wouldn't have done it otherwise. Because hardly any farm people owned cars, there was little need to learn car protocol. Two other women clambered into the back seat with their groceries, packages from town, everything.

Susanna was not her real mother. Catherine had just asked Marina earlier that day about her own mother.

"Dead, Missus. For a long time now. She knew she was very ill. Susanna is her cousin, and she asked Susanna to care for me if anything happened to her. We lived far away."

"She loved you a lot, to do that. They both did."

"Ja, Missus."

"What did your mother die from?"

"I don't know, Missus." Catherine understood that answer. She wondered if it was a death from AIDS, the death that came without clear causes, because of the social stigma.

"And your father?"

"Nee, Missus. I never knew him."

"Are you their only child?"

"I think there was an older brother but he disappeared long ago."

"Oh my. But I think you are very lucky to live with family. I can see that Susanna loves you."

"Ja, Missus."

"Do you get along all right with Reuben?" The violent, insect-hallucinating druggie, son of Isaac and now Susanna's husband, had morphed into a solid family man, with a solid cottage to house his family and a solid vineyard job. He'd agreed to take her in. Catherine's question was indirectly whether Reuben respected her person, without hidden requests for favours, so to speak.

"*Ja, Missus.*"

They drove up and up for many kilometers, past farms growing peppers and beans and cabbages, farms growing roses, farms growing, of course (it's the Winelands) grapes. Their little community of workers at the Arendsvlug farm sat high up, at the very end of the road, on a steep slope. The cottages clustered around a shared dirt *werf* with stones, weeds, and trash. One cottage, however, looked lush with greenery, with an entrance arch to their own yard covered in climbing roses. A few chickens and lots of curious children in the *werf* stepped aside leisurely to make way for the car.

"Marina, are you using that table and light that we got you for study? Do they help you?"

"*Ja, Missus.*" She looked at her ma, then said, "Would you like to come and see?"

They carried purchases into the cottage, met by the smell of old cigarettes and unwashed dishes. Just like Bellezicht's cottage, thought Catherine.

Marina showed her the spacious but dark bedroom where the table and lamp were. They stepped over a long extension cord for the lamp. In the corner was a large bed, hers. In the opposite corner, two bunk beds, for her cousin's two sons, 19 and 12 years old.

"Can you really read here, write here?" Somehow Catherine had to ask.

"*Ja, Missus.* It works well." School notebooks and papers lying around evidenced her reply. The wall sported a poster that Marina had made for Life Orientation class, showing herself as a hairdresser. Susanna smiled.

Catherine noted curtains on the windows held by a loose string, but at least there were curtains. The house was cool and solid. Exiting through the lounge, she noted a low table with one leg wired into it. The table held a modest hi-fi set, with large speakers standing on either side. The interior walls sported dark blue paint. Children of neighbours wandered in and out. Susanna's son Jaco ran in to get his football shoes for an afternoon game nearby, nodded in greeting and was gone.

As Catherine thanked them and turned to go, Susanna said, "Missus, I want to show you something." She moved the group onto the stoep, a happy light in her eyes that otherwise seemed perennially tired. She produced a jewellery box. They gathered round.

"A ring! How beautiful!" The diamond flashed light this way and that.

"It's for my son Danie. He's going to marry his girlfriend. She's carrying his child. She studied and has a job teaching little children."

"My goodness. This is quite some news. Does Danie himself have a job?"

"He's looking for one. He worked for a bakery and he's waiting for them to call him back." Susanna said it proudly. Don't wait too long, Catherine thought. She saw the signs.

Danie, the boy who dropped out of seventh grade. The boy who sucked his thumb into his mid-teens. Soon to be a married teenager.

"So you are going to be an *ouma*, a granny," Catherine said with a smile. Too late for intervention now. Susanna flushed with pride.

Marina walked her back to the car.

"I wonder, Marina; where are they going to live?"

"Right here," replied Marina. "The girl is already in."

"Really?"

"*Ja*," replied Marina. "She sleeps in the bed with me."

The girl was already in, already living with the family of the boyfriend. In a short time that family would have another one, the baby, living there.

"Does the farmer at Arendsvlug allow you to take her in?" Catherine couldn't believe her ears.

"He doesn't care what we do. He doesn't help us with school things. He doesn't know who stays here, and he doesn't care. He lives way on the other side of the hill."

As Catherine drove back home, she realised that she had just been given a lesson for the future. The lesson came from, of all places, a farm at the ends of the earth, at Arendsvlug. Susanna and Reuben had two teenage boys, and there were two teenage boys at Bellezicht. Danie's girlfriend was pregnant. Who knows what she saw in him, but ... . Soon the two teens at Bellezicht would become sexually active, and there would be pregnancies. Then the arguments would start.

The family at Bellezicht would say, "How can you not let the baby live with its father? The mother is far away, she has other boyfriends, so the baby must live here."

The next step would be, "How can you not let the baby's mother live here? She's changed, you know. You mean, separate the baby from the mother? No way!"

The adults at Bellezicht would keep on toyi-toying. There would be demands for more rooms. There would be more babies. The population of Bellezicht would keep on growing; there would be no end to it. There would be more overcrowding, more tension and even less quality of life.

As she pulled in to Bellezicht along the driveway through the vines, the lesson Catherine had just got from taking Marina home hit her like a clap of thunder. It was so obvious!

She could see clearly what was happening at a neighbouring farm. Now at last, she could see what would happen at Bellezicht. But maybe it wasn't too late. Maybe this was a chance not just for André and herself but for everyone who was caught up in this mess.

The question then was: Could she convince André?

~ 22 Braai ~

The phone call came in late afternoon on a very rainy Cape day. "Hi, Catherine, this is Frans. I've had to make a sudden trip from Joburg and I just landed in Cape Town. I'd like to come and stay overnight with you and André at the farm, if possible." Frans was a long-standing friend and a fellow economist.

"It should be okay. Let me check with him and I'll phone you right back."

"Okay. I'll organise my rental car in the meantime."

"Of course!" said André. They were both fond of Frans.

Say yes first, then decide what to serve. It always worked out. Although André was a stickler for fresh food, the spicing recipe that he used for his chops seemed to cover any freezer taste. Catherine knew Frans Brown liked an early start to his day; that meant an early braai. André would have to get home early too.

The October day should have been spring-like but winter persisted. She heard thunder, unusual for the Winelands. Lightning, more thunder, and then rain, rain, rain. Heavy grey rain. It came down faster than it could drain away. Pools connected with other pools to flood away parts of the road and to collect at the exit point of the donga. She looked out from under the ribbed plastic roof of the veranda. No mountains were visible; just a wall of grey rain and the snap of pebble-like raindrops against the roof.

Luckily for her, the rain came down straight, so her basic farm anorak was more useful for warmth than for being waterproof. She leaned against the side of the braai fireplace, which was built in at table height and upwards with its own chimney. It was actually built into the veranda at the same time that the roof was erected over that outdoor space in the week before their wedding, the reception being held at Bellezicht, to have a roof for their guests in case of rain.

The rain somehow made it a good evening to braai. It created an intimacy to the veranda, as if the rain were canvas and they were safely tented within. Catherine scratched around under the *braaiplek* and found a dry newspaper, several pine cones and a few twigs, along with a packet of firelighters (cheating, but hey, it made things simpler). She covered the tinder with small wood logs leaning against each other. It took several matches before the fire took hold, first tentatively, then stronger, and then the blue-orange flames shot up.

She gradually adjusted the wood with long tongs and smiled as she coaxed her full braai fire into being. Dancing really did describe it. It would take a while, forty minutes maybe, before there were enough coals. One could always prolong a fire by adding more wood. She was grateful for the wood, which came from invasive vegetation. Such trees and bushes had been brought from other continents and grew so readily in South Africa that they were crowding out indigenous plants and it became government policy to remove them as much as possible. The farm could use the firewood too; two birds with one stone, or better to use the Afrikaans and say *twee vlieë met een klap* (two flies with one swat), because it felt better to Catherine to eliminate flies than birds. At least they could remove the unwanted plants from the little piece of earth that was this farm.

She stared again at the wall of rain and felt its pounding. Then she looked back at the fire and its leaping warmth. The contrast struck her – how the kaleidescope of bright colours contrasted with the steely blue-grey rain. I wonder if this is us, she thought – André and I. Am I the light and André the dark? Am I warm and is he cold? Will I dance away from him? Will he dance away from me?

Then a loud knock on the door and in came Frans, laughing at himself dripping pools on the terracotta tiles. She laughed too as she gave him a big hug. "Welcome to the Cape! We don't always arrange such a liquid red carpet."

"André phoned," he said, "to tell me he'd be just a little while, until he finishes his newsletter and gets it in the email to his clients."

"Great. Just get settled – you know where everything is. Then put on something warm and join me on the stoep. How about a glass of 1998 Hartenberg Shiraz, to start?"

"Just the thing to go with your stunning fire."

She retrieved the wine from the wine cellar and opened the bottle with a winged opener, the easy way, and set it there to breathe.

It was too cold to sit so they stood by the fire, the rain still beating down in sheets in front of them as if they were behind a waterfall.

Frans had majored in the economics of civil engineering with a speciality in roadworks. The kind of huge machines they needed for excavation and levelling, with all the planning such projects demanded, gave Frans something in common with André's approach to the building industry. Both he and André had trained as economists and they spoke the same professional language.

"Let me take over the fire," said Frans. "It's a man's job." As he rearranged it and added two logs, he asked about the farm. The events of the past few months came tumbling out.

Frans listened with great interest. He himself had grown up on a farm near Swellendam. It was a family farm producing grapes, peaches and apricots.

"It's now my brother's farm," he said. "He bought me out, and our sister, and he is still there running the farm. He's got a group of workers living there, and they also gave him problems recently."

"So then you've heard this story before."

"It sounds familiar," nodding his head at the coincidence. "People gathering and shouting, but it was even more serious because they refused to work for a week at a time."

"It hasn't gone that far here. Yet." She thought for a moment. "Anyway, Godwin doesn't do vineyard work. So your brother can understand what's happening here."

"Yes. When people refuse to discuss matters, it opens up an even bigger gap. It can get dangerous, because there are always people around, usually those who don't work for you, ready to exploit any difference and make it into a political rally."

"Hmm. That's exactly what I am afraid of. There seem to be politicos here too but they are shadowy. Our people won't identify them. But they are welcome to come talk with our people. And with us."

"Well, they will probably have plenty of time to talk, because they usually don't work much. They are 'community leaders'. Farm work is quite beneath them."

"But our people won't talk to us. With or without 'their people,' as they say." She thought for a moment. Back to us and them.

Frans looked at her, braai tongs in hand. "I have a suggestion for you."

"That's good news. After months of this stuff, we need to try something different. André thinks it will just go away. But I think it can only get worse."

"I agree with you."

"You just told me that, when a gap like this opens up, like at your brother's place, someone can jump in to fill it. Then your problems only get more complicated. I would guess that the problems can then multiply."

Frans sipped his wine. "It's even more important for you, because you are a small farm and the people are right here, scant metres away."

"So what did your brother do?"

"He got in a facilitator, someone to go between you and them. Someone who understands the situation. Someone who can speak their language."

"Where does one find such a person?"

"Someone in labour relations, perhaps. Maybe you could ask around."

"Yes, we've been asking, but our neighbours don't seem well informed either. No specific laws that they know of."

"Just try again." He looked out at the rain, gathering his thoughts.

"Well, now you have a new situation, it seems to me. And that is, no one works for you in the vineyard. How can you be expected to house people who don't contribute to the economics of the farm? Check it out, but I imagine that it would not be difficult to get an eviction order."

"Frans, we don't want to evict people. That seems like such a brutal process. Can't we just get them to go? The visitors, I mean. Besides, court orders take years. They cost money. As do lawyers."

"Catherine, I really don't know. This is why you need someone who knows your specific farm, your specific circumstances."

"And there's another twist. That twenty-year law, or is it ten years? It guarantees people a place to stay the rest of their lives on the farm. Some of the people have been on this farm a long time, Certainly Godwin. He was born here, before we bought it."

"That's another thing to check out."

"Okay, Frans. It scares me. Anyway, thanks a million for your thoughts. We'll just have to keep trying."

First Jonty and then Lola barked into the rain and then they also heard the sound of an engine. André.

"Frans, please do me a favour. Tell André what you told me, okay? A facilitator will cost money and André is not keen to be paying."

"I'll do my best." Their eyes met and she knew she had an ally.

~ 23 Point ~

"André. Mind if I join you?" She sat down on the bed as André sat against the headboard reading his latest issue of *The Economist*. He had thrust his legs under the duvet against the persisting winter cold.

"Fine. Just let me finish this article. About five minutes."

"No hurry." Ah, this was a good chance. She went out to the bar and poured two small glasses of Frangelico. She used the new cut crystal glasses, a gift from a good friend in America. The crystal diffused the light into a rainbow of colours. They looked beautiful on their small silver tray.

The tray balanced easily as she set it down on the bed table. She'd brought the bottle too, just in case. Her legs curled under her as she sat down at the foot of the bed facing him. She freed her hair and gave it a finger comb.

He closed his magazine reluctantly but kept his finger on the page he had been reading. She knew she'd better be very careful. She had to be proactive and keep him from putting up his usual defences. She had to prevent him from invoking his mantra, "we need them for security." Once people get their defences up, you might as well stop wasting your time. Especially true with André.

She kept her voice soft, deferential. "My darling, there is something special I'd like to discuss with you. Would this be a good time? " She held out the tray.

"It must be really something, for you to go to all this trouble."

"Am I that transparent!" She laughed.

"It better be good, to drag me away from my *Economist*. Cheers." They took a sip.

"Well, it's been brewing for a while and at last I think I'm ready." She took another sip. The hazelnut liquor gave her a bit of courage. "I've been thinking about all the trouble we've been having … ."

"Whoa, let's not get into that again."

She got up and put on the bedside light and turned off his reading light. "We need a little atmosphere."

She went back to sitting on the bed. "Well, we have to –"

"Come on, Cath, it's a waste of time. Give me a break! We just have to wait them out."

She took a deep breath, then softened her voice again. If he really didn't want to talk about the farm right then, she would give him an escape, but just for the moment. He would then have to find another time to hear her out. Also, maybe she could tweak his curiosity. "My darling, it's just that I've realised something important and I'd like to share it with you. But if this is not really a good time ... ."

He put a disgusted look on his face. "Okay, you've started now. But please, make it quick." He glanced at his magazine, then refilled their glasses and sat back against the bedpillows.

"Okay. The heart of the matter is this. All this shouting at us, all the ranting, all the rudeness – it just may be a blessing in disguise." She knew that to be one of his favourite quotes, about Churchill, and now she was right on the money.

"I feel the way Winston did – then it is very well disguised."

"Oh, you think you're so funny!" she laughed quickly, but tried not to be deflected.

"How can this aggression possibly be a blessing?"

Stay calm, she told herself. She thought of her classroom communication courses, where she learned something about how to persuade an unwilling audience: save the big request until last.

"We have to end this conflict if possible, right? Because otherwise they win. Their visitors just stay on. Then nothing changes."

"Not an option to stay on."

"No, but it will happen if we do nothing."

He was silent.

"Waiting them out at this point is really not an option. André, it could drag on for years, and then things could even get worse." She tried not to plead with him; best to keep her even tone.

His eyes went to the ceiling but she felt he was listening.

"Besides, a gap like this, between us and them, opens the way for someone to exploit them – and us – politically. For example, the shadowy ones will say to them, 'You don't have to take this, trust us, we will force them to let you all stay on, we know how to harass them in subtle ways, we'll take it to the unions, these farmers think they are God, but not anymore,' and so on. André, you and I – we have to act."

A stubborn face. "So what do you suggest, Miss Know-It-All?"

"Come on, no sarcasm please." To get less confrontational, she stretched out on the bed, facing him but with her head at the foot of the bed. She put her hands under her head and crossed her legs.

"André. It's beginning to dawn on me that there can be a good ending to this conflict."

"Get to the point."

Ah! She had him. She hoped.

"André, all of them – they all have to go." She took a deep breath. "Because there is no end to it. And for their own sake."

"What? What about security? Who will be here when we go away? Who will be here when we even go to work? We need a presence here on this farm and you know it." His face got grim.

"Yes, we have to think about that. Long and hard." Then she plunged in. "But you can surely see that we've had this same issue over and over for all the years that we've been here. It's never going to go away. It will only get worse."

He frowned but looked at her.

"The teenage boys will soon be parents. Despite all our efforts, they are not doing well in school and it's just a matter of time before they lose all interest and ignore all authority. Drop out. And become fathers of babies."

He shook his head.

"Then the grandmothers, Neela and Sheryl, will demand that the babies live here, so that they can take proper care of them. Then someone will demand that the mothers of the babies live here. Here we will sit, watching it all, powerless to do anything about it. No, André. It's no longer just about the visitors. It's about the whole family – they all have to go. All. Here at Bellezicht we have to make a big, big change."

He was silent. His eyes glared at her.

She picked up the thread of her argument. "André, it can become an opportunity for them. They need the chance to make their own decisions. To take people in if they want to. But on their own terms, at their own expense, independent of the farmer. They will have some autonomy. It will be new and it will be freeing, I'm sure. Eventually."

He stayed silent.

"André, there is another good thing for them as well. They need the chance to have some kind of an investment to work toward, to protect. Maybe to pass on to the next generation. Neela felt it was already happening, when she told us that her father had given her the cottage. Except it wasn't his to give."

She went on. "Even very poor people these days own homes. The government has been building low-cost homes for some years now. Remember that friend of Henry, who owned the small home that Neela and the family lived in for some time? He was a homeowner. It was small, and it was not in good repair, but it was his."

And then, the closing argument, the *coup de grace*. "Remember what Marina told me, about Danie's girlfriend at Arendsvlug? The girl is already in. 'Already in.' Just like that."

He still glared, lips tight. She lay there in the soft light. She'd given it her best shot.

He was silent for several minutes. She knew to wait, just wait. She sat up and sipped at her drink, something to do when one needs quiet time to think. She looked at the photos on the wall, the enlarged one of him, André, opening a bottle of bubbly on their last holiday, his eyes sparkling like the coming bubbly. She looked at the bedroom curtains, rather limp and there for years but still functional. Anything to reduce pressure on him. Anything to stay with him but keep down the confrontational atmosphere.

He sipped his drink and took a deep sigh. Then he spoke. "What's happening at our neighbouring farms? How are they dealing with their workers?" Ah, some interest at last.

"I've phoned around a bit. It varies. Three farms don't have anyone living there anymore."

"Really? How can they manage?"

"Well, the winemaker two farms down the hill said that when a cottage of theirs is vacated, they raze it to the ground. Eventually all their workers will be living somewhere else. He didn't say where, but the message is clear. No more tenant farmworkers."

André shook his head but said nothing.

"Two of the larger ones, Peacemaker Farm and Bayview Farm, have relocated all their workers. They've come up with creative solutions."

"Such as?"

"Peacemaker Farm bought four houses, one for each worker, under bond, but in the name of the worker. The farm pays the bond as long as the worker is their employee. The farm also pays transport for the workers to and from the farm every day."

"What about Bayview Farm?"

"At Bayview, the boss makes life so miserable that the people just leave. Or so he claims. I think he may have bought them off a few years ago with cash. So no workers live there anymore. I ran into the winemaker at Bayview the other day, at the bank, and he said it's such a relief. They pick up and drop off workers every day. Weekends are now blissfully quiet, he says."

"Security?"

"They both have open properties, like ours. The farms are too big to fence, or so they say. Thus they have the same security that we have, and they are doing all right."

She could see that he was thinking hard. She continued.

"Peacemaker gave us another clue about our situation. The owner suggested that we do what he did."

"And that is?"

"After the workers moved out, he had four cottages open. He renovated them and he rents them out. He says there is a big rental market out there for the romance – yes, romance – of living on a wine farm in Stellenbosch. The cottage can go from an expense to an income. He uses that income to pay the bonds of the workers, who now are homeowners. So it's win-win."

"Amazing."

They sat there a while. "But Catherine, where are we going to get the money to do all these things? A house for Godwin and Esta? What about Neela and Henry? Sheryl and her sons? Not to mention the visitors. How can we afford to renovate the cottage? If it is even possible, because they keep it in such a bad state."

"André, I've just made a bold suggestion and we can think some more about the financing part. Remember, you are not financing things all by yourself. I work too."

"I know. It's just that it's the man's job."

"Was. In the past. André, it's not all on your shoulders anymore. I've got a bonus coming and we can use that. Maybe we can increase our bond on the farm … . I'm just brainstorming now. We can discuss things later. So please, André, try to relax for now about the money."

He made a face, as if she were asking him to fly to the moon and back. "More debt. Just when things were getting a bit easier. I don't know about that … ."

"We will find a way, André. I'm sure we can."

For a moment he looked like a sailor in a small boat that was just swept out to sea without a sail.

She went on in a soft but urgent voice. "In the meantime, Bayview gave me the name of a facilitator who is well experienced in matters involving workers on farms. Frans also suggested that we bring in someone to facilitate. Bayview recommend him highly. We can ask his input. Shall I phone him tomorrow and see if he is available, and affordable?"

"A facilitator? That psychobabble stuff to get people talking?"

She ignored the put-down. "Well, Frans said it worked on his family farm. It's a risk but why else do we have language, but to talk? We have to talk to one another sooner or later. This waiting game opens too many wormholes that could be disastrous. Frans warned us about that too. We have to act."

"Besides," she added, "a facilitator is likely to cost a lot less than a lawyer."

André got up from the bed, stood there a minute, and said, "I need a glass of water. Can I get you some as well?"

"I guess so, thanks." She knew he needed a break. He came back and handed her a glass of water with a bit of lemon in it. He stayed standing beside the bed.

She didn't want to let go of this opportunity; he was listening at last. He had come back to the bedroom, a good sign. Usually when upset he stomped away. She took the glass of water from his hands and tried to catch his eye, but it was not on her. She sipped the water and then pushed her luck.

"Also, André – why don't I stop by the Legal Aid Clinic in Stellenbosch? They offer free help to poor people, and most of their work seems to revolve around the farms. They should be able to tell us our options."

He took a long look. "Well, I guess … I guess it can't hurt. As long as it doesn't start costing me money."

"I wonder if they will ask us a fee. It would be understandable. But let me go find out first, okay?"

He nodded.

"André, there is one other thought. I was thinking about the whole farm setup in South Africa. It seems to me to be so outdated. It reminds me of the lord in his castle with the serfs all around him. So medieval. So dependent. So undemocratic."

"So what!" André laughed.

"Times have changed. South Africa has just lagged behind."

His eyes deepened. "Well, as an economist, I can see that workers living on the farm will never have a way to get themselves a home. They will never be able to make enough money to buy a house."

"The whole model has to change. Don't ask me quite how, but the time for workers to get housing on farms, generation after generation, is long past its sell-by date."

She smiled, they toasted with the last of the Frangelico, and she stood up and gave him a hug. "I suspect that we will need all the strength we can find."

They stood there, for a moment, arms around each other.

~ 24 Legal ~

"André, I wonder if you would make us one of your delicious omelettes. You always get them just right."

"Hah, I see right through you. You just want me to do the work!"

Catherine chuckled. "I'll make the coffee and the toast. And fry the tomatoes."

That Saturday morning, she felt a lightness of being so different from her burdened, responsible self. The early hours had brought them a spirited encounter in bed, like what happens when an overnight stay in a grand hotel brings respite in the midst of a long journey. The road ahead still seemed long but less daunting. Alone, the journey felt desperate, even impossible; but with André moving to be by her side, the challenge seemed invigorating.

They sat in the kitchen at the breakfast bar. The sun came through for a while, though indirectly, perhaps just to reassure them that spring was not far behind. As they finished their coffee, talk turned to farm matters.

"Cath, see that paper? I found it under the door this morning."

"Let's have a look."

"It's an appointment for Neela with a back specialist at Panorama Medical Centre, near Cape Town. She is asking you to take her."

"Oh my. I thought it was woman things that were troubling her, even from several months ago. But her back. Poor thing. I'll see what I can do. I doubt she wants to ask us, but for this appointment, she doesn't have much choice."

"So the public health service is not all that bad, if they send her to this specialist." André took his own cue. "Speaking of specialists."

"Yes?"

"I think we need to follow up on getting legal advice. About the farm housing situation. Who has a right, who doesn't, and under our specific circumstances. Every farm is somewhat different."

"Let's start with getting a facilitator, and with Legal Aid too. We should at least to try to get some names and maybe more direction. Seeing we have lost our own lawyer."

André's eyes drooped but he nodded. "We've heard that Isaac might have had a right, after having lived here for about 20 years. Laetitia seems to have had a right too, something about living at the same farm for a while after the loss of a spouse. Does that right extend to adult children? Grandchildren? Other family members? And to their partners? What about their number of years? We just can't be sure. If they are going to get a lawyer, then we better know what we are dealing with."

"We've been asking them to bring their lawyer, or their people, or whoever they want. They just ignore us."

"Esta claimed she has a lawyer; seven of them, she spat out."

"Does this seven-lawyer story ring true?"

"No, it doesn't. Maybe one of the reasons they ignore us is that they can't get those lawyers to work for them." André frowned.

"Maybe. Why don't we encourage them also to go to the Legal Aid Clinic? I've been meaning to stop by myself."

"Yes. The law is the law for all of us." André brightened up. "I'll even write their letter for them." Catherine regarded him with pleased amazement.

"But André, remember that time with Sheryl?"

Sheryl had gone to the legal clinic once, one of the times that André had been pressing her to leave and make her own way. She told them a pack of lies. *Al die jare,* she said. Living here so many years, poor abused woman, how badly they treated her, and then they wanted her to move. Stop them.

"*Ja,* I recall something like that." He scratched his head. She had never even worked for them beyond a bit of casual work for pocket money.

"She obviously thought that she had some kind of right to stay here. It shows that we are all confused about who has what rights."

"But the people at the Legal Aid Clinic weren't born yesterday." They had phoned to hear Bellezicht's side of the story.

"That was the end of that complaint," Catherine said. "Did she really think that they would not try to verify her story?"

Catherine remembered that André had been outraged. He had gone to see the lawyer at the Legal Aid Clinic that Sheryl had spoken to. He took a diagram of all the people on the farm that showed how they were related to one another. He even showed her the photos of when Sheryl and Reggie moved to Tulbagh, to show that they had left the farm. There may have been some law about rights contingent on people living on a farm continuously. André had driven her and Reggie, with all their belongings in the back of the bakkie. Two trips, even. The lawyer even complimented André on how well he knew the farm family.

André sighed. "I guess many farmers don't know and don't care who is living on their farm."

"You know, Marina told me just that. She said the farmer there at Arendsvlug doesn't care."

"He can't be like that much longer. If something bad happens there, he will be held to account. He could even be harbouring drug pushers, for all he knows."

She thought for a moment. "But he lives far from his workers, and our farm family is right here, just a few steps away."

"Still."

"Besides, that's not my style. It's not my way to treat people, unless it's what they want, or … ."

"Do the farm people there pay their own utilities?"

"To some extent. Each cottage has its own electricity meter. For prepaid."

"Well, that's the utility that costs the most. At least it's under their control. Then they can decide what to use it for, and when."

"If only for that reason, it's a good thing. That tradition of dependency has to go. That way, they have a chance to make their own decisions."

After breakfast, Catherine took their plates and set them by the sink. She felt a tap on her shoulder. As she turned around, he took her in his arms and put his face against her hair. She could feel his beating heart.

"Catherine. This whole thing has been hard enough for us, and I know I've made it even harder for you. I didn't mean to, but I did. In spite of all that, you had the vision and yes, the courage, to find a way."

She pressed her body tight into his. He kept speaking.

"I'm still worried about how it might all pan out, but somehow … with you by my side … somehow I'm starting to think that it just might."

Despite the issues looming between them, Neela and Catherine focused on directions to the specialist's consulting rooms, which Neela had written out very carefully. Neela also showed herself to be quite an accomplished back-seat driver. "Turn here. Move into that lane. Watch out for the police car behind you. Stop at the red light." Surely she was just trying to be helpful. Catherine had experienced back-seat directions from Godwin as well. She didn't make an issue of it.

Neela had expected to be sent to a government hospital for treatment, right from the specialist's office. She had a plastic bag with her containing a change of clothes.

"I put together a few things in this bag for you," Catherine said, indicating another bag in the back seat. "Toothbrush, washcloth and snack bars." She just nodded. The specialist sent her for two weeks.

The following Friday Catherine found herself very busy at the school, with the usual teaching plus organising a field trip for the Grade 7 learners. She phoned Neela in hospital, not expecting there to be any air time on Neela's phone, and to her surprise, Neela answered.

"*Kom jy vandag uit?* Coming home today?"

"*Ja, Missus.* Two o'clock."

"I'll be there as soon as school is out. At Door C."

"*Ja, Missus ... Missus?*" There was a long a pause. *"Dis goed om Missus se stem te hoor.* It's good to hear your voice."

Catherine teared up. In spite of all the conflict, Neela said something positive, right from her heart. Being separated from the familiar, especially when ill, is not easy. We are all just human after all.

The next Friday morning, Catherine drove into Stellenbosch to pick up Anna for her weekly work in the house. She asked Anna if she'd mind waiting in the car while she made a quick stop. She explained she just wanted to make an appointment at the Legal Aid Clinic, in order to find out what the law says. She took a letter on the farm's letterhead, with all the contact details. She started explaining at the reception desk that she just wanted an appointment, if possible.

The receptionist said, "I've seen this letterhead earlier today."

As she said it, one of the lawyers walked by. He said to the receptionist, "No new clients until next year." It was November and they would be closing down in early December for the holidays. Nothing would happen again until the end of January.

For some reason the lawyer had a glance at the two letters. He saw that someone had been there earlier with a similar letterhead. It was the one André had written for Neela. He saw that Catherine was standing there, with another message on the same letterhead. What did he think? Perhaps that here was something urgent? He beckoned to Catherine and she followed him to his office. Who knows why.

"Look," he said. "You want to know what the law says? I'll tell you quickly."

The lawyer pulled a book off his shelf. "Farm residency law is based on the Security of Tenure Act 1997." He read from the book, then spoke. "It says that a worker has the right to live on that farm the rest of his or her life, where he or she has lived, if there for 20 years and – this is important too – is at least 60 years of age."

"The worker. That makes sense."

"You can't take away housing from a retired person just because housing goes with the job, in theory anyway. Where could such a person go?" He went on. "This law is to counter the old apartheid law which required retired people, people no longer economically useful, to go back to a homeland. There are political as well as human overtones to it."

He went on. "The law is not so clear at this point about just who has a right to live with the retired worker. There is a right to the 'comfort of family,' the latest buzzword. It will take some time for this point to be legally clarified."

She listened, then added, "But now, we don't have any retired persons on the farm. Just their family and some visitors who won't leave. Just one person works for us, and he doesn't even work in the vines."

"Well, you might move them off the farm; it's not so clear. It's likely to be a long process. But still the question is, where can they go? It's not to anyone's interest to have homeless people. The onus is on the farmer to provide a place for them to go."

"Are you serious?"

"Yes. You can't put people on the street. That's what all these new laws are trying to avoid. Especially when there are children involved."

"So … the farmer has to provide a place?"

He nodded.

"We'd never, never just put people on the street." She sighed in resignation. "What kind of place would we have to provide?"

"The law doesn't say what kind of place. It can be a rental place. You can ask people to leave the farm, and you don't need a reason. But there is one other big consideration; you need their consent. That's the tricky part."

He discussed several ways to provide housing. "First, just go to an area where they are likely to be comfortable. There may be houses ready for a quick sale. If you can come up with the cash, then you can find a place.

"Second, look where they are building. Don't look to Stellenbosch, though, because they build only 300 low-cost houses per year, against a waiting list of 25 000 families, mostly people new to the Cape. Farmworkers are only beginning to apply for Stellenbosch housing."

He went on. "There's a government subsidy scheme available but it's not easy to manage. The government wants people to own homes. They offer a qualified first-time home buyer R84 000 against the new home."

She took notes. "That is something to consider. How does it work?"

"First, you identify a house. Then, you make an offer on it. That reserves it for you. You then submit all the details of the offer with an application for the subsidy. When the subsidy comes, you can conclude the sale. This step can take a lot of time, and most buyers don't want to wait that long. It can take up to a year.

"Most farmers buy the house outright, move the worker into it, and have the subsidy reimburse them. It's cumbersome, which is why it's not better promoted, and someone with capital or at least access to credit needs to put the money upfront.

"Now, I need to get on with my work. You say you will get a facilitator. Then you don't need us anymore. But if this case does come back to us, I will recuse myself." He nodded and left her still sitting in his office.

Catherine returned to the car, her head reeling. "My goodness, Anna. Poor thing, I'm so sorry. I didn't expect a meeting but it happened, and it was great."

She pulled into the traffic. "I feel as if the Lord has just now given me a great blessing." She tried to explain. Anna smiled bravely. That brave smile drew Catherine into Anna's world and she could imagine Anna's thoughts. Anna and her family had to scrimp and save their whole lives, and Godwin and his crowd may be about to get a big something just handed to them. Like those golden handshakes: goodbye and don't complain and don't come back. How could Anna deal with unfairness like that? Whatever she was thinking, Anna had no comment.

They drove into the farm *werf*. Anna settled in for her day's work. As Catherine readied herself to leave for school, later than planned, who came walking into the *werf* but Neela, sweating and out of breath. The taxi had dropped her at the tar road and she had walked up the last half-kilometre to the farm.

"Neela!" Catherine exclaimed. "You must have been at the Legal Aid Clinic too this morning. Why didn't you say something? I could have dropped you off when I went to get Anna. You know we go to pick her up on her work day."

Neela gave her a long look, put her nose in the air, and walked to the cottage.

"She's showing you that she can manage on her own, thank you very much." Anna understood.

Back to Square One, Catherine thought.

~ 25 Arno arrives ~

Arno Landman unfolded himself from his white Toyota Hilux bakkie. He was very tall, very well built, with a shock of white hair, and he spoke flawless English.

"Mr Landman." She extended her hand. "Welcome to Bellezicht. We need you in a big way. It's great that you are an Afrikaans speaker, like the farm family. I can speak some Afrikaans, but the nuances often escape me. I'm afraid my Afrikaans is like a third-world country, always developing."

"Something is better than nothing," he smiled.

André led the way to the dining room, which in the less comfortable weather, doubled as the conference room. Coffee of course. "Black," said Arno.

"We've got five hectares under vines, and yet nobody here works in the vineyard. I've had to outsource the care of the vineyard, can you believe it." André got quickly to his frustrations.

"It looks decent. Who farms it for you?"

"There's an enterprising chap who saw the gap in the market to manage small farms like ours. He's gathered a crew of steady workers. He pays them decently, even with vacation and sick leave, and brings them to prune, weed, spray, pick, whatever. For a substantial fee, which goes up like everything else."

"Why didn't you get a neighbour to help you instead?"

Catherine spoke up. "We tried that. A neighbour did help us for a while, but then he bought more land and became too busy to help."

"I understood from your phone conversation that the farm family is threatening you."

"Not physically, of course, but they can surely smear our name in the tabloids. They threatened to go also to the *Eikestad News*. God knows what they would tell these people. Neela said that her father died because of sprays and he didn't have a mask to wear – safety violations, our fault, she says. Never mind that he smoked lifelong, and to boot, smoked chewing tobacco rolled in newsprint."

Arno nodded. "That was an earlier age, before there was much safety awareness."

"Our trouble started with visitors who never left. Then the farm family got the idea that we wanted them all to go. Just jumped to that conclusion. But we never intended that at first, nor even thought it. They were just so paranoid."

"And now? What do you want them to do?"

André spoke up. "We're not sure. We do need them for security. But … maybe times have changed."

"What are you willing to give, from your side?"

André and Catherine looked at each other. She could feel her anxiety rising like phlegm in her throat. "We're not rich, and the farm has been losing money for several years now. Old vines didn't yield much at the end; then we replanted, without a harvest since then. Not until next year. But … it's uncertain what we have to give."

"Well, it's certain that we'll still be losing money." André looked away.

"So you keep going thanks to the jobs that you both have." André nodded.

"There are lots of ways to address your situation. Let's start with the easy way. Sitting down and talking things out."

"We invited them to this meeting, but they won't talk to us. Not even informally. That is how they are being advised."

"Try. Try again. Try to avoid the courts; and try to avoid force. That could take years and cost a lot of money. You still will have to provide some place for the people to go, the ones that you get to leave. No escape for you, unfortunately. Unless you all just make peace and go on."

"That seems less desirable. The overcrowding will just keep getting worse."

"Call a meeting. Invite them and their people, as they say. The ones who are advising them. Their lawyers; anyone. Give them directions to the farm. I'll be here. Let's see."

He took down names and ages of the family members. Because they had closed up, there was no way that he could meet them. He decided not to have André go and knock. That was his first visit, getting acquainted, sort of.

The next day, Catherine found a date and a time that should suit everyone, a week later, at 18:00, after the work day. André gave the farm family a written invitation, at Catherine's urging to write everything down.

"It's important," Catherine told André, "because then we escape the you-said-no-we-didn't business, and besides, any court – horrible thought – will look for a paper trail."

On the planned day Catherine set up the table with coffee and tea and cookies. Esta would be back from her char work, Godwin's workday ended at 17:00, and Neela was always there anyway. So was Sheryl. Henry showed no interest at all.

Arno came. He and André and Catherine sat around the table, door open, and drank coffee and waited until 19:00, a full hour after the requested time. There was activity at the back, children and dogs, but no adults came out. "Try again next time," said Arno.

André had to go to Johannesburg on business, so about ten days later, they gave another written invitation. Arno and André and Catherine waited again. Again, no one came. Arno's hourly fees, on the high side but still reasonable, were piling up.

"This is getting old," Catherine said. She drafted a letter for a third try. It said: "We have asked you to meet with us twice, and twice you have ignored us. We are asking once more. If you ignore us again, we will proceed without you."

André liked that. "Put it to them!"

186

"But let's not be officious. In fact, let's be humble. Let's beg."

She wrote: "Please come to this meeting. It is to your advantage. We need to work together, for the good of us all. Don't miss this good opportunity."

"You should have been a marketer." André duly translated into plain Afrikaans and delivered the letter. Arno came, and they sat around the table and waited. Just before 18:00, a taxi, one of the mini-vans that serve as private local buses, drove up into the *werf*.

"Is it their people?" asked André.

Catherine studied the situation from the window. "No. Seems to be just them. Getting out with grocery bags from shopping." Her hands trembled. What if this doesn't work out again?

The taxi drove off. Obviously "their people" were nowhere to be seen.

After a few minutes, she bit the bullet and walked to the back. They were out but with stony faces. She smiled anyway and said, *"Wil julle nie 'n bietjie tee kom drink nie?* Won't you come for a cup of tea?" No response.

"Please come, when you are ready. You'll be glad," Catherine said, not taking no for an answer. Where did she get this strength? she asked herself. Maybe from Arno? As she walked the few steps back to the house, Arno stood inside the window, watching.

Half an hour later, Esta came to put something into the refrigerator in the garage, on the *werf* where paths crossed. She was getting closer.

Arno and Catherine kind of wandered out. "There's tea when you are ready," said Catherine. Esta turned away but did not leave.

"Take it easy," Arno whispered to her.

They all just stood around, casually, no rush, take your time. Catherine could hear the fees ticking up even though she knew that was not Arno's goal.

Then Neela came around the corner, meat in her hands for the freezer. To make way, Esta moved, toward the house. Arno also took a step toward the house. It seemed like a delicate dance, one for which

Catherine didn't know the moves. Neela put the meat away and stood at the garage door.

Arno took another step, followed by his dance partner Catherine. Esta turned slightly toward the house. Neela took two steps away from the garage, steering a middle path that could have taken her to either the cottage or the house.

Arno ushered Catherine toward the house, stepped lightly through the door, and held the door open like a butler welcoming the Governor. It didn't need holding open, but it seemed polite. Esta slouched her way toward and through the doorway. Neela dragged herself along, as if each foot had a 100-kilo weight attached. Arno sat down first. He and André and Catherine all smiled brightly and said, *"Welkom!"*

Both women sat beside each other like cold stone statues, skew in their chairs, bodies angled away from Arno, angled away from the table. Arno sat at one end of the table, with André and Catherine along the other side.

"Welcome, again. My name is Arno and it's nice to meet you. You are ... Esta?" Esta gave a slight head movement. "Neela?" A barely perceptible nod.

"You live here, at the cottage?" Small talk. Of course they lived at the cottage. They didn't reply.

"Your families, too?" A wary glance at Arno.

"I hear you are from Robertson, right?" he said, looking at Esta. A slight nod.

"And you, Neela?" No answer.

"I think someone mentioned that you were from there, over that hill." Neela jerked her head sideways.

Arno kept it up. Not taking silence for an answer. But not pressing them, either.

"Neela, you have a child here, right? A boy, still in school? And a granddaughter – is that right?" *Klein* Henry had grown up and found a girlfriend. Arno looked at Neela with genuine interest and listened. With the mention of the children, she began to bring her eyes around. She gave a nearly imperceptible nod. "Your man is here as well? What kind of work does he do?" No answer.

"Esta, is it going well with Godwin?" A pause. "Going well with your own job?"

No answer.

Catherine's hand shook. She tried to be unobtrusive as she poured the tea for Esta and Neela. Lots of milk, three spoons of sugar. She stirred their cups and set a cup near each woman. Each one eventually reached oh so slowly for her cup. The cookies, however, remained untouched.

She sat down and thought they should get down to business. She felt her voice give a tremor so she used her most professional manner. "We've asked you here today to discuss the housing situation." Arno gave her a look and a slight wave. Shut up, Catherine, or you will mess up everything. Just shut up. She felt herself getting flushed and tried to smile graciously. She definitely shut up.

Arno continued making small talk. When will he get to the issues, she wondered. André sat there with his tea, listening, looking, and saying nothing.

Then Arno said, "Well, it's been very nice to meet you both. I hope you have a nice dinner." That was it. Meeting over.

André and Catherine looked at each other. Everyone sat there quietly for a while, sipping tea. Eventually Arno stood up, and everyone followed suit. The women finished their tea. Catherine packed up the cookies "for the children," and Neela couldn't refuse.

Arno waved them off on a genial note. Then he came back in and sat down. "It was a good first meeting. That's how it goes." They knew he'd handled negotiations with workers at the huge mushroom company in the area. Successfully.

Catherine felt frustrated. "But we didn't get anything done."

Arno smiled. "Oh yes, we did. These things take time. Just call another meeting."

~ 26 Payback ~

In the meantime, André and Catherine discussed matters furiously.

"It's very clear, André. They won't go unless there is secure housing for them."

"The law doesn't say that."

"I know, but I know them too. Renting a place won't work for them. They know they could be thrown out and then it would be back to the same situation they are in now."

"Maybe not."

"How could they not be vulnerable? Neela of all people knows it well, having to leave their friend's house. Esta and Sheryl are more streetwise and they want security."

"I think that's you talking, not them. You would give away the store just to feel better about yourself."

"Not fair, André, and you know it. Feeling better and living with my conscience are two different things. I just cannot let them be that vulnerable."

"You want to take responsibility for their lives?"

"No, not fully, but yes, I want to protect them as much as I can. I think we have a moral responsibility to them."

"What?" André turned fully to her. "We didn't put them into the situation they are in."

"No, we didn't. But we have benefited from their presence, and we have benefited from the work of Godwin and his grandfather. The farmers in general have all benefited from the farmworkers who have gone before, even from the 1600s. Just read your own history books. It started as cheap labour for everyone's survival, and now, here we are."

"So you see it as payback time? We have to pay?"

"I know it's not really fair to us, but who else will pay?"

She continued. "If we haggle with them about renting for them, we will lose any hope of good will coming from their side. I don't want to risk it."

"Are you saying you want to buy them a house?"

She took a deep breath. "I don't know where we will find the money, but that's the only way I can see."

"You are mad. They will sell it and spend the money."

"I doubt it. But if they do, then they do. It will be clearly their own decision and not ours. We have to let go and not try to boss them around. Of course we don't want them to make such a mistake. But … ."

"Maybe we should just cut to the chase and offer them the money. Then they can buy what they want."

"Not a bad idea. It would make it much easier on us."

They took a break.

"Catherine, maybe they want to separate from one another. There are four family units now. Can you believe it, all living in that small cottage space."

"Maybe. They are presenting a united front but there is no love lost between Sheryl and the rest."

André looked thoughtful. "Maybe others there could qualify for their own subsidy and house, such as Sheryl and her boys, Neela and Henry, and of course the visitors."

"Yes, it seems so." She gave a deep sigh. "I just can't take on those matters too. It seems up to them at a later stage. I think we have enough on our plate now, just to see this process through. Because it's not just about housing. It's also about separation, starting on a new path, transferring responsibility. Lots of other issues mixed in."

"Us too. We will have to rethink our lives here without them, especially security matters."

"Then if we find the funds for cottage renovations, and rental, and all that. It is uncharted territory for us."

"I guess you're right. We should try to keep it simple now, at least as simple as we can."

"The next question is, what can we afford?"

"We have to do some serious study of our own finances. I know it's money that won't come back to us."

"But won't the value of our farm go up, by releasing it from future housing claims?"

"That could be. We need to investigate that with our town and regional planner. Maybe check out your colleagues who are property experts, André. So maybe this effort to house the farm family will help us after all. Not that it's our prime concern."

"No. Our prime concern is to help this family get onto a modern track, one that gives them autonomy and legal protection. One that takes a giant step toward independence."

"I couldn't have said it better."

There seemed no option but to secure some kind of permanent housing. Rental housing would not really solve the problem, especially for Godwin and the other members of Isaac's family around him. Surely they knew that. There would have to be some ownership, somehow. But what? For whom? What could Bellezicht offer? Perhaps Godwin and the family would prefer cash, and a lot of it. They could use it to buy a modest house for most of them. After all, there were four family units there, and perhaps there was an auntie or someone who could take in some people, along with the cash, of course. What about Henry's brother and that side of Neela's family? What options could they bring?

The day before the meeting, Catherine approached Neela tentatively at the garage. Neela looked off-putting.

"I hope your people are coming to this meeting, at last." People who would support Neela and Esta. People who would keep them from making a mistake and agreeing to a proposition that might not really be in their interest. People who would prevent the white people with their smooth talk from exploiting the farm people, yet again. People who also probably had their own political agenda. "We will all sit down together and talk."

Neela scowled. Her eyes screwed up and she looked as if she were battling tears. Head tilted back, she looked down her cheeks at Catherine. "We don't have people."

It was a gut-wrenching admission. The support they'd heard about at rallies, the backing that those organisations promised so fervently, wasn't there for them. They were alone. They had to manage the destruction of life as they had always known it, by themselves. This, after all the threats, all the bold talk.

"Oh, Neela." Catherine's heart went out to her. She wanted to put her arms around her. But something in Neela's bearing said no. Catherine just hoped she could hear the empathy in her tone of voice. It seemed strange that she felt empathy, when it was to her interest not to have Neela's people here. But that didn't matter; Neela must be feeling very, very alone. They both knew there was still a long and winding road ahead.

The next meeting wasn't so difficult to get started. Arno knew he'd laid the groundwork.

"We need to look at possibilities for the future," he said. "There are many of them. We need to ask ourselves some tough questions. Which options are possible for us? Which ones fit us the best? What are our choices?"

Esta and Neela, this time joined by Sheryl and Godwin, listened. Who knows why Sheryl decided to get involved. Up to now she had been a passive bystander; now she was a player on centre stage. Godwin as well. He was ultimately a gentle soul. He did not like conflict and either agreed or kept a distance. But now, he was also coming to the party.

It seemed clear enough to them that one of the choices not offered was the choice to stay on. It was as if somehow, this did not come as a shock. It did not even need to be said. It seemed they had assumed this course from the start, unlike Catherine and André. It had taken the owners a long time to catch up. Another indication of life in two different worlds.

The farm family knew they could oppose all offers. That meant they could stay on, for a while, during the process. It might even take years. But in the end, there was no way they could stay on forever. Things could never return to the normality of life before that fateful meeting many months ago.

André explained the property law relating to cottages on farms. "Even if I wanted to give you the cottage, I couldn't," he said. "The law stops me. This is a farming area and we cannot subdivide even into smaller farms, let alone cut out a place for a cottage. Otherwise, we'd have a housing estate and the law prevents farmers from doing that."

"Maybe we can find something even better," said Arno, smiling. "Who knows. We all must try."

Catherine waited for Arno to explain that everyone can see that no one in the cottage works in the vines. Godwin does garden work, and he is like a foreman on the farm, seeing to things, but the vines bring in the money, at least potentially. Besides, the cottage would be needed to house a new vineyard worker, not a gardener. But Arno was cool. He left most of it for messages between the lines.

He continued. "Think about it," he said. "Talk it over. There is no pressure. We will meet again and continue our discussions."

This time, the ladies had the cookies along with the tea. But they remained aloof.

Early the next morning, Neela came to the front door. *"Ek wil met die baas praat.* Is he still here?" She used the old word more familiar to her, *baas.* Catherine ran to get André who had just gotten dressed. "Neela is speaking to us!"

Neela stood outside the door like a pillar. Her hair was combed back neatly. She spoke her proclamation in a loud clear voice. *"Baas. Ons het onder mekaar gepraat. Ons stem saam met the baas. En bring daai kêrel terug."* She turned on her heel and was gone.

Catherine, standing behind the amazed André, said, "Quick, tell me! What did she say?"

He spoke slowly and with some disbelief. "She said: 'We've discussed matters among ourselves. We agree with the boss. And bring that man back.'"

Catherine felt tears well up, tears of relief, tears of amazement. At last! The turning point, after months of anger and uncertainty.

"I feel as if I could fly up and buzz around the mountains like a big bumblebee," she burbled, stumbling over her similes, "and land back softly as a dove." She choked back tears as André hugged her so hard she could feel his every bone.

It had happened quickly. Subtly. Between the lines, with a logic of its own. Not the force of powerful ideas. Not the force of threats. Not by abuse. Not by manipulation. Was it Arno's presence, his understanding of farm people? Was it through no politicos supporting them? Did they finally understand the nature of the situation they were in? Was it that they retrieved some level of trust, remembering that Catherine and André had tried their best to deal honestly with them all along, through the years? Persuasion could be mysterious.

"It's amazing. But now," cautioned André, "now, the real work starts."

The next morning, Catherine turned over in bed as sleep oozed away. Four-ten in the morning. By 04:30 she gave up and got to her feet. Lola and Jonty rose as one from their own beds next to André's side, greeted her with wags and licks and led the way for her to open the doors.

The spring morning spread out to her, calm and pleasantly warm. She caught her breath to see the mountains. They ranged from north to south as they always did, as viewed from the Bellezicht veranda. But now they stood outlined darkly against the eastern sky. From somewhere behind the peaks light threw out a brilliant gold. It could have been a deposit guaranteeing that yes, today, the sun definitely will rise, and rise in style.

There were clouds. They reminded her of a huge oriental fan emanating from one small point and spreading itself across the whole visible sky. Brilliant purple on the spines of the fan, fleshed out in between with shades of charcoal. Gold and purple, the colours of royalty.

As she turned her head to take in this sweep of majesty, she caught her breath again. To the northeast hung not one but two shining planets. Jupiter and Venus, looking not far from each other. Big brother, little sister. Or maybe the farm and the farm family, other worlds, not so close but not so far. Jupiter and Venus, come to visit us on this little hill.

There in the outer reaches of the fan a large full moon smiled down. Catherine's eyes filled with tears at the greatness of it all, of our neighbours in our very own solar system, come to say hello. She thought she saw the fan give a slow flutter, as if blowing her a kiss on the morning breeze.

Ten steps below the dogs sniffled around the grass and bushes, doing their doggy thing, oblivious to the tears slipping down her cheeks.

As she watched, the whole fan shifted ever so slightly northward. Jupiter disappeared. Then Venus went right after him. The moon was nowhere to be seen. The celestial visit was over. But the grace, the courage, it had brought to her heart.

~ 27 Next ~

The three witches of Bellezicht, Catherine thought, not unkindly. Neela, Esta, and Sheryl sat across from André and Catherine at the dining room table for the next meeting. Arno as usual sat at one end and Godwin at the other. Catherine imagined the three women in the cottage, stirring the cauldron, thinking up all the nasty things they would like to do to farmers who make them move. In her fantasy they were cackling with glee.

Arno began. "It seems that we can now discuss the way forward." They nodded. Catherine served the usual snacks. There was finally a bit of cheer, a bit of relief. They went for the cookies. Their bodies angled toward Arno, not away as in the past.

He posed the question to them. "The Steenkamps have thought long and hard about the next step. They know that you will need a place to live. That is not easy to find. The first decision is how to go about it. The basic houses that are built by the government cost about R80 000. You could buy an existing one for even less than that, and you could extend it yourself with the extra money. Godwin has some skills needed for building. Or maybe you could think of another plan.

"The Steenkamps are offering you cash. R100 000. This is the first possibility. They will transfer it to you promptly, at a time and in a way that we can discuss. There is also a housing subsidy that you can apply for and it seems very likely that you will get it. Like all government matters, it takes lots of time and lots of paperwork. But you will be getting lots more cash. Then you can buy as you like."

Eyes focused on Arno. Listening takes a lot of energy, Catherine observed. She now knew to shut up and let Arno handle things.

"The other possibility is that the Steenkamps themselves will get you a house. They will supply some cash, and they will apply for the subsidy of R84 000 with Godwin as a first-time homeowner. A person can get this subsidy just once, the first time you own a home. That subsidy will then be used by them to help pay for the house.

"They want to work together with you, whichever way you choose. So would you like some time to think about these choices? Or perhaps suggest other ways?"

Catherine and André had discussed the issue of what they should offer Godwin and his family with a group of close Afrikaans friends. Most of them had had a family farm somewhere in their background. The friends predicted unanimously: they will definitely take the cash. It is much more immediate, you can spend it any way you like, for a vehicle, for clothes, and just to enjoy life for a while. Tomorrow is very far away; they will definitely take the cash.

The four of them looked at one another.

"No pressure," smiled Arno. "We can arrange another meeting."

Esta spoke up. "We'll take the house."

"Are you sure? Don't you want to think about it some more? Talk it over?"

"Nee, Meneer, ons is doodseker." She repeated, "We'll take the house."

The other three nodded.

Arno wasn't quite ready for such a clear and unambiguous agreement. He paused to remember the next thing.

Sheryl lobbed in. Her face changed to a pout. "The house must not be small. It must have all the things we have now – three bedrooms, two bathrooms, kitchen and lounge." She gave a curt nod – or else, it seemed to say.

"There must be ceilings too," added Neela. Apparently some low-cost houses came with roofs but not with ceilings.

He quickly caught up. "All right. And, in order for Godwin to have transport to come to work, the Steenkamps will contribute the bakkie as well."

"Just remember," André added, "it's an old bakkie. But we've maintained it well, and it's well built. It's a tough little Ford; an American. Like my wife."

"My first bakkie," said Catherine, after the farm people had left. "I remember driving it home one evening, shortly after I bought it, on a very stormy Cape winter's night. It was after a rather late parents' night at the school. It was before cell phones so I couldn't assure André I was on my way, not to worry."

Arno nodded.

"The rain came down in sheets and I drove in and out of fog. At a traffic light just out of Stellenbosch, I recognised Henry also making his way home to Bellezicht through the merciless rain, but on his bicycle. I hooted twice but he didn't look. I had to pull over in front of him and hoot again as he drew near. I leaned over to wind down the window before he recognised me.

"He threw the bike onto the back of the bakkie, clambered into the passenger seat and wound up the window against the horizontal rain. He then looked straight ahead, and intoned solemnly, 'Missus, go to the house.' His version of "Home, James."

Arno shook his head, smiling.

"So on we drove, Henry and I, through huge puddles, through the mist, creeping along, taking splash from passing trucks, and trying to stay safe. The Ford waded up the farm road leading to Bellezicht, its front-wheel drive holding on against muddy water flooding down. As we approached the farm itself, the rain abated somewhat. There at the driveway through the vines leading to the main house stood a worried André, flashlight in hand, glad to see me. And there at the second driveway above, through the rows of vines ending at the cottage, stood Henry's worried wife, flashlight in hand, glad to see him."

~ 28 A dop ~

André's brother Frankie was incredulous. "Have you got your head up your collective ass? What do you two mean, just give them a house? Surely they will have to pay you back at some point." Frankie, tall and blond and ponytailed, swirled and savoured his current wine favourite, Jacobsdal pinotage, dark and luscious with muted berry and a flash of spice. "Ah, a *lekker dop*." He smiled at the glass. "A very nice drink." His blue eyes smiled too.

He and André and Catherine sat on Bellezicht's veranda facing the sweep of mountains, mountains whose ridges and gullies showed up in great crisp edges as the evening sun reflected off their western-facing slopes.

"Catherine, you can't be serious," he said. André nodded and shifted in his chair.

"No, no payback from Godwin and his family," Catherine said. "Definitely not. We want to just give the house. They will never be able to pay us back anyway."

André chimed in. "We have to cut the dependency ties. We've had it the whole time on this farm, that, whenever anything came along, they have been so dependent on us. We did our best to help. Then, if things didn't turn out the way they wanted, they blamed us."

"Frankie, it's about moving toward greater independence," said Catherine. "People have to stand up and take responsibility for themselves. We are ready to help if they ask, but the responsibility must lie with them, not us."

Something the colour of emeralds flashed from around the corner and flew right to left in front of all three of them. Catherine half-stood as if to escape, releasing her grip on her glass. It splintered down the steps, spraying shards of crystal, like droplets from water falling into light.

"A sunbird," said Frankie, unperturbed. "It wants to drink from the flowers in that vase."

The array of large brick-red pincushions flowering against the veranda wall had drawn the bird in. But it hadn't bargained on people being that near. It got a fright and flashed away, flicking its iridescent feathers.

André sat Catherine down again, seeing the distress on her face. "Relax. Here's another glass. We can sweep up later."

As they settled down, Catherine picked up her train of thought. "There's another huge factor here as well, Frankie," she said. "Godwin and Esta and Neela and Sheryl, the children and whoever else they want, they will have housing for the rest of their lives."

The men turned to look at her. "They won't ever again have to fear being evicted. It will be Godwin's house. Godwin's own house."

Frankie, however, was still preoccupied with not giving it away. "Why don't you get a bond, and charge them a modest amount, for example R200 per month? Surely they can afford that. I mean, just to GIVE it away, to part with all that hard-earned money ... it's just not at all fair to you. How can you still be considering it? Are you mad?"

"Mad, maybe. And you're right, it isn't fair. But do you think they will complain? Most people complain when life makes them suffer, not when it's generous to them."

"So? It's still not right. You are even the ones setting it up to be unfair toward yourselves. I mean, you don't have to give them a house."

Catherine looked into her new glass as if hoping to find a clue for making Frankie understand.

"Frankie, I can't believe that you really expect life to be fair. It just isn't that way. We can't expect it to be fair. If we do, we are in for huge disappointments, over and over."

Frankie was silent for a moment, then spoke softly. "That's for damn sure."

"One more thing goes along with it," said Catherine. "There are no guarantees. If I can remember those two principles, I won't expect the wrong things. I can keep my balance in this uncertain life."

Frankie turned his blue eyes fully onto Catherine for a few seconds, then shook his head. "So now, how can you do it? It doesn't make sense. I mean, you can control it. You can structure any deal you wish. But you aren't keeping any advantages for yourselves."

"That may be how it looks to you. Maybe we want the joy of altruism, even though I know there is no such thing. But there are definitely advantages to us."

"Such as?"

"A certain freedom. For one thing, they are not likely ever to be able to pay." She thought for a moment. "Or to want to pay, if they can get out of it. So we are free of the burden of always trying to get money from them."

André added, "I wonder if they would feel they don't have to pay; after all, they might reason that they are here, already living in the house. Already possessing it. They could just get tired of paying."

Frankie nodded. "Money for debt. It creates so many problems."

"Even now, like most South Africans, they spend beyond their means," said André. "In fact, I just read a statistic, about the bottom-income group that makes up over 80% of South Africans. People in that group spend about 110% of their income. So payment would always be a problem. You know the story, especially of many farm people: get in debt, miss payments, make them come after you, try to disappear, hope things will change so that you eventually don't have to repay."

"Not everyone," said Catherine. "Our Anna is very serious about repaying her debts. And she does."

"True," said André. "However, she is a townie, not a farm person. Not repaying worked on the farms, when workers borrowed from the farmer. But even that doesn't work anymore, now that farmers have stopped lending. If farm people want to borrow, they have to borrow from the bank or a microlender, at exorbitant interest rates."

Catherine agreed. "Many people, not just farmworkers, don't even know how much interest they are paying. My friend's char borrowed R2 000 from a microlender at Christmas for six months and she had to pay back

R2 800. That's R800 down the drain. Just for extras on top of her bonus. My friend saw her bank slip. When she asked her char how much the interest was, she said, 'R200?' She didn't know herself and her guess was way off in the end."

"Can you imagine," said André, "trying to collect from Godwin and his family every month? There are always reasons not to pay. They owe someone else, the cell phone has packed up, Neela needs to take two taxis to the hospital to get treatments for her back, visitors are here long term and you know how much food costs. How about payments on that expensive home entertainment system that some salesman long ago sold to Godwin? It shouldn't be legal, to saddle a farmworker with a debt of R15 000. But somehow, the salesman did it."

Catherine kept trying to persuade Frankie. "A third problem of giving a bond would come up if they seriously defaulted. How can anyone repossess a property in a poorer area?"

"Well, I suppose," admitted Frankie. "I've heard that trying to repossess is to take your life in your hands."

"I've heard of people hijacking an apartment building in Johannesburg. A building! If enough people in the building refuse to pay their rent, there is not much that the building owner can do about it."

Catherine watched a sparrow splashing in the birdbath. How simple life could be. Why did it always seem so complicated? But we are working at simplifying now, she thought. "There's one other thing. If we are the bondholders, then, when anything goes wrong, they phone us. Say the drain clogs up. A small crack appears in a ceiling. A light fixture stops working. We'd be over there all the time. We'd be responsible. No, that won't work. Not for us, anyway."

She sat for a moment lost in her thoughts.

"No, Frankie, a bond won't work. Better just to make everyone's life simple and give the house away. We pay, and it will cost us more interest because our own bond will be bigger, but then strife with Godwin and his family will be over. Over and done. Finish and *klaar*. The end."

"I need another dop," said Frankie, holding out his glass.

"There's one thing I've learned today, after all this discussion," said Frankie. He looked directly at André. "You both really do have your heads up your collective ass."

~ 29 Look ~

"Start with the phone book," advised André. "Everything is there. You can use the online version." He made it clear that, from now on, this was Catherine's project, not his.

"That's the problem," she said. "It's just too vast." She thought for a moment. "I've got a friend in the business."

The friend sent the names of agents in the low-income property market in this area. There weren't too many of them. In fact, there were just three names.

"*Ja,*" said André. "Maybe because there's not much money in it for them. It's probably difficult selling to people who don't have money."

One agent said he knew about relocating farmworkers to an area that would be comfortable for them. He came to the farm. Catherine organised a meeting at the farm for after working hours to suit everybody. Neela, Esta, Sheryl and Godwin sat down on the veranda shielded from the full January sun.

"They are building in Macassar," the agent said. Arno had said that was the only place in the whole area where any serious building was going on.

Stony faces. "We don't know where Macassar is."

"It has lots of grey areas, not just for black people, or coloured people, or white people. It's close, over that way, just eight kilometres." Stony faces.

Macassar was clearly not going to work.

"We don't want to go to Eerste River," declared Neela, "or Wembly Park, or Blue Downs. Too much crime there, too many drug dealers, not good, not good for the children."

The others nodded. At least there was agreement on what they didn't want. The field was narrowing.

"We may have something for you by next week," said the agent.

"Next week!" Catherine said. "Too long."

Another friend had given her a contact at an estate agency in an area that might be acceptable. She phoned. Lots of negatives, no, no property in that sector of the market, nothing available. She just kept asking more questions, feeling desperate. She didn't want to be put off with negatives.

Finally the agent said, "Oh yes, there's Tony. Give him a call." And Tony had a house. Just one.

Catherine approached André. "It sounds good – several bedrooms – and the price is even lower than we expected. It's R200 000."

"I don't have work time to lose," he complained.

She went to see it and then dragged him anyway to see it the next day. It had been built up by the owner. With the granny flat it totalled not three, but five bedrooms and an extra bathroom. It had walls around it, a spacious paved yard and a gate. The neighbourhood showed signs of wear and tear but it was alive. It was just the ticket for Godwin and his non-nuclear family.

André was so taken with it that he put in an offer on the spot.

"Step Two," said André, "Godwin and the group have to agree to move to that house, in that place. Arno said it's crucial. It can be delicate."

Catherine felt the tension coming in between her shoulders. "You know how hard house-hunting can be. If they start playing games with us now, it can be very delicate indeed."

Anyway, she arranged for the three women and Godwin, again freed from his garden work on the farm, to go meet Tony on the next day available and view the house. See what they think. Sheryl had growled, "We're not taking the first one we see."

"No, of course not," Catherine said. "We can look around, decide. No rush." Taking Arno's words, she added, "No pressure." Despite Sheryl's negative talk, Catherine felt that the faces on the farm people looked guardedly optimistic.

The morning came and they assembled to drive out. Godwin held the car door for everyone there, Neela and Esta and Catherine. But where was Sheryl?

"It's pension day, Missus. Sheryl went to the payout point at the cash store."

Catherine held her tongue. She was getting good at shutting up. She phoned the agent, asking for a thirty-minute delay. They drove down to the cash store, in the opposite direction. People milled around. Mainly older people queued for their cash. A security guard, contracted for pension-payout days, stood near the entrance to the store, armed with an AK 47. The rifle pointed to the ground but the guard's eyes swept the crowd.

"There's Sheryl," said Neela. She had walked up from the store a bit off the road.

Relieved that she didn't have to drive near the crowd and the AK 47, Catherine made a U-turn and drew near to Sheryl, who put on a resigned smile and climbed into the car.

The agent was waiting by the bridge. Catherine pulled over and they all got out.

"There are some houses over there and we can see later if any are available." His arm waved toward the beehive of houses on the north side of the road. They were RDP houses, tiny little boxes, but if one had nothing, it was something that could be called home. As well, it was something, finally, to own.

They strained to see. "Small," said Esta. "How can our people all fit into one of those hob houses?" They probably had a floor plan of about 45 square metres. They had plumbing and electricity; the idea was that the new owners could add on rooms themselves.

"All of them look small," said Neela.

Godwin said, "I can do paving and some bricklaying, but not building extra rooms."

Sheryl just shook her head.

They climbed back into the cars. Tony wove into another neighbourhood and pulled up at the house he had for sale. It sat in a short cul-de-sac. There was a Vibracrete cement wall around it. The wife of the owner came out, smiled and opened the gate. "See what you think," Catherine said and stepped back.

Esta walked in behind the wife, eyes everywhere. The kitchen was small but with built-in cupboards. There was a lounge area. "Here's a bedroom. Another bedroom." The wife opened a third door. "And another one."

Catherine trailed after the group.

The master bedroom seemed huge, with an orange spread over the queen-sized bed. It had just a few pieces of furniture and long, high curtains over the windows. Burglar bars protected the windows on the outside.

Neela's eyes opened wide as she looked but she said nothing.

Everyone wandered through. "Why are you selling?" asked Sheryl.

"We are following our daughter to Durban," she replied. "We are sad to leave. My husband did so much work on this house." She was a slender, neat woman with greying strands in her hair, which was tied back in a bun. She wrung her hands every few seconds.

"Is this the whole house?" asked Esta. What a question, thought Catherine.

"There's a granny flat outside." Inside the granny flat they greeted an old woman, definitely a granny, with a little boy. "They are renting from us but will move soon too," explained the wife.

Tony said goodbye to go to another appointment.

They noted two bricked areas enclosed by the walls, under roofing. Some laundry hung under one area. The other could be for parking or braaiing. There was still more enclosed space if people wanted to sit outside on a warm summer evening.

"My husband put in a shower connection," the wife pointed out. "But he was still building the base of the shower." The bathroom was three times the size of the bathroom they had at the cottage. I'm sure we could help fix that shower, Catherine thought.

"The electricity meter is over there," the wife said. "For prepaid." Neela nodded. That will be a new experience, thought Catherine, with sympathy. At Bellezicht electricity for the cottage was free to Godwin and his family. Were they ready for the expenses of being homeowners?

They wandered around outside of the house. Sheryl waved her hand and pointed. "My grandmother used to live over there by the church."

"There's the school," observed Esta. "Now we wouldn't have to pay taxi fees to get the children from the farm to school."

"*Ja,*" said Neela. "They could just walk."

Catherine detected a cautious excitement in some whispered comments as they wandered around the house, the granny flat and the walled-in areas. They were not being open. They seemed to feel it was still them and us.

The street outside was tarred but it was dusty and strewn with things. An old shoe, a few crushed soft-drink cans, pages of newspapers moving in the mild breeze, an apple core, empty chips bags, cardboard boxes. Not to mention pieces of brick and old bent nails, probably rusty. Numerous children and uninterested dogs wandered around. The occasional car rattled by.

The scene reminded Catherine of the cottage *werf* at Bellezicht, except for the car. She admitted defeat in getting the farm family to sweep the *werf* daily. They seemed quite content to sit in the sun amid the trash. An adult would explain, "The children dropped it there." Without making a move to dispose of it, let alone resolve to teach the children better.

"Well, you need to teach them to put their trash in the black bag. It's just two steps away."

"*Ja, Missus.*" But it never seemed to happen.

Catherine could feel that the new house had possibilities. But they might want to play games. It surely was reasonable to look around some more. After a rather long time, the group was ready to leave. No more houses to see that day, even if they had wanted to. Catherine had to come up with alternatives so it would be back to Tony for another appointment, another house to view.

Everybody piled back into the car. "Missus, could you stop at the Spar in Kuils River? We'd like to get a few groceries."

Catherine was always ready to stop for groceries anyway, understanding a woman's duties. Today she was the epitome of graciousness. Self-centred graciousness.

She waited outside, joined by Sheryl, along with the fruit sellers and the vegetable hawkers and the soft drink merchants. The shoppers took quite a while but the sunny day made waiting easier.

Eventually Neela and Esta and Godwin emerged with packets of things. "Sorry to keep you waiting."

"No problem," Catherine said, today especially, the model of patience. "Take your time. No rush," as they started for home.

Godwin sat in front, with the women in the back. There was a modulated Afrikaans buzz in the car. Catherine couldn't quite hear words. She just drove.

In due time they came to the turnoff for Bellezicht. Catherine drove up through the lower gates and approached the little bridge. Legend had it that the previous Scottish owner of Bellezicht had had Scotch stashed in the little stream under the bridge and had imbibed freely as he walked from place to place over his farm.

As they crossed that bridge, Esta called out. "Missus – we'll take it!"

Catherine hit the brakes there and then, and called out a loud "Whooopeee!" She laid on the hooter, on and on, and they made all the noise they could. Everyone whooped and laughed and chatted with great excitement as they drove up the road and into the *werf,* laughing and hooting.

As they got out of the car, Catherine said, "I'm so glad there is a decision. But just think about it and we can decide tomorrow, or later."

Tomorrow would bring just confirmation. It seemed like there was no better house in the world for Esta and her people, Neela and her group, Sheryl and her boys. If the kingpins in his home were happy, who was Godwin to disagree.

André drove up to the farm around six o'clock. He found Catherine waiting for him on the stoep with a cold bottle of South Africa's best bubbly.

~ 30 Why ~

The farm family started immediately making plans for how they would manage, how Godwin would get to work, how the children would get to school. The same school near Bellezicht, because the current fees were lower, they said. Catherine didn't argue; the reality of travel would come later. No matter that school fees were abolished some time ago; just some administrative fees were asked, but in the farming community, not demanded. It felt good to have such a positive spirit, after months of enmity. How long could it last?

The lawyer phoned. They all attended a meeting with the estate agent, a silver-haired lady with a lot of patience. She explained the process to Catherine as well as to the farm family in the same meeting, using both English and Afrikaans.

There had been unexpected recognition of Catherine's efforts to keep all the meetings open and inclusive. At those tense meetings with Arno of a month ago, Sheryl had said that Catherine told her this or that.

Catherine had said, "*Nee, Sheryl, ek praat nie agter mense se rug nie.* I don't talk behind people's back. I don't speak for just one person to hear. Everyone must know what is said."

Of all people, Neela had spoken up, loud and strong and clear. "*Dis waar,*" she said. "That's true." In the midst of conflict, still the truth came out, and Catherine felt immensely gratified. Her respect for Neela was confirmed even within those delicate negotiations.

Now, a few days later, there was still more work to be done. Godwin needed to go sign more papers to continue with the process. There were actually two processes, one of Godwin as worker taking ownership of the house, and one of Godwin as first-time homeowner applying for the government subsidy. Catherine had arranged the appointment for two o'clock with the estate company's lawyer. Godwin came to work that day in a smart shirt and black jeans.

Before she and Godwin were to leave, Catherine went back to the cottage *werf*, no longer such foreign territory, and asked Neela, who was sitting outside, for her ID book and that of Sheryl too. These were the two dependants, his mother and his auntie, who would help to qualify Godwin for the subsidy. He also needed to bring his payslip showing the modest wages of a gardener, which André had printed nicely for him. Godwin also would need to declare that he had not owned a house previously. This all had been discussed with everyone by the estate agent at their meeting.

"Why our ID books?" said Neela, as she stood up to face Catherine. "Why does Godwin need them to get a house?"

Catherine stood there in disbelief, while also realising that this process was foreign to this family.

"Because of the subsidy," Catherine explained. "Sheryl is his mother and he has an obligation to her. Neela is his auntie and he has been housing her too." All to hostile looks.

Godwin came out, accompanied by Sheryl and Esta, but under protest, it seemed. Catherine kept trying to explain.

"There are so many people out there who are not honest. They want houses and they make up lies to get them. The lawyer and the government officials have to check and check to be sure that the person getting the subsidy does exist. And that his or her dependants exist. We've all heard of the ghost workers? These are people who have died but other people go on pretending to be them and getting their social grants, and other benefits. The government needs to be careful."

Scowls.

"It's the lawyer's job to see that all the information is correct. Otherwise he is not a good lawyer." The young lawyer in particular felt happy to be part of this positive process, whereby he was helping someone to actually own a house.

"We've never heard of this," said Neela.

André sensed some tension and joined them at the cottage. "As the lawyer explained it, it's part of the process. Neela and Sheryl are dependants and they fill the requirement for Godwin to have dependants. They don't give the subsidy to someone who doesn't have other people to take care of. He doesn't have children, as you know."

Esta looked away.

"We've never heard of this," repeated Neela.

"Well," André said, "Godwin has to prove these people really are his auntie and his mother."

Still scowling.

"We have to have these documents. Otherwise, they won't give the subsidy, and then André and I cannot afford such a nice large house. A house for everyone," Catherine added. "You all can come along too, if you wish."

They produced the documents grudgingly.

Godwin and Catherine drove over to the lawyer's office minus the others. Godwin produced his ID book and theirs too. Catherine asked as many questions as she could think of, for Godwin's benefit as well as for her own.

There were lots of headings and tables and blank lines and places for Godwin to sign. He just signed away, page after page as anyone would, trusting to those who know the law. Everyone has to play the game, so to speak. Godwin and Catherine returned to Bellezicht, one to the computer and one to the garden.

Then there came a loud knock on the front door; a very loud knock. That was already not a good sign. The anger in the knock gushed in through the keyhole and under the door.

There, at some distance from the door, stood three women looking even more like the three witches. Neela's nose was in the air, Esta wore a deep frown, and Sheryl glared at Catherine with open aggression.

Neela spoke. "What's all this, papers and signing? And why is it taking so long?"

Catherine stood there incredulous.

Neela went on. "Someone we know bought a house in Oostenberg, signed all the papers, and it went through in a month." Body language was smelling a rat.

Respectful of their mistrust, Catherine did the best she could. "The house costs a lot of money, R200 000. We can afford it only if you help, and that means the subsidy available to Godwin. He needs to ask the government for the special subsidy for people who get a house for the first time. Remember?"

No answer.

She continued. "So how do you ask the government for money? You fill in papers, more papers, and more papers."

She was getting nowhere. "They take their time to check everything, no hurry for them, no rush for government bureaucrats. The lawyer said that the papers have to go to Cape Town, then to Pretoria, then back to Cape Town, then back to the lawyer, and only then, back to us."

Catherine had just spent the whole day preparing Godwin plus collecting all the documentation for the meeting, getting him to and from the lawyer, sitting there beside him, asking questions on his behalf.

Still the disgruntled looks.

André had told her that her reservoir of patience could sometimes be enough for all of Cape Town. She felt that explaining, with listening, was an act of caring. However, this time it did not reduce the negativity flooding toward her.

Catherine recalled that these same people use the government health care system with all its bureaucracy and documents and messages of "come back tomorrow." Every visit costs them the day sitting and waiting for the folder, waiting for the nursing sister, waiting for the doctor, waiting for the medicine. More papers to give the farmer, if they need to be booked off for a while. More papers to be signed for the next step in treatment. Why is today's procedure, part of the once-off procedure for getting a house of one's own, such a burden?

Scowls, scowls, scowls. For once, she'd had enough. "That's what we're doing for you!" For good measure she lobbed in, "I'm helping you!"

And finally, she threw up her hands. "Then do the work yourself!" She turned and stalked back inside the house and slammed the door.

How could they be so suspicious, as if she and André were playing games with them? As if she and André were trying to hurt them. As if they were withholding information, or trying to trick them into something they didn't know about. As if "Just sign here" and all rights disappear. But then, they weren't so wrong; such things had happened in the past.

Catherine paced the passage. She stewed for a while. Slowly she began to calm down. She began to reason with herself. "I don't know myself like this. But I guess we all have a breaking point. This far, and no further."

She sat down at her desk. "Am I dealing with centuries of mistreatment of farmworkers by the farmers? Am I dealing with generations of disenfranchised people? Am I again the 'lucky' one who gets to confront it face to face? Furthermore, are we the 'lucky' ones who get to pay for the wrongs of centuries?"

She put her head in her hands. The anger slowly became a great weight. She looked out of the window and saw the mountains with patches of sunlight at their feet. She saw the trees in the middle distance, different kinds, in rows and clumps. She saw the row of bougainvilleas along the boundary, entwined in their reds and brilliant pinks. Her study filled with the fragrance of frangipani which she only now noticed.

It took some time to find again the "yes" in her heart.

~ 31 Moving ~

A lorry and a one-ton bakkie with a trailer, in one trip – that's all it took to move the worldly possessions of 12 people from farm to city. Beds, each giving rest to three or four bodies. Tattered cabinets. A large green-painted, padlocked chest inherited from grandparents. Black plastic bags full of clothing and sheets and blankets. Large plastic paint cans that used to hold R2 000 worth of high-quality paint, paint which had waited two years to be smoothed against the cottage walls. Where had it gone? Not on the walls of the cottage, that's for sure. Now the large cans held cups and plates and glasses.

The farm people were ready for this move. They had their things set outside the house, in the *werf*, for two days before the moving day. They were asked as part of the agreement to leave the place clean, inside and out, and they took that commitment seriously. They washed down the walls, cleaned out the corners, and left the windows shiny. They even offered to come back the next Tuesday and do more, if not satisfactory. It was amazing to see the place cleaner than it ever was while they lived there. The heavy smell that was in the house, and on everyone who lived there, was nearly gone.

Where had that heavy smell come from? Years of dirt build-up in the corners? From the furniture? From beds and clothing? From overcrowding? Years of airlessness couldn't have helped. Nor could years of smoking. Suddenly, it was history.

Once the furniture was loaded up, it was time. But where was Sheryl? She was never an easy customer. Then it came out that she had threatened not to move, for unknown reasons.

"Everyone must move or no one moves!" Catherine exclaimed. Anyone staying behind would just prolong the situation they had worked so hard to resolve.

"We'll talk to her," said Esta.

Whatever they said, if it was cajoling words or threatening words, it worked. Somehow, Sheryl came around from the cottage and waited, ready to climb into the car. Then, where was her son, Quinton? Not on the farm. Sheryl didn't seem concerned.

"He's over there, at the next farm," said one of the teenagers. They always knew.

Catherine drove by herself over to the next farm. On the way she thought about Quinton's little life, bisected into two planes: one the everyday life of school and home with extended family, and the other, a life of wild and free possibilities through crime. Mainly stealing, along with the money and friends it could get him. He had even asked Sheryl to buy him a gun; surely not a typical child request.

Lately he had been reached emotionally by a teacher in the government school, a man who understood 12-year-old boys wanting more. Catherine had asked Sheryl to make arrangements for him to stay with friends for a few weeks, to finish the school term with this Meneer. But Sheryl refused, maybe nervous about leaving him without enough supervision.

As Catherine drove into the manor area of the neighbour's farm, sure enough, there Quinton was, with a school friend. No problem, he just climbed into the car. Like mother, like son. Maybe it was a coded request, or maybe just a bit of extra drama to make one feel alive.

The final stages. Catherine opened the cottage door one last time, just to see that everything was out. Every item of furniture was definitely out, including all the light bulbs. She noticed something in one corner, something moving. She stepped in to investigate and there were some inhabitants who were not leaving this cottage today. They were coming out of hiding: cockroaches. They can stay here for another day, thought Catherine. She stepped out quickly and went back to the people milling around the werf.

André stood around watching. "This is really something," he told Catherine. He folded his arms across his chest in the stance of a patient man. "How could we have come this far? It's actually amazing."

"How so?"

He shook his head. "When all these troubles started almost a year ago, I wanted them to do things my way, just get the visitors to leave. Then Godwin and the ladies fought because they were sure we wanted them to leave. Now, they are leaving, and with lots of open possibilities." He shook his head in wonder. "We wanted them to move to our way of thinking, and today, we have moved to their way of thinking. Isn't that like the eighth wonder of the world, or of our little Bellezicht world?"

"It feels like a miracle," said Catherine. "However did it happen, that 'us and them' changed to 'we'?"

The loadmasters covered the piled-up furniture with blankets and tied it down with a network of ropes.

André had backed out both vehicles, the bakkie and the off-road vehicle that Catherine drove. People piled into that old 4x4, so useful for farm roads, according to rank. Neela sat in front, Esta and Sheryl and the visiting girl in the back. With each woman came a child on the lap or squished between knees. Catherine hoped that there would be no police today to check on overloading. At least there were seatbelts.

One of the teenagers just managed to squeeze into the carry space at the back, along with his dog Ringo. Godwin rode in the bakkie with André, in the front seat. The visitor fellow and Quinton rode in the open back, along with boxes and bags of household goods. Just as the procession was about to begin, Henry rode up on his bicycle. He was ready to cycle alongside the rented lorry but they found room on the lorry bed and hoisted him up, bike and all.

Godwin had managed to pile still more items on people's laps and at their feet, including his own. Backpacks, bags with food, other sacks. He had managed to keep track of his ID book and other documents through this difficult day.

Catherine had her own bit to contribute. Godwin, through years of living on this wine farm, and having helped André to move to a new office, had picked up a sense of celebration and even mentioned it earlier, about something special, and she thought yes; she loved it. She had packed a special basket herself and added a few extra touches.

It took about thirty minutes for the drive to the new house. As the men offloaded, she stood keeping an eye on the children and the dog. Poor stressed Ringo! On the leash, he had nowhere to go. When the boy went to buy chips, he whined and pulled, but then accepted his fate and lay down. But his tail wagged strongly when the boy re-appeared. Ringo kept looking at a certain box, and of course it turned out to contain his dog food.

Furniture came off the vehicles. The ten-kilometre trek had not been kind to these very modest things. A few boards had pulled away and left nails sticking up. There were scuff marks on the standing kitchen cupboard. At least it was still able to stand.

The movers were a story in themselves. It seems that the grandfather had started the moving business, which was now run by his son and then, the grandson as well. White fellows and not so well off, it appeared. They manoeuvred the vehicles into the *werf*, along with three isiXhosa-speaking men, probably casual workers, to unload. Those men seemed happy enough to have this job and they put themselves seriously into it. While the offloaders worked, the son and grandson disappeared, popping around now and then to supervise. One of them sent Quinton over to the little shop nearby to buy him four cigarettes, just four. When all was offloaded, they appeared again and worked the vehicles out of the yard.

Although André had organised the movers, he stood to one side and let them do what they had to do. Now it was time for Catherine to swing into action.

"Help me unpack this basket, please," she asked André. She read his body language – today, ask him anything and you've got it with a smile.

They set the items onto a cabinet standing outside: a cloth, twelve tall long-stemmed glasses, some blue plastic cups for the children. And, in the best international tradition of celebration, a bottle of bubbly. Drinks were poured and distributed, with grape juice for the children and others who didn't drink, and in the classic way, everyone, even the little ones, raised their glasses and cups in a united cheer.

André stepped forward. *"Gesondheid vir almal* – may you have health, peace, good luck and many blessings in your new home!"

~ 32 Sun and moon ~

As Catherine followed André driving back into Bellezicht, the *werf* seemed larger than it felt just a few hours ago. For the first time since they had moved in, all those years ago, there was no child to come from the cottage and have a look, no report of the day's activities from Godwin, no warning bark. At least the ridgeback Lola and the little white terrier Jonty wiggled a welcome.

"Now what do we do?" asked André, looking a bit lost.

"What any respectable wine farmers should do," she replied. "Open a bottle of wine."

He grinned and found, in a corner of the small wine cellar, a lonely bottle of very pricey De Toren Fusion V Bordeau-style blend, a gift from friends.

They sat side by side on the veranda, glasses in hand, watching the evening shadows move from the foot of the mountains and up the steep slopes, until the peaks muted into a lonesome blue-grey.

André spoke first. "It's not the end of our relationship with them. Godwin will still be here on Monday to go on with the gardening."

"Oh, the irony of it," Catherine coughed as the thought hit her. "All these months and nobody went off to Robertson after that first horrible meeting. Nobody even talked about it. Godwin is still here. As things would have been for him, without all the drama."

"Still here," agreed André.

'We'll still be here for them if they need us," Catherine went on. "But I don't think Esta will need us much. She likes to be in control and now she is. She won't give that away easily."

"In fact," she added, "she'll probably tell us to keep our nose out of their business."

"Suits me just fine."

"But we'll still help them. I'll go on buying school clothes and pencils and things. And rewarding the children with a bit of cash for good marks on their reports. If the parents want us to, that is."

André laughed. "They will, don't worry."

Catherine thought for a moment. "Well, they are now their own unit in society. They have their own place to live, as owners, just like us." She sipped the wine.

"It's a lifetime home, and a good investment too," added André. "I hope they see it that way."

"So far, so good. They did choose house and not cash, when we offered the choice."

"So there is hope. If they thrive, then there is hope for the country. What we need is a nation of homeowners, not *inwoners*, people who just stay. Owners have a strong stake in the future." He sighed. "That's the economic theory, anyway."

"Well, we've done what we could do. We enlarged our bond and cashed in on another investment too. From our pension money."

"You can say that means we are still investing in South Africa."

Catherine gave a wry smile. "At least they can't shout at us any more."

André also smiled. "So it's cheers, to them and to us."

"No," she said. "Cheers to everyone, to all of us. They will always be part of us, part of who we have become."

As they raised their glasses, they turned toward each other and their eyes met.

André poured them more wine. He knew how to pour many times from the same bottle; she smiled again in awe of his measuring skill.

Catherine studied the wine in her glass and gave André a sidelong glance, with a bit of mischief in it. "André, I wonder what we are going to fight about now, with the farm family gone."

André shrugged. "I'm a lover, not a fighter."

"You could've fooled me. You put up quite a few battles in the last year."

He adjusted his chair slightly away from her.

She saw it. "Come on, you know it."

"I can't help it if I was brought up in the old South Africa."

She softened her voice and touched his arm. "Of course not. My darling, I think you have done an amazing job of getting past all that."

He was silent.

"As I think about it now, you have come so far. Including all you were willing to pay, in the end. And still are paying."

"You are paying too." He gave her a nod, like a bow of deference. "It certainly isn't the farm that pays."

"No, we are lucky if the farming side doesn't make a loss." She turned directly toward him. "André, I see this whole moving thing as a kind of social justice. People were disempowered through no fault of their own. We've done what we could to help make things right."

He sighed a very deep sigh. "You know, Catherine, so much of the credit goes to you."

"I had to let go too," she said quietly. "I had to learn. People don't always rise to the occasion the way I think they should."

"But we didn't give up. Neither of us. So here we are, older and wiser. We'll make it, Catherine. We will make it."

The evening stayed warm long past sunset. The sniff of autumn drifted through the air, and they heard the turtle doves calling, undisturbed.

"Look, Cath, there's a plane coming in from Durban," said André. It was a pinpoint of light between two mountain peaks. They expected to see the pinpoint come toward them and fly overhead, as the plane circled behind Bellezicht's hill toward Cape Town airport.

But the pinpoint grew. It became a wedge of light. As they watched, it just grew.

"It's a … a … the moon!" They stood up and stepped to the veranda wall.

In a few minutes, quickly it seemed, there emerged a huge full golden moon, the biggest Catherine had ever seen. She seemed to feel the earth turning toward the light. Behind them were their shadows, moon shadows. They turned as one to clink their glasses and take another sip of beautiful Cape wine.

~ 33 Really ~

What a Hollywood ending. "And they lived happily ever after," as the cowboy rescues the girl and they ride off into the sunset. Alas, despite the best of intentions, despite what she thought was a shared vision, Catherine was devastated that things didn't work out as she had hoped. Hopes were one thing and reality was another.

The story went on for about five more years after moving day. Catherine and André still had contact with the wider family, still bought school things for the youngsters in Kuils River and for family at nearby farms, gave some Saturday jobs for the older boys if they asked, and sometimes gave lifts as possible. Catherine kept notes and added to the file of Godwin and the farm. She supported everything at the schools, as usual.

In four of those years Godwin still held his job at Bellezicht. In the first two he would drive to work, which took about 20 minutes, but that was before big changes happened. Until then, they all just carried on, not seeing that assumptions and expectations in one world differed dramatically from assumptions and expectations in another world.

Life in Kuils River settled down. When Godwin, Esta, Neela and Sheryl chose this neighbourhood, they saw it as a peaceful place, where they had relatives and where grannies lived. Godwin's house gave enough space for everyone, and he had a job and a bakkie. The school was close by; no more school taxi fare to pay. They could easily get to the shops. Life had definitely improved.

Esta kept house and did not get a regular job. She would frequently come along to Bellezicht with Godwin and sit all day in the bakkie while he gardened. Though Catherine felt a bit hemmed in, she provided not one but two lunches and a lot of coffee, plus a place to come in out of the rain.

André took care of three big repairs to Godwin's new house, thanks to Catherine insisting. He had contractors build a shower base, connect the shower head to the water supply, and fix a break in the perimeter wall with bricks and cement. It was not what he wanted to do, because the house was sold *voetstoots,* just as it was, but it was a way to help Godwin take ownership without a backlog. It was also a way to achieve finality. Of course, it eased the consciences of Catherine and André. They were doing the right thing, the best thing, the Christian thing, to empower previously disadvantaged members of the community. It was a way to reduce the inequality gap that was beginning to emerge in the national narrative.

The learning curve for Godwin and Esta was steep. They complained to André that their drain got blocked. André was glad he did not have to take responsibility for that. He told them to phone the City of Cape Town. The City found that many drains there were blocked and sent a big truck and fixed the problem. Esta asked what to do about the water bills that they kept getting in the mail.

"What have you been doing with them?" asked André.

"Putting them in a file," replied Esta.

André checked with a friend who served on the Cape Town City Council about what options Godwin and Esta had. In the end, the friend said they should claim indigence, what most people were doing these days, he said. So safe municipal water was piped to them for free.

Godwin had received training as a paver. Catherine helped him to develop calling cards so that he could perhaps make extra weekend income. A neighbour asked Godwin to pave his driveway, and wanted to know how many bricks he had to buy. Although Catherine tried to help from a distance, it was a calculation beyond Godwin.

It seems that no one, neither "them" nor "us," anticipated how different life in the city would become, after they moved from rural to urban living. No one had thought to tell them or even ask if there would be adjustments, let alone what kind of adjustments. They now had to care for the house and keep it secure and keep it in repair. Godwin had to maintain the bakkie. No one had thought to tell them that there was a huge lesson waiting: that it costs money to own something.

Neighbours, instead of being helpful, seemed a problem. Someone jumped over their wall in the middle of the night, and Godwin had to chase him away. The boy next door threw stones onto the roof. When

Esta complained, the parents shouted abuse at her. There was no farmer to run to when family fights broke out. With 12 people under one roof, just as at Bellezicht, fights in the house were inevitable.

There was one conflict that no one saw coming. Godwin's mother, Sheryl suddenly claimed that Godwin's house was her own house. Esta said she became impossible. So Esta insisted on marrying Godwin legally, to strengthen her position as wife to the owner of the home. They chose to go to the magistrate in Paarl, and asked André and Catherine to take them. Catherine photographed Esta in her white dress and a long string of pearls, posing in the park along the Berg River.

But marrying didn't help. Sheryl got worse. She laid a complaint with the police against Esta for "emotional abuse", citing screaming, tearing the curtains down from the windows, other things. Esta was unhappy about having to go to court, and it was the last matter that she went to André and Catherine to ask for advice.

"Well, did you do those things, Esta?"

"Nee, Missus, dis nie die waarheid nie." (No, Missus, it's not the truth.) Catherine did not feel fully convinced by her denial but she knew the court would decide. Esta had a poignant comment, in English: "I wish I was back at the farm."

"Show the court your copy of the deed of the house, which is in Godwin's name. Then that shows that Sheryl can tell lies, even in a sworn statement." It would also probably reveal Sheryl's perjury but Catherine knew things would not go that far. Godwin later told Catherine that "Esta won."

Those consultations were exceptions. In general, Godwin and Esta stayed independent. They refused any comment or input. They refused help from a social worker. Catherine could understand this in a way, in that they had been so dominated by others most of their lives, and by their own poverty. There were generations of disempowerment. Everyone needs to seek advice at times; but they didn't ask. So Catherine stepped back.

They didn't have a clue how to get an income from that big house. They had even seen the previous owner's tenants, a granny and a small boy, renting the outside two rooms. But they just could not think of doing the same thing with their asset, using it to make additional money. Catherine had told them before the move how in the USA she had rented out part of her house and shared it, and that had helped financially and had worked out well. But they didn't take the point. Anna, who dropped by their home from time to time, said that they had come to see their big walled house not as an asset but as a liability.

"They aren't managing well," Anna said. "They didn't use the cash you gave them for things like a ladder, light bulbs, curtains for the windows, or cleaning materials. They just spent it at Truworth's on clothes for the children, or so Esta said."

Catherine felt that was true, because Esta loved buying things on credit. When she repeatedly did not pay her bill, the credit department would phone Godwin at his job at Bellezicht. Some requests were for garnishee orders against Godwin's salary, but André always refused. He tried talking to Godwin, for him to talk to Esta, to no avail.

As time went on, Godwin told André that there were gang fights near them that left them huddling in their beds, with bullets flying. It seemed that the once-decent area was getting infected by Cape Flats gangsters and getting worse by the day. News reports confirmed it.

In the third year after their move, Godwin came asking for the deed to his house and went to the lawyer and got it. Such a subsidised house was not to be sold for five years, but they sold it anyway, and for the same price André and Catherine had paid for it. There was no consultation. Catherine wondered if Esta was insisting because there would be cash and plenty of it.

It was a huge disappointment for Catherine and André, especially after they had withdrawn serious money out of their retirement investments, money now lost to generating future income. The real cost would only hit them when they had to retire and start withdrawing. It made them miserable not to see it used as intended, not used to house this poor extended family, to offer them security, to bring stability to their children. What a waste of so much that they had worked for.

What happened to the money? André confirmed with the conveyancers that it had been paid into Godwin's own account. How could it now be used to build a better life? Could Godwin and his wife even imagine how to manage R200 000? It was a fortune in 2005 money. A large portion of it, R84 000, was government subsidy money intended solely for housing. Esta had talked about buying a better house but André said it was just a deflection. Somehow the money disappeared.

Godwin still came to work every day, even by train and taxi, into the fourth year after their move. He said they now lived in a decent area in Paarl but the address he gave was not to be found. He started calling in sick, or Esta would make the call. It became a day or two every other week, and then every week. He would miss two days, just at the limit before needing a doctor's note to book him off, come to work for a day, and take the next day off. Godwin would rub his stomach and say it's running; he was nearly every hour at the toilet. Catherine supplied him with Imodium but it didn't seem to help. There was never any visit to the clinic even though she offered to take him there in a work day. Finally André and Catherine woke up to a pattern of absences and they sensed that something was not right.

Meanwhile, the gardens lost their health and their beauty. Hedges grew untrimmed, weeds sprouted happily everywhere, and long grass and dandelions took over in serious patches.

One day in September Godwin asked to speak to both André and Catherine. He told them he was resigning from his job, effective in December. After some discussion, and a few days for him to really think about it, Godwin was adamant. Time to move on, he said. André was more than ready to accept, after all the absences and excuses and lie after lie. The next day he drafted a letter in Afrikaans, of resignation in three months as requested, which Godwin happily signed.

Godwin's last day arrived. As did Esta. Amazingly there were still some unused sick days from previous years. Even though Godwin's work had deteriorated in the last year, André was relieved to have an end in sight and paid him out fully. Including the expected (but unearned) year-end bonus, plus Christmas money. Plus *vakansiegeld,* insisted Esta, extra pocket money for the year-end leave. André gave a wry smile and complied.

"Wat van die R9 000 vir nege jare se werk?" spat Esta. (What about the R9 000 for nine years' work?) Her sunny face in an instant flashed like lightning. André and Catherine were taken aback. Suddenly a generous, amicable parting spewed hairy hissing things.

Catherine responded, "We've never discussed that, in all the years. It was never part of the agreement."

"It's not right! We want our money!"

André's face reddened with anger. "It's not your money. It's not an agreement and it's not a right. I've paid and paid, all the wages, all the benefits, extra money too. Now you demand more?"

"Pay us now!"

André shook his head. Catherine tried to reason with them but Esta flared up and her rage took control. Godwin threw down the keys, and as they clattered on the glass table top, everyone stood up and Godwin and Esta stormed out of the gate and off the farm.

After all the investment in Godwin and his family and his house and his bakkie, all the meetings and paperwork, the specialised training in paving and tutoring for the driver's test, retaining him in his job. After the caring, non-judgmental attitude of Catherine and the basic patience of André. This payment was not law; some employers paid it just to avoid a conflict, but not all did. André refused.

Of course that wasn't the end. One morning at 06:00, Godwin and Esta appeared at the farm gate, all smiles, wanting to talk. Catherine felt something was brewing and luckily, they had house guests to wake up and to ask them to observe the meeting on the veranda.

After the first pleasantries things got rough. Esta demanded an immediate payout of R9 000. André stuck to his earlier refusal. Then Esta jumped up from the table and ran down to the lawn, shouting abuse.

"You are garbage! You are rubbish!" She ran behind the hedge and back to the lawn, shouting the same thing in Afrikaans. *"Julle is vuilgoed! Gemors!"* She went into a tantrum, shouting it over and over. Godwin stalked right behind her, a terrible expression on his face, one they had never seen from him before, and looking daggers at André and Catherine. Despite his gentlemanly nature, Godwin had become her clone.

They headed for the gate, which André gladly opened for them. As they stormed out, she glared at André with hate in her eyes.

She shouted, *"Ek gaan iemand kry om jou dood te maak! I am getting someone to kill you!"*

André and Catherine were in shock. A death threat! From the sale of their house, Esta and Godwin had money to pay for anything. Of course, it is against the law to make such threats against people. It was a case of intimidation that could go to court, confirmed to Catherine by the police. There were witnesses.

Esta phoned and phoned and phoned, many times per hour. She made not just a pest of herself but a terrible pest. Such behaviour is aimed to wear people down, and that is exactly what she did. Finally, to get rid of her, André said, okay, half that amount. She agreed. He paid R4 500 into Godwin's account.

That agreement meant nothing. Esta continued with the harassment and abuse. She even made a case with the CCMA, the Commission for Conciliation, Mediation and Arbitration, set up to resolve labour disputes. She just wanted money, money, money.

André was ready to fight that, and Catherine too.

Esta still harassed André and Catherine both. They learned how to block her phone calls. She then took to using other people's phones. Finally they engaged the labour consultant Arno Landman, who had helped everyone resolve the initial long-standing fight. He was ready to support André if it came to a hearing. As the days wore on, neither Catherine nor André found the stomach for ugly and lengthy contact that such a case would bring. So poor André, feeling extorted, forked out the money.

This saga of the farm in Africa is drawing to a close, thought Catherine. Contact remained, however, between the Steenkamps and other members of the extended Jacobs family that lived not far from Bellezicht. Their children still received school clothes and supplies from

Catherine and André, and there were occasional requests for transport, food and money to buy electricity.

From time to time, sightings of Esta and Godwin were reported. They were in Worcester; no, he was working in Robertson; no, they went to Paarl. Someone had recognised Godwin in a church service there and told his half-sister Trina, who told Catherine.

"He was unshaven and uncombed," said Trina. "His shirt was not ironed and his shoes carried mud. And to church like that." She'd heard he and his wife were living in a cottage on a farm there, without electricity. There was no communication between Godwin and Trina; Esta had seen to that, with a history of jealous shouting matches even at Bellezicht and blocked phone numbers.

These events, especially the final ones, affected Catherine deeply. Through 20 years of being involved, she felt more understanding of how complex it was to make real contact over wide unseen gulfs. She felt from the day they moved in that it was the responsibility of her and André to work together with the farm family for their prosperity and independence. After all, she and André had worked long and hard to create their own prosperity and independence. They had delayed marriage and family; they had even delayed the sexual experimentation of youth as their homes had taught them. Both Catherine and André had held down two and sometimes three jobs, saving money, building up a few assets; sacrificing good times to study and build credentials, to write assignments, teach classes and produce economic reports. Couldn't they – they – delay a bit of gratification as well? For a better personal future?

She was beginning to suspect that prosperity and independence may not be things that can be given to others, much less imposed on them. If the others do not have a sense of how it works, if others do not do their part, there is no gain.

Though depressed by events, Catherine thought she would try to sum up and see just what happened to all the people involved. She wanted a sense of closure.

She started with Isaac and Laetitia Jacobs and their four children, Reuben, Sheryl, Neela and Tommy. Isaac retired at Bellezicht and André paid him a full pension until he died. Laetitia also, until dementia made it impossible and her family asked help for her to go to an old-age home. She lasted there about two months. André and Catherine paid for both of their funerals. Oupa had passed on a few years before.

Sheryl had moved along with Godwin and the others to the big house in Kuils River, along with her two younger sons Quinton and Jannie. She seemed to be living somewhere in Kuils River. Her two older children, Trina and Godwin, were estranged from her because she was never there for them as they grew up; Laetitia and Isaac raised them. Trina lived with her husband and two children on a nearby farm and she still had a special path into Catherine's heart, with occasional visits. She's a story for another time, Catherine thought.

Quinton, Sheryl's third child, dropped out of school at the move to Kuils River and then tried to go back to school at the one in Kuils River. Sheryl told Catherine how one morning he got up, dressed in his school clothes, and walked to the school. One can imagine him making his way down a long passage feeling uncertain where to go. He turned around and walked away from school and from any more formal education. How could Sheryl not have gone with him, Catherine had thought. Quinton continued his stealing, was charged in the gang rape of a smaller boy and he just got worse. Little Jannie stayed with Sheryl and was doing well enough in Grade 4. He sometimes visited his father, who included him in the activities of the wife and family which he'd had all along.

Neela fell ill and the problem seemed more than her back; she declined to show her medical papers to Catherine, who was ready to help. Even Esta seemed not to know the other problems. There were different stories, maybe even cancer; but of course she was seeking medical care and her privacy had to be respected. Six months after the move, she passed away. Her husband Henry had family in Kuils River, a brother, and though he had moved to the big house, he hovered on his bicycle between his brother's family and the big house. *Klein* Henry, never very strong, had fathered a child, became ill and weak and passed away at age 21. The younger son stayed close to his father.

After a decent time, Henry found a woman he wanted to bring home. Esta would have none of it; another irony, as she now rejected new people, actually just one new person, coming to live there, the very thing she had fought for with Catherine and André. Eventually Henry and his son went to live with his brother's family.

Reuben, formerly the violent druggie, got himself together and with Susanna, produced two sons. Son Danie still lived with his parents at Arendsvlug, finding only casual farm work. The teacher he was to marry went off with someone else. Despite decent school marks, their other son Jaco made it to the high school but liked only the sports there, became a disciplinary problem and did zero schoolwork. The school recommended a special program for skills and training but he dropped out just before the end. He married a young woman with a child and they had a child and he got a farm job and settled down.

Tommy dropped out of high school. The principal himself came to the farm looking for him but he literally ran away into the vineyard. Catherine served coffee while he waited but finally left. It turned out Tommy had slipped into the cottage and the family covered for him, because it wasn't yet known that he had a pregnant girlfriend. He got a job and a cottage also at Arendsvlug, married the girlfriend, took a mistress for a while, and had five children.

Anna Solomons retired from domestic work after 20 years with the Steenkamps, who paid her a modest pension.

Marina was the only one who actually finished high school. She went through all the motions, as did the school, and wrote her matric exams while under quarantine from measles. Catherine supported her special dress for the matric farewell, and the next special dress for her party when she turned 21, meals and gold key and all. After some months she was hired by Shoprite to pack shelves and she later became a superintendent. Eventually she moved to a place of her own, found a boyfriend, and had a child while still keeping her job. She had made the move into the first world. She remained close to Susanna and went into debt to give her a big 60th birthday party. She remained close at heart to Catherine too.

The Baby, the one who didn't eat much, grew up at Bellezicht, left school and was in and out. She had a son and left to find a Muslim husband in Kuils River, with whom she had three more children. Her son was taken in by Susanna.

The visitors remained a mystery. Once they moved to the big house, neither Catherine nor André saw them again. When asked, Godwin said they had both taken a week's course to become security guards and that they still didn't have work. It seems they slid even more into the margins, as did the child which may not have been theirs. Catherine did not really know them. They had been there and not there. She never heard about them again.

One evening shortly afterward, when Catherine and André felt that the fighting and abuse were finally over, they went out on their veranda to regain a measure of calm. André held a chair for Catherine and then opened a bottle of Credo Shiraz and poured each of them a glass. His silver temples shone in the waning light. As he sat down beside her, he gave an appreciative smile as they raised their glasses. "To you, my darling wife."

"How could it end like this," said Catherine, with a smile though feeling downhearted. "I was so sure we could make a difference in the lives of that family. Those families."

The sun sank behind them into the west. They watched quietly as the line of steel-blue shadow moved up the mountain range across the valley, pulling dusk behind it.

"We sacrificed a lot," noted André, shifting in his chair. He looked mournful but managed a philosophical tone. "Especially you, with your caring nature. Of course, the American funds helped."

Catherine looked at him. "No, you too, André. Your savings seemed to evaporate. We will never recoup them. At least we still have each other. Though there were some moments … ." She caught his eye. "We learned to understand each other better."

"I know we had … I know I gave us some tough times but here we are, still together."

She adjusted her chair closer to his, with a flicker of a smile. "I've learned a lot too. To open my thinking. My ideals are fine but my way is not always the best way. As hard as that is to admit."

André sighed. "This conflict with the farm family could have been avoided. But one could probably say that about most wars, I guess."

"Other forces were just too strong for us and we may never know the real reasons."

"Well, we got close; we almost did it," he said with a rueful smile. "It could have ended amicably. And after all that," said André, "after all the strife and pain and fear, after all the time and effort, even after a mountain of dialogue, it is so ironic." He shook his head and looked at Catherine. "We and they – we are still, still, worlds apart."

GLOSSARY

aarde: earth; *my aarde*: exclamation as in my heavens

agterplaas: back yard

alles: everything

almal: everyone

baas: old word for boss, now less acceptable; newer word to use: *meneer*, sir

bakkie: small pickup truck

bergies: people living in the bush

beskuit: rusk

bietjie: a little

bly: happy

boep: paunch

boer: farmer

braai: South African barbeque

braaiplek: fireplace for cooking

daar onder: down there

daarso: right there

dagga: marijuana

dankie: thank you*; baie dankie:* thank you very much

diefstal verander alles: theft changes everything

doek: headscarf; plural *doeke*

gemors: garbage

groen vingers: a green thumb

hierdie: this

hoes: cough

huismoles: domestic violence

inwoners: occupants

ja: yes

jaar: year

kakkerlakke: cockroaches

kies: to vote

kiewiet: plover

klaar: finish   •

Klein Henry: Henry junior

knopkierie: knobkerrie, club

koeksister: Afrikaans speciality like a donut twist

koeldrank: soft drink

Meneer: sir

Mevrou: Missus; for mature woman

Missus: Mrs; title of respect

moeilikheid: trouble

nee: filler word like "well"

nee, wat: expression "oh well."

nie: not

nies: sneeze

ou: nice fellow

ouma: grandmother

oupa: grandfather

pad: street

panga: large machete-like knife

puisies: pimples containing pus

rooibos: a bush whose leaves make rooibos tea

senuwees: nerves

sjambok: whip

skool: school

skelmpies: on the quiet, no one seeing

stywe vrou: woman with a solid build

tjaila: quitting time

vakansiegeld: vacation spending money

verkiesings: voting

vis: fish

voetstoets: condition of a house sold just as it is

vuilgoed: garbage

was my: wash me

welkom: welcome

werf: yard

TRANSLATIONS OF DIALOGUE

p. 2   *Ons is hier oor my ma.*   We are here about my mother.

p. 3   *Ons wil net seker maak.*   We just want to make sure.

p. 3   *Meneer, hoe bedoel Meneer?*   Sir, what do you mean?

p. 3   *Julle het my gehoor.*   You heard me.

p. 3   *En as Godwin trek, dan moet almal trek. Dis hoe dit is, en klaar.*   And if Godwin leaves, then everyone leaves. That's how it is, end of story.

p. 3   *Ek wil nie! Ek kan nie! Nooit nie!*   I won't leave! I can't leave! Never!

p. 4   *Wag, asseblief!*   Wait, please!

p. 5   *Dan moet almal ook trek.*   Then everyone has to leave.

p. 7   *Alleen in die wêreld.*   All alone in the world.

p. 14   *Baas, jy moet ons help!*   Boss, you have to help us!

p. 15   *Baas, Isaac raak mal!*   Boss, Isaac is going crazy!

p. 15   *Isaac het 'n knopkierie en hy maak ons bang!*   Isaac has a club and he is frightening us!

p. 15   *Nee, Baas. Kom ons aangaan met probeer.*   Well, Boss, let's just keep trying.

p. 16   *Baas, ons is moeg. Bel die polisie.*   Boss, we're tired. Call the police.

p. 16   *Meneer, u kan vir Isaac kom haal.*   Sir, you can come get Isaac.

p. 45   *Die baba bly hier.*   The baby stays here.

p. 45   *Ek is klaar met die kombuis.*   I quit working in the kitchen.

p. 47   *Dis my pa.*   He's my father.

p. 48   *Daar's nou baie mense hier.*   There are a lot of people already here.

p. 48   *Ons sal 'n plek maak.*   We'll make room.

p. 49   *Oupa, jy is baie welkom hier by ons op die plaas. Ons hoop alles is gemaklik genoeg vir jou.*   Grandfather, you are very welcome here with us on the farm. We hope everything is comfortable enough for you.

p. 65   *Het julle Jannie gesien?*   Have you seen Jannie?

p. 71   *Het jy die foon gevat?*   Did you take the phone?

ACKNOWLEDGEMENTS

This book came out of a true story on a South African wine farm. Many people encouraged and assisted me in writing this story and I thank each and every one.

Dr Ronald Irwin, for his short courses in creative writing at the University of Cape Town and for bringing his numerous contacts so generously into my writing life.

Prof Jenefer Shute, for her constructive guidance at several early stages.

Pamela Jooste, for her many brutally honest discussions and her shining moments of kindness.

Leann Hornung, for lending me her lovely apartment over some years for writing solitude.

Linda Rode, who through her publishing skills gave me thorough feedback on every page.

Ydalene Coetsee, for feedback and editing the raw manuscript.

Marida van der Merwe, for spontaneous responses to story and style.

James Dennerlein, for insightful feedback at an early stage.

Sharon Colback, for prose writing instruction and consultation.

The many friends who kept bugging me to get on with this project.

My understanding husband Dr GJJ (Johan) Snyman, who believed in me from the start and freed me to write.

Cover photo and design by Ydi Coetsee Carstens

Photo of author by Llewellyn D Duim

SOURCES

Barnard, Chris.1972. *Chriskras*. Cape Town: Tafelberg.

Giliomee, H. 2003. *The Afrikaners*. Cape Town: Tafelberg.

Hughes, D., Hands, P. & Kench, J. 1992. *South African Wine*. Cape Town: Struik.

Small, Adam. 1975. Poem: *Die Here het gaskommel. Kitaar my Kruis*. Pretoria: Haum.

www.sahistory.org.za The San. Accessed: 13 Jan 2014.